CRAWLING BACK

VAMPIRES OF FATE BOOK THREE

JULIE HUTCHINGS

inked entertainment

Vampires of Fate

Running Home (Book 1)

Running Away (Book 2)

Crawling Back (Book 3)

The Harpy Series

The Harpy (Book 1)

The Harpy 2: Evolution (Book 2)

The Harpy 3: Damnation (Book 3)

Betty Bedlam Series

with Connor Ashley

Damned (Book 1, coming soon)

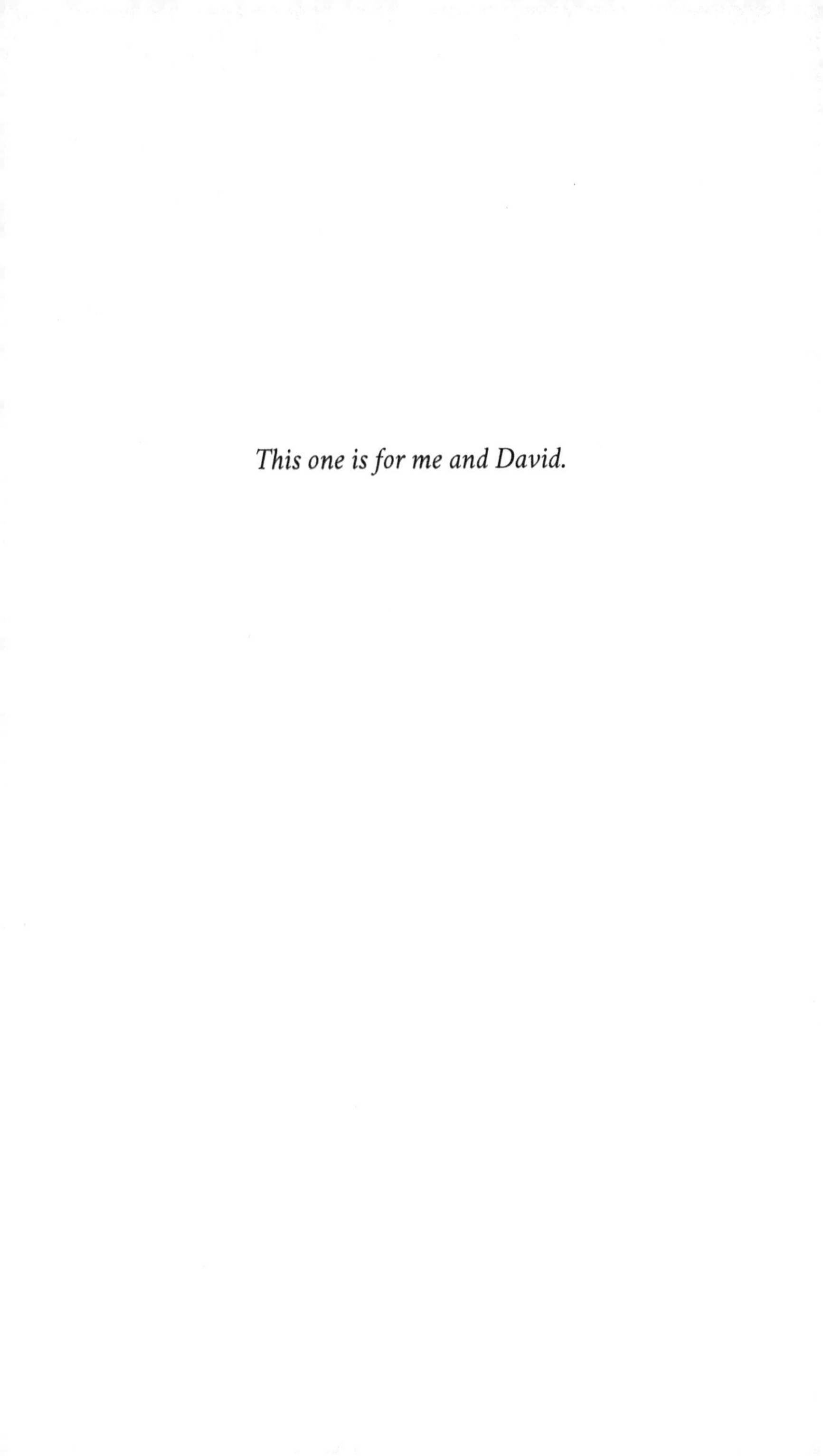

This one is for me and David.

CHAPTER 1

The crows followed me back to the woods of New Hampshire, and I was met with the form of living death that I despised.

Chris Lynch glowed with life, even behind the cobwebs in his eyes. The tragedy of Kat's death was all over him, but there were others. So many others.

"Time for some emotional sword swallowing. Can I come in?" I asked as I pushed my way through the door.

The Great White Mansion appeared darker through my vampire eyes. Or maybe through any eyes—clearly he'd dismissed any cleaning staff he'd had. The cobwebs weren't only on his soul, if he still had one, but on the high crown molding meant for mimicking classic elegance to lure in easily-impressed victims. Dust rolled across the marble floor as I came in. I'd never noticed until they'd wilted and died, but Lynch had always had fresh flowers in big, expensive vases on tables nobody ever used. Lilies, I think. Now they were corpses.

Trailing my finger over one of the crunchy petals, I knew without question that it had been Kat who kept the fresh flowers.

I'd have known it without the lightning-flash image of her carrying in an armload of them, kicking the door shut behind her, striking me with an electricity that burned in my brain.

Pink dress. Then jeans and my stolen Batman T-shirt. Then green raincoat.

Layers, prisms of pictures of her smiling, arms loaded with the blooms. Something a person would do in a *home*, not at this miserable castle. But everywhere Kat was had felt like home.

I whipped my fingers away, holding them to me as if burned, my heart instantly scorched by the vision that jumped into my psyche without warning.

Never before had my mind's eye given me a vision from a mere touch, and of an inanimate, dead object. I fell back against the wall, panting. Me, the most frightening and unpredictable of the *Shinigami*, frightened. My eyes shot to Lynch to see if he'd noticed my reaction, but he toured the room aimlessly, a ghost in his own home.

"Do you even wonder what I'm doing here?" I asked him, more gently than I'd intended. Abomination or not, he was still *cracked*. To attack him now would have been horribly cruel, though I couldn't say why I cared.

"Why aren't you with Nicholas?" Lynch monotoned as he roamed the cold room, eyes never resting on me.

"He doesn't want me there right now," I said. To say such a thing to this monster, to open up to him so easily didn't feel as foreign as it should have, as it would have before his blood called to me across nations and oceans. His blood had something to show me, and I was okay with giving a little to take a little. Or a lot. He was, after all, the man who undoubtedly loved my best friend, and we'd both lost her. The light of both our lives, snuffed out.

The Lynch I'd known would have taken that opportunity to make a vicious comment, but this Lynch was too far away, too lost to feel vicious or anything else. Anything but sadness, pain. The vision that dragged me here, of him crying in this very room, tearing at his hair, then rushing out the door, letting it hang open behind him as he sought a woman to kill burst into memory.

This was a man who was more dangerous when he was sad than when he was angry.

"Lynch, sit down," I said quietly, and with only the urge to be there, I was suddenly beside him. Moving more quickly, Nicholas had said once in Japan, than any vampire he'd ever seen. I put my hand on Lynch's elbow in his wrinkled shirt. Nothing about him was as polished as it had been. The look he gave me, wide-eyed, shocked and afraid, made me lean away, but I kept my hand on his arm. It was as if he'd just realized I was there. I steered him toward the sofa I'd always hated, *Miami Vice* white leather, and pushed him onto it.

"You came here," he said, utterly blank. "Why would you come here?"

"I have my reasons." I shook my head, and sat beside him. "Sorry. I won't pull a Riddler on you. We'll save that for—" My throat constricted. I couldn't say his name, didn't want to think of it anymore when he was so close and so far away. *Nicholas.* "I came here because your blood called to me from Japan."

For the first time, he really looked at me. The supple skin, the healthy shade of his lips—it didn't match the utter madness of his eyes, the hollowness of them. I could only imagine the vitality of the woman he'd stolen this latest glow from—

...how her blood must have sparkled on the tongue.

I growled at myself, the way my thoughts became so gruesome with the blood craving. How could I condemn this man whose own kind called him "the Abomination" for acting on urges I was barely controlling myself? I'd found that since leaving Japan, since knowing that I was my own higher authority among the death gods, since confirming that I had a choice in who I killed, that I saw everyone as a potential victim.

Lynch still had his eyes on me, waiting for me to speak more. Again, a new trait for the forked-tongue attorney who'd been too quick, always assessing, always on the hunt. This waiting...this was a new hunting tactic that I recognized as a vampire, one of his own kind.

Subtle, intimidating in the most calm and cautious way. He didn't even know he was doing it, which made it even more blood curdling. Even to me, a dead thing like him, in so many ways.

I thought of myself as dead in that moment, but in truth, I felt completely alive. Unhindered. Strong. Purposeful and determined. Invincible. I was *Shinigami*, wandering this world as I saw fit, like a bird of prey, swallowing down every sense, every bit of knowledge, every taste with renewed vivaciousness. I didn't feel dead. I felt, for the first time, entirely my own. Not owned by the lingering spirit of death—I *was* death. Not beholden to the shadows to avoid humanity—I owned them, if I wanted them. Not tortured by a mystical connection to the man who delivered me to this fate—it was my choice. For as much as I loved Nicholas French, it felt damn good to not feel owned by him. And I'd known it as soon as I'd gotten to Japan; my path was mine to carve and I needed to do it alone.

Dokkoudou, Izanagi had called it. *The path of aloneness.*

I drink the blood of a god, I thought, and found myself sneering.

"You're a vampire," Lynch said as I let my mind wander into its own depths. I found I was far more inclined to dig deep into my subconscious as a vampire, that one second of thought suddenly became the unlocking of a treasure chest I didn't wait to explore.

"I'm a vampire," I said back.

"I'm sorry," he replied.

"Wha—what? What?" I stuttered, unable to comprehend his words. "Why are you sorry?"

Blood-tinged tears glinted pink in his bloodshot eyes. "To live forever without her…"

I took his hand in mine, and waited in silence with him for darkness to come, when we could wash away the haunting of Kat in someone else's blood.

CHAPTER 2

I didn't ask where he was going; I already knew. Another Eliza, a human Eliza would have had a pang of sadness for the life—or lives—he would take this night, but the Eliza who had a world of choices opened up to her didn't. Human Eliza would have been racked with guilt over the loss of an innocent life, convinced it had something to do with her. But *Shinigami* Eliza saw all too clearly that it wasn't a matter of when, but how a person would die.

I could be that death.

Lynch could be that death.

I'd spent most of my life thinking about death. Now as a vampire, my mind moved so fast, thought so deep, I thought of all new aspects of death. Probably not good for me. No wonder Nicholas had been so torn apart when we met. A thinking man with too much time to think. I'd never concentrated on what Lynch did to his victims, how he delighted in and drew out their murders, hardly any of them having been "fated" to die. Because I'd seen how short-sighted even the *Shinigami* had been under the Master's leadership. They'd blindly followed a calling to kill with the knowledge that the human's alternative fate would have been worse for the whole of humanity. But not once did the vampires question what the fates of those who *weren't* chosen would be. Certainly there were horrendous tortures, deaths, enslavements and the waking nightmares people suffered every day. Unless some higher power told his vampire clan to do it, they weren't supposed to drink from anyone else, even though any one of those victims could be suffering every minute of their lives, in their own minds for that matter. It was for the better of *humankind* that we drank. That's what the *Shinigami* told themselves. Gods indeed.

If I was to be a god, I would be the death god I was meant to be. One that didn't follow senseless orders, or let fate decide for me. If I wanted to be a humanitarian that sucked blood, I'd do it with the mindset that everyone suffers, and suffering is a detriment to humanity in all its forms. Even vampire.

Kieran Coughlin would have stood cheering at this most recent foray into my subconscious. He would have burned as brightly as the sun.

While Lynch hunted to take his mind off his own suffering for as long as he could, I wandered the mansion, taking in all of its quick decay. In such a short time, he'd let the home he'd taken such arrogant pride in deteriorate. I could hear bats, birds and squirrels in the attic. I felt the pungent wetness of mold, the dryness of the balls of dust. The smell of dried blood and sweat in the piles of clothing in his bedroom reached me in the great room where he held parties, where he "lived." My vampire senses didn't need to give me *everything* in high definition.

My fingers hovered over the dead flowers I'd touched earlier, and they shook wildly. As much as I wanted to touch them, see what I could see again, I abhorred the thought of glimpsing a living Kat just to have her taken away again. I should not have to relive that over and over.

The unfairness of it made me want to take a victim, let someone's loved ones feel the pain I would feel for eternity. And that thought didn't make me feel guilty either. Misery loves company is right. But Nicholas wouldn't agree. Nicholas would look at me like a stranger if he knew what I was thinking, how I felt. It stomped all over the ideals he'd been raised as a vampire on, the ideals of a power-hungry ancient liar that stole the *Shinigami* from their true creator, Izanagi. Left him alone for eternity again.

I plunged my hand into the center of the flowers forcefully, petals crumbling to the floor. I howled in rage when I saw nothing. Nothing. Where before I had seen her, felt her, now I came up empty, and I hated...*hated...*

that I didn't control this new sort of vision. I hated not knowing what I would see next and when.

Aggravated, I envisioned myself upstairs, just to get away from this room and all its memories. I'd never been to the second floor of Lynch's house, and he wouldn't care if I was there now. He cared about nothing now. He hadn't even said goodbye when he left the house to hunt as he pulled his hand from mine.

Upstairs was the wreck I knew it would be from all the things my senses showed me before. It was hard to imagine the sharp attorney that had so enchanted my best friend living in this hole. Standing on the white carpet, now stained with filth and blood from coming in after haphazard hunting, a new fear welled in me.

What would I see if I touched the things in here?

Morbid curiosity got the better of me, and I perched on the very edge of Lynch's bed. It was also gross, and I didn't really want to touch it. The blankets were in a ball, the pillowcases stained, and the worst of it all—the fitted sheet was coming off one corner. Placing my palms on the mattress on either side of me, I let out a long breath. But I saw nothing. I did the same thing on the chair in the corner, and the ottoman at my feet, but saw nothing. The knot in the pit of my stomach unwound as I realized that I wouldn't be assaulted with memories of Kat everywhere she went—but when would I? When I least expected it, of course.

Memories. The place held memories. That hadn't been a vision, when I touched the flowers—it had been a memory. But surely there were more in this mansion where she'd spent her last days. Why would I not discover them everywhere, in everything I touched that she'd touched?

Again I let my mind delve into hidden possibilities, losing track of time and forgetting the space I was in. Two things stuck out for me—two things that I probably wouldn't have picked up on in my human life, and for a second I reveled in my abilities. First, Kat had personally brought those flowers into the house. They were there because of her. And second?

They had been alive.

I don't know why it troubled me so, made me grit my teeth and pant until the protective red mist that shielded me seeped into the room from my fingertips and toes, taking over until it was the only thing that mattered anymore, soothing me. I don't know why I would be so goddamned *afraid* of the idea that living things Kat touched held a piece of her memory.

I was one of those living things she touched, and I held her memory powerfully myself. Too powerfully. Though really, I was no longer living, I was no longer that emotional corpse I'd been in the days following her death, before getting to Japan. The kinship I was feeling with the dead flowers in my hometown showed me how much I'd changed.

How little was left for me here.

The marble floor split with a *crack* when I ground my feet into it, as if rooting myself there, refusing to leave, to be forced out. Not when blood called me there, back to my home, not when death itself turned me in this direction.

I screamed, stomping the cold floor over and over, shattering it like an earthquake, shaking the walls.

"It's MINE!" I growled, hunched over, wraith-like, waiting to defend myself against the world. But the world wasn't coming after me. I wasn't prey any longer. This was my home, New Hampshire belonged to me, and unnatural thing that I'd become, I still had the right to come home.

"I'm home," I whispered to the white walls, the decaying room. And I pounded the floor once more. The door fell off its hinges.

~

He stumbled through the door, banging his head on the frame and falling to one knee.

He didn't even swear. Not once. I would have sworn at least three times. That's how I knew he was dead inside.

I glided to his side instinctively, as anyone does when a person needs help. "Lynch, what happened to you?"

He raised his face, blood wet on his chin and throat, ruining his already filthy shirt beyond repair. His eyes were blank, emotionless. "Nothing," he said, voice guttural. *Nothing.* He'd drunk the blood of a living, breathing, complex creature, and felt nothing.

The mess that he'd become sent me a memory of Roman in that asylum attic, withering away in every way he could. Then to Kieran, black as ash, only partly hopeless; the part that knew I loved Nicholas. And Nicholas, alone, a flash away, may as well have been in the next room for as fast as I could get to him, and still… alone. Immortal, all of us, the eternal gift of life, and we'd squandered it so young. We were all still so *young.*

Eternity promised a lifetime of hurt, but infinite time for redemption.

I led Lynch to the stupid white sofa as easily as a kitten to milk. The sofa wasn't white anymore—nothing was pristine around us. I'd hated this man with every breath in my body, blamed him for the end of my friendship with Kat, known what horrors he was capable of, felt the deaths of those who hadn't deserved it, having seen through his eyes in my visions. But now? I felt only pity.

Pity for this vermin. Soulless murderer, the Abomination to his own kind, the only family he knew.

My dearest friend had seen unparalleled beauty in this despicable bastard.

He sat immobile, but he was listening. I sensed the tiny hairs in his ears moving ever so slightly. But he stared straight ahead as I faced him at his side. "I'm not here to kill you, though I'm sure that's what you think. I don't think you'd care if I did. I always hated you, from the moment Kat told me the crap you spewed to her while trying to...*date*...her. Before I had vampire senses I knew you were a monster—I just knew. Given the chance then, as confused as I was, my whole world changing around me, I wouldn't have killed you. You symbolized everything I knew being taken from me, but I wouldn't have killed you. Now? Now I could kill you in the blink of an eye, less than the blink of an eye. And I don't want to."

"Why, then?" His voice crackled with age, as neglected as this home he'd built. Everything about him was surface, so easily ruined, despite its appearance. The thinnest of skins. "Why are you here when you belong in Japan?"

"Your blood. I need to drink it."

He looked at me, incredulous, the first real feeling I'd recognized in him since I'd arrived. "I'm a vampire, just like you," he said simply.

We are not alike, I ached to say, but stopped myself. Now was not the time to lean back on my human resentments.

"What use could my blood have to you?" he said. He hung his head, surely thinking that he was of no use to anyone. I'd felt that way for too long, before my purpose was put before me like a home-cooked meal to the starved.

"Let's find out," I said, fangs protruding, dimpling my bottom lip. Fear flickered in the wells of his eyes, riling my not-so-inner predator. I pulled him to me by the arm with one swift tug, and buried my teeth into his exposed neck where his shirt was torn. He was silent as I wrenched my head back and forth to get the vein right where I wanted it, though the pain had to have been extraordinary. My eyes unfocused and rolled back with the first deep drink. Moments passed like years as I waited for knowledge to fill me with every drop of blood.

The first mouthful caught me unawares. It wasn't Chris Lynch I tasted, but that of a girl—always a girl with him—visiting the slopes for her last snowboard run of the season. She had a creaminess, a soft vanilla flavor, pure but rich. But there was another personality deep in her recesses, one she didn't know yet. One that would torture her for the rest of her life. One that was capable of hellish things that this brilliant young lady would never dream of; until she did. *Shayla.* Shayla's recessive personality was a dark, terrible thing, one that she hid from without knowing it.

When I'd drunk her story, I pulled away, wiping the wetness from my chin with my sleeve. "Nothing!" I roared, mist flooding out of me as red as Shayla's blood. It churned for a moment, confused, upset, before mummifying Lynch, straightening his body and covering every inch of him but his face. I relished the panic in his expression. I wanted him to answer for whatever he was hiding.

"Eliza, what is this?!" he whimpered. Coward. The mist constricted more.

"What are you covering up, Lynch? Huh?"

"I don't know what you're talking about!"

"Stop squirming, the mist won't let you go. I saw nothing important just now, no reason for me to be here, drinking from you, what are you *hiding*!"

"I have nothing left to hide, Eliza! I killed the girl, it didn't help! I don't know what you mean!"

Calming my panting, the anger swelling in my throat, I unclenched my fists and the mist dissipated, releasing him. He lay gasping, holding his arms around himself in a hug that didn't comfort him.

Pacing, running my fingers through my hair, getting it caught in a knot on one side, I rambled. "Your blood *begged* me to come here, it had something to show me, and I listened, of course I listened..."

"I don't know what you're saying!" he screeched in a panic. I stopped and spun on him, and he leaned back as far as he could into the sofa.

"I can see your fate if I drink your blood. Human, vampire, I know what's going to happen or could happen, and I get visions of things that matter, but this... Shayla's life story wasn't what I came here for. You have something *in there*," I hissed, leaning over him and pushing my index finger hard into his forehead. "There's something in there that you're keeping from me, and I want it. Do you hear me? I want it, Lynch."

Gently, he pushed me away from him, and with a sad smile said, "I have nothing to give you. But maybe you can do something for me."

"What? No. I'm here for one reason, and then I'm gone."

He closed his eyes. "Do you remember coming to me, asking me to kill you?"

"Not the sort of thing you forget."

"I wanted to do it, but I wouldn't because I hated you so much. Your reason for being here is to torture me, and finally kill me. I deserve it, but because I *want* it, you won't do it. Even if it's the real reason you came here, you won't do it." He wasn't making much sense, and it made me wonder what someone so confused could really show me.

What if my visions, the call to feed, all of it had failed me? What would my purpose be then?

"I'm not here to do you any favors, Lynch. One of these days, your blood will give me the answers I need, and I'll act on whatever it tells me. Until then, sulk, rot, cry, do whatever you need to do, but keep your self-pity away from me."

I left his house slowly, letting him hear every footfall that would leave him alone once again.

CHAPTER 3

The idea was preposterous, that Nicholas was the equivalent of footsteps away for me, and that I was trying not to go to him. No matter that we left on terrible terms, or that I told him to go away for so many reasons. No matter that Blue was living with him at that very moment in the cabin that was *my* dream house, with my dream lover. No matter that the pain we'd both suffered when apart was an elaborate thrall that the Master had managed to create. Pain was endurable. But this… I missed him. I missed him too much to stay away.

No sooner than I'd thought about it, I was in the woodsy front yard, fully aware of how terrifying I would appear to human eyes. Standing unnaturally still, staring at a little cabin with eyes full of fire and red mist and ice, betraying my feelings. My confusion.

The sun was coming up. Barely touching the trees, but I felt it on my neck, my back. It reminded me of being alive. My mind went down one of its whirlpools, remembering the beach and how fast I'd burn, how I'd refuse to go to the beach again until Kat begged and I'd burn all over again. I'd worry about skin cancer, and Kat would make me go to the doctor but there was nothing to worry about. I always worried about the burns until winter anyway. Winter, when I met Nicholas and it would turn out the burns wouldn't matter anymore.

The thoughts came so fast and plunged so deep, the sun burning holes into my flesh, my scalp, hotter than when I'd been alive. Vampirism and vivid memories—vivid everything, especially pain—but it was a memory.

Except it wasn't a memory. I stood in full view of the big bay window, horribly still, my reflection in the glass screaming as I burned.

Terrified, and stupidly stubborn to admit I'd done something so careless and *while* going to blubber about missing Nicholas, the screams tore from my throat, but I couldn't move. Hoarfrost tickled my fingers where the prints had certainly burned off. Cold brushed up my arms, across my throat, a personal blizzard engulfed my feet, but I could see nothing, only feel. Cold battling the fiery sun, my body the killing field.

All at once the unbearable touch of the slightest breeze on my body, as if I was naked to the elements, flesh burning and freezing, my veins surely exposed with my skin eaten away—

"What the hell were you doing out there!"

Nicholas. Nicholas. Nicholas. I could say it over and over in my mind until that burned away, too.

The scent of the cabin took over the scents from outside and the merciless searing of my nostrils. Old wood and freshly cut wood mingled, traces of dirt tracked in, the wool of the blanket on the back of the sofa, the mustiness of the books in the loft. And the flowers that were my friend, Blue. Better than any of it, the peppermint brownie I needed. I needed it more than blood. But when my eyes healed from the sunlight, I saw Nicholas, and I wasn't ready—the sight of him hurt more than the sun.

He looked healthy enough. Dark, tousled mess of gorgeously styled hair, lips pinker than any other man's in the world, laugh lines and perfect creases framing the eyes that swam with mocha and cocoa and cream in a constant vortex. But it was his inner health that shocked me. I sensed it, felt his peace just by laying eyes on him.

He was happy. And I was crushed and confused by my own head.

"I said what the hell were you doing out there?" he repeated calmly, running his fingers through his hair. Tendrils of steam rose from them where my fire had met his ice moments before. "What are you doing *here*?"

"You…you look great," I murmured, my voice hoarse from the heat.

"Yeah, thanks, but no thanks," he said with an angry confidence.

"I needed to see you," I said, my voice as tremulous as his was strong.

"Why?"

Blood tears formed in my eyes, the pink sheen making me feel weaker than the sun ripping my body to shreds. I looked to the floor. "Didn't think I'd need to say why."

His silence gave me hope that he'd soften toward me, but it ended soon enough. "I think you should get a hologram of me, Eliza, for when you feel like seeing me. And then you can just, you know, blink it out when you're in a mood."

"It's not my fault—"

"Don't say that!" he shouted, surprising me into looking at him, and God help me, he was *smiling* this scornful, wicked smile. "What can you possibly expect to say isn't your fault? Actually, I changed my mind. Say it. Finish your sentence, I need a good laugh." He raised an eyebrow in that genuinely amused way I'd loved, always loved. Until now.

"You said yourself time and again that I would be different when I became a vampire—you had no idea how different, how could we ever predict *this*?" I rambled, gesturing to myself. As I looked over my pants and plain T-shirt, I noticed there was no sign whatsoever that I'd been on fire when the sun rose. My clothes were unaffected, but my body was covered in sores underneath. I laughed. *Just like me. Okay on the outside; inside, an open wound.*

His chin was still tilted up in that condescending, snarky way I loved, but his eyes were glassy and his smile gone. "I would have loved anything you became."

"You don't now?"

"You. Sent. Me. Away."

What was I now, really? Who? I resembled nothing of the girl I'd been. Sitting on this couch, watching horror movies, talking books, sucking in her stomach and noticing the bulge of second-boob over the top of her bra. I was nothing now. No one.

"There were so many reasons for that. I'm pretty new at this, Nicholas, and I think I'm doing okay! I don't know which path to follow—"

"You were crystal clear when you told me to go. You needed to be alone."

"I know what you're thinking, and it's not true!" My voice cracked, the blood tears flowing freely, hissing where they touched my cheeks. "Now that I see through eyes like your own, you think I don't want you. That I think you're a monster because—because I'm one, too."

"You could never be a monster," he said, certainty returning to him instantly. "Even if you were, you'd be my monster. I would always love you." Blood tears streaked down his own cheeks now, and I sobbed at the sight of them. "I would always love you, Eliza Morgan, monster or not."

I was in his arms, making him stumble backwards as I bowled him over in the rapid movement of my body. I was more confused than I thought a being ever could be.

My mind reached to depths as a vampire that I was totally unprepared for, reminding me of the patients at Bethlem, drowning in their own mind disease. But there was no confusion to the utter satisfaction of feeling the heat of my body hiss against his coolness, of his arms around me, the scent of Christmas kitchen enveloping me. This was where I belonged, fated or not. I couldn't restrain myself any longer.

"I'm sorry about what happened with Kieran—" I said.

"—what you *did* with Kieran," Nicholas snapped.

"Yes. What I did with Kieran. I'm sorry I betrayed you, because that's what it was. I called it a lot of different things, but that's what it was, no matter how I *felt*. No matter what I needed."

"I'm barely a good man, let alone perfect, El, I can't—"

"Neither of us are. We don't even have to be good, really. We aren't human. We just aren't."

That went a different way than I'd expected. And once again, feelings from a place I was just beginning to discover erupted in words I didn't want to mean. Nicholas was clearly taken aback, head tilted at me as if he wanted to run, but was afraid to.

"You don't mean that."

"I don't say anything I don't mean. Please, don't give me that face, and don't be all silent. I have to be able to say things to you that aren't...perfect."

Something sank in him that brought down his face,

his eyes, his spirit. "You keep me human. If I lose that in you, my heart can't survive."

The tenderness vanished quickly at those words, dissolved into anger at being given such a responsibility as to keep him grounded for eternity, but even more so...

"You made me a vampire! I am *not* human, I am *not* the same as I was. I don't want to be loved *despite* that, like I did something wrong by becoming what I was meant to be. Finally, I have my place, and you want me to stay the same as I was? Dull, chubby Ellie who bored you to tears?"

I only saw red. Felt red. Anger, venom, rage, rage, rage.

My head felt every fiber of the ceiling's wood when I rose into the air, propelled by my crimson mist; my protector, my lifeline, my instrument, my emotions come to life. The smoky tendrils wound around my legs and I felt all traces of the sun's burn disappear. I sighed with relief, relaxed into its arms and let it heal me, even as the anger boiled from inside, threatening to incinerate me.

Anger at Nicholas. Nicholas French.

Memories of him beside me at the pond in his backyard, of the pain that connected us, of sharing the shield bubble with him in the growing sunlight, of his lips, of the teacup in his hands, of his T-shirts and his laugh and the way he balanced a mug on the arm of the couch instead of the table, and of him petting the stray cat that moved in. Of his *katas*, how he made the fighting movements into a work of art, how the *Shinigami* adored him, how he put everyone at ease, how he carried me in every way through the mountains of Japan, how he nearly became nothing but ash to spare my feelings and my best friend...

I hit the floor, the red mist retreating into my soul with a hiss, Medusa's snakes recoiling. I lay there, my cheek sensing every particle of soil beneath the cabin, the rings on the worms moving them along.

I was going mad.

And Nicholas didn't come to help me up.

I got to my feet like a human, clumsy and pained. I brushed my hair out of my face. My boots felt too heavy, my clothes like scraps wrapped senselessly around me. But it felt real, like me. Like I was. And I wasn't that anymore. There's some comfort in being imperfect and powerless, lost and with death chasing me down. But I left that mediocrity behind when Nicholas French entered my life. I took death by the hand when it offered me a place by its side. And the comfort I'd had was gone. I had to create my own all over again. It had to come from within me, not dependent on Nicholas, or Kat. I was *Shinigami*. Death god. I'd been trained and acclimated to this afterlife by the oldest death gods in Japan, the creator of vampires himself. I was given the means to a fount of strength that only martial arts could infuse me with. I didn't need anyone to make me feel valuable, powerful, myself. But I wanted Nicholas there.

I met his eyes. I saw his hurt and his fear, but more than that I saw his love and concern. It entwined with every whirl of cocoa and cream. He remained rigid, waiting for what I would do next. Because things didn't *happen* to me. Not anymore.

It was me that changed everything for a race of vampires.

The blink of thought of my hand in his, and it happened. I grinned when the speed of it made even Nicholas jump.

"You are such a wild creep," he said, combing his fingers through his hair with his spare hand.

"Oh my god, all I want to do is watch a Rob Zombie movie right this minute, now that you said that."

With speed matching my own, his fingers were in my hair, his lips hot on mine, his hips pressed against me, and we were one.

He pulled away too soon. "That," he said, "is the humanity I'm talking about."

CHAPTER 4

House of 1000 Corpses was halfway over before Nicholas and I even looked at the screen. Red sparks and puffs of my crimson mist erupted every new place I touched on him, followed by trickles of blood as we fed from each other in love bites. My body healed along with my heart each second, wholeness overcoming me like a tsunami.

Nicholas's hair was soaking wet as he brushed it off his glistening face, eyes wild, chest heaving with breath he needed only in memory. He collapsed against the arm of the sofa, head hanging back. "God, I've missed you," he said.

I crawled on top of him, our flesh sin-slick against each other. "We haven't been apart very long," I murmured, running my fangs along his jawline.

"But we have been far away."

"Too far away," I agreed. As he put his swollen lips to

mine again, I pulled back snarling, whipping my head back and forth, searching. I leaped up, throwing a stray hoodie on and pulling on my panties. "Another," I hissed, the animal in me taking over.

"Another what?" Nicholas gasped, unsettled by my sudden alertness after the sleepy urgency of our lovemaking.

"Another vampire." I'd reared back on my haunches, crouched and ready to pounce, no thought whatsoever in hindsight, only instinct.

A shadow slipped past the window, jerkily, graceless. I was at the glass in a scarlet burst that disappeared immediately so as not to give me away. My armor, my guard. I zeroed in across the distance, through the trees, everywhere my mind wanted to see at once. I felt the unknown creature. It was still now, and I saw nothing.

Wheeling around, I caught Nicholas's expression: terror. Once again, I was terrifying him. But there was no suppressing the soul of the thing I'd become, a *Shinigami* unlike anything else.

The Japanese god of creation's blood still flowed in mine, forever there like the very marrow. Beyond taming.

"Eliza, what's out there?" Nicholas asked.

"Vampire," I hissed again. I couldn't have formed a sentence if I'd tried. I was not a person then.

My head spun at the pulse of the creature on the move again. Closer. "Closer."

"Jesus, El, I think I'll take my chances with whoever's outside," Nicholas muttered. I ignored him.

The front door burst open, and a cobalt ball of material rolled inside, steaming and shrieking. *Weakened. No match for me.*

The creature unfurled, waves of heat emanating from its body as it came to standing.

"Blue!" I cried.

"Gah, Blue, for crying out loud, you made Eliza turn scary."

Even I was shocked as I came back to lucidity, when I found myself at Blue's side, sniffing her all over like a hyena. I met her eyes, this seemingly delicate flower of a woman, yet such a powerful fighter, so fiery. Also the same vampire who'd been terrified to leave the mountaintop to hunt her own fated victims, leaving it to her creator to bring the *unmei nashi* to her, worms to a fledgling bird.

I saw nothing of that complex woman here.

Her cheeks were sunken, raven hair in knots, rosebud lips curled back and trembling. Blue's dark, inviting eyes had become fathomless, *evil.* It snapped me back at once to who I was, hoping to find who she'd been.

"What's happened to you, Blue?" She gazed at me with a crushing hollowness. I was hyper-aware of the vampires I knew, even ones I'd spoken with briefly at the temple—but Blue was utterly unrecognizable to me. I hadn't even known it was her soul outside the cabin, when before she'd had the aura of exotic flowers and polished gemstones. It broke my heart to see her as such a shell of herself. Blue had been the only friend I'd made among the *Shinigami* whose vitality and warmth reminded me of Kat. This was not the same vampire. "You don't even smell like you."

"Oh. Yeah," Nicholas said, feigning boredom. "Blue's been feeding on real bastards."

Human blood leaves a residue on the *Shinigami* soul. An essentially good person gives us sunlight, love, happiness complementing the fullness of their blood. But drinking from the broken, the wretched, the cruel and vicious left us the same. Left us in darkness in every way.

Nicholas continued as Blue and I stared at each other appraisingly. "Some of her personality quirks have been really exciting," he said, dripping sarcasm. "Our little Bluebird tried to poison my coffee...what was that? Thursday?" he said mockingly to her. But Blue only stared at me, shivering occasionally. I winced at her state. She was so *lost,* not a hint of her refined fierceness apparent. I wanted to touch her, hold her to me and let my mist wrap around and heal her, but one snarl from her was enough to stop me.

"What happened to her?" I whispered. "Why would she do this to herself?"

Nicholas approached her easily, took her hand and disappeared with her down the hall, certainly to the room that had always been mine when I stayed here. So long ago. Moments ago.

"She's acting out," Nicholas said, suddenly beside me like a warm cup of hot chocolate I'd waited too long for. He plopped on the sofa where we'd been alone, before I saw what Blue had become. Nicholas rubbed a hand over his face, a dad lamenting his troubled teen. "It started with one *unmei nashi*." He saw my eyebrow rise when I heard it. When I'd become one of the *Shinigami*, I brought to light—or more accurately, took away—the illusion of having victims fated to be ours. The entire idea was created by the Master, a thrall he put the *Shinigami* under to keep them in his control. But when the Master was destroyed, his influence wasn't. Not for all of the vampires who'd been reborn and raised with him. And not for Nicholas, his most trusted and trusting. Truly, his son.

"You know *unmei nashi*—"

"A figment of our imaginations, yep," Nicholas said with a huff. "But imagination has been pretty good to me. A little imagination broke you out of cashier land."

"Don't. Start," I warned, sensing the oncoming critique of my mundane former life as gift shop lady. I smiled, the memory of all those conversations warming me despite myself. "Imagination is a powerful thing, I know." In truth, I was becoming more and more certain that imagination and the *unmei nashi* were a self-fulfilling prophecy. The *Shinigami* believed in them, and so it became real. Wasn't that the start of anything great? An idea that turns into truth?

The irony wasn't lost on me that my truth, the purpose I'd always searched for by hiding where I didn't belong, was to take the purpose from those who *did* want me. Unmei nashi *aren't real, and the man you consider a father is a fraud, and you're not just a murderer, but now you're a murderer with no higher reasoning to blame.*

I missed not knowing my purpose.

"Earth to El." Nicholas's eyebrows were raised.

"I slip away sometimes." Vampire thoughts wrapped around me, enveloping me and dragging me away.

"Don't get lost in there. Anyway, Blue had one *unmei nashi* that was really dark. She wouldn't talk about it, just spent days in her room—your room—silent. When she came out she just sucked all the light from around her. I've never seen a human leave a residue like that, turn someone so vibrant into a Dementor."

I snickered. We'd missed too many Harry Potter weekends on the Freeform Channel recently. I hoped Freeform would exist for eternity.

I sat with him on the couch, throwing my legs over his. My vampire senses felt every sinew, the blood pumping through his veins, the blister on his toe. "So after that one dark human she drank from, she went looking for more." I knew. I didn't have to ask. Dark called to dark. Someone as buoyant as Blue would fall, trusting the darkness to show her something wonderful. She'd come to New Hampshire without a plan, her excitement leaving her open to every new experience, every new feeling and side of herself. She'd been lost as soon as she'd left Japan.

"She'll be okay," Nicholas said, patting me on the leg with one strong hand.

"We don't know that she'll be okay, sweetheart." I almost said, *You didn't see Roman in Bethlem. You don't know what it looks like when the bulb burns out in a loved one.* I recognized my own arrogance right away; Nicholas had lived through the Master's death.

And he'd been there with me those long weeks after Roman killed Kat, leaving me as good as dead.

Blue was a sister to Nicholas. They were so much alike, and different in all the right ways. If their relationship hadn't been so clear and magnetic I might have worried that I stood no chance of him loving me over her. I'd thought that for a time, when her effervescence was so overwhelming that I couldn't see myself in her presence. But Nicholas did. Always. As reassuring as it was, it left a lot for me to prove. A lot that I couldn't handle.

Darkness called me even now. The stench of death was wine and roses to me, and I longed for it as much as I'd wished it away when I was alive. It was something I wouldn't share with Nicholas, not if I ever wanted him to see me as this human he insisted I was.

If only either of us knew what I was capable of, maybe I could have been saved.

CHAPTER 5

I t was all too easy to avoid talking about—anything —for days. Blue hadn't come in the house more than once in her dark state, preferring to prowl the woods with the wolves and bears. Though uneasy when we knew she was peering in at us sometimes, we felt alone in the cabin. The more Nicholas and I touched, the more my mist encircled us, the more my burns healed and the living tissue strengthened. In that short time my body became even stronger, my skin still fair, yet toughened like a lady who'd seen one too many tanning beds. I'd never entered a tanning bed in my life and if I ended up with second-hand leather skin I'd be pissed.

I'd like to say those days were blissful, but they were merely pleasurable and ignorant. Bliss comes with a certain carefree peace. We were immune to such things. We hadn't earned it and we'd never get it now. No, those stolen moments in the cabin were just that—stolen. Ignoring all the things that forced us apart. The roaring god blood inside me begging me to be alone as a vampire, to find myself like some underage hippie. The same blood that showed me Nicholas was supposed to be here with Blue, and I was supposed to be with Lynch, and that was the only way Roman would return to us. And I so needed him to return to us and allow Nicholas to feed from him. That alone would restore Nicholas to his complete health. But all these mystical elements had very little to do with the problems in our relationship. Problems that we needed space to sort through.

It didn't change how much we loved each other. It didn't stop our wanting and needing and hurting and obsessing and hoping.

We'd been curled under his old afghan for hours. So many times we'd wiled away hours on that couch, surrounded by the scents of Christmas, the blinking tree lights, the hush of the snow on the windows, the clinking of tea cups, the feel of his old sweater that I'd stolen on my arms. Some of my favorite human memories.

Then Kat died.

"You got up," Nicholas said with surprise. "Get me a cookie?"

I shook off the memory of Kat, the hole that she'd left. "I'll never not love that you still want cookies," I said.

"Yeah, got that sleepy craving for something sweet, so it's cookies or I eat that pharmacist downtown."

My laugh came out as a sudden bark, one of those that hurts a little because it's such a surprise. "Oh my god, how can you say things like that?" But I was grinning.

"If I can't say it to you, who can I say it to?"

I relished the familiar feel of my feet on the wood floor, the creaks and groans. Nicholas had left as much of the knots and roughness of the bark as he could when he built this cabin. He said he wanted to keep nature on his side and leave as much death as he could at the door. Through a battered, red swinging door, the wood gave way to black and white kitchen tile in need of a polish it would never get. As I unwrapped the cellophane on the cookie plate—chocolate chip—and glanced at the coffee pot. It was unnatural not to have coffee, to pick up that pot every time I was in this room with its wood stove and the memory of the black stray cat curled up in front of it.

"Where are you now, kitty?" I whispered. We'd left for Japan in such a fog, wrapped in ourselves, we'd barely given him a second thought. I twisted my face in disgust at myself, that I hadn't even wondered about him until this moment.

I returned to Nicholas with three cookies in one hand and one in my mouth, and handed him two.

"I didn't say *you* could have one of my cookies," he grumbled.

"Two, and then one more in the kitchen."

"Which means you ate two more in the kitchen in Eliza Cookie Terms. Why that face?" he asked, wagging a finger.

"Where's the cat?" I mumbled.

"I don't know." He sighed. "I was hoping he'd be here when we came back. Ships passing in the night, we were."

"No. He loved it here. He loved you guys." The trouble it gave me that the cat was alone again, abandoned after he'd found security and happiness, made me nauseous. "If we can't keep one damn cat safe, what hope do we have for eternity as do-gooder murderers?"

Nicholas rolled his eyes. "The cat was never this existential whenever we talked."

"I'm not kidding," I said, elbowing him. "We have to find him. He picked this house, you and Roman"—Nicholas winced—"for a reason. We owe it to him to take care of him."

"Okay, let's find him," he shrugged.

"You said you tried."

"I did, but you didn't. You have super aura-ra-ra powers, so use them."

In the heat of a late night or early morning in front of the fire, Nicholas asked me if I'd found any less torturous vampire abilities since we left the temple in Japan. I tried to tell him about the sensing of auras, knowing no other way to describe it. I hadn't noticed it at the temple; being enslaved by an all-powerful ancient vampire and subjected to visions of thousands of humans and inhumans alike hadn't left me much room for dawn-of-the-dead exploration. But once I left that place and knew I wasn't going back, I saw colors around everyone. Not just crayon box colors, but hues from other planets, from times more ancient than the Master himself. Colors of tastes and memories, and heat and light. The hues were smoky as campfire around some, as clear as stained glass windows over others. They tasted like dungeons and carnivals and the first breath of life and violence that throbbed like a bruise. In my growing ability to control the visions that had assaulted me mercilessly, I gained this glancing sense of people and I reveled in it.

"You think I can find the cat this way?" I hadn't noticed the aura around animals yet.

"Yeah, I do." The way he looked at me, as if I were some storybook character with a crystal ball sent my heart fluttering. "I think you've found ways to do the most incredible things, stuff I never even dreamed of, and finding a *cat*," he grinned, "is one more thing we can add to your afterlife resume."

"I guess I should get to it, then," I said, smiling.

"Right now?"

"Sure. Why not?" I walked, human walking, to my favorite window, the one where Nicholas had put his green sweater around me so long ago.

I tried to breathe through ignoring everything

around me, but it was sorta tough when I didn't actually need to breathe. Ended up concentrating more on that than focusing on the cat. When I stopped thinking of breathing or the cat, everything else piled on top of me —the memories. The things I wanted away from.

"I can't do this. I'm focusing on the wrong things."

"Then stop focusing on the wrong things," Nicholas said with a shrug.

"Why are you this way, who do you think you are?" I said, shaking my head slowly, forever unable to believe that he was always so right when he was pompous like this.

He watched me expectantly, a scientist waiting for his beaker to bubble.

I concentrated on shoving the errant thoughts and memories away, clouds of red crowding them out until there was only the crimson sea and my own non-breaths.

And I noticed. I noticed the aura of the spring-fresh trees, as old as time and promising of futures. Tiny, flitting auras of gold and berries that were the humming-birds around the feeders Nicholas had carefully hung. When I looked to the soft ground, I saw beats of light where life grew underneath in worms and moles and grass seeds. I saw the very air's brightness as more than sunlight now, but something else entirely; what Heaven really must look like.

I could always see, and I could recently see better

than any other vampire, but now I let myself notice. Nicholas had given it to me.

"He's there," I murmured, awed by the ease in which I found my mark. Instead of taking in the glory of the air surrounding every good and evil and gray matter, I gave it mine. I let my own aura, venom red and mourning gray and forest green and buttermilk yellow; warm, vanilla-scented and tinged with spiders and sharp crow claws. I pushed it forth like a peace offering, a request, and the world gave back to me what I asked for.

"You found him?" Nicholas asked, flickering to my side like a firefly. "Already?"

"You were the one who said I could.'"

"Yeah, but come on. You're so *weird*," he said under his breath, searching the woods outside through the window, then shaking his head when he saw nothing.

The cat ran across the yard, fast like he was chased by something terrible, right to Nicholas at the window. Nicholas put his fingers to the glass in disbelief and the cat meowed at him.

An imperceptible movement, so fast it left Nicholas's mumbles about weird cats and women trailing behind him, and he was outside, lifting the cat in his arms and back in the door before a human could have seen. But I saw. I saw his lips nuzzle the cat's fur, the twinge of his smile as he held the cold kitty close, the sigh he let out at its softness.

I felt like the Grinch; my heart grew three sizes that day. I loved this man so much.

And just as fast that feeling soured in my stomach and a heat replaced it, a vengeful heat that told me I had no right to such innocent pleasure. "*Shayla,*" my insides hissed at me. I gasped at the foreign name, only barely recalling that it was the name of Lynch's last victim.

Now her blood ran in mine, in its briefest traces. It wasn't her residue I felt, not some endearing little habit of hers that joined my own as a last tribute to her life. No, this was a second-hand blending of that innocent girl's life and Lynch's perversion of it, the vitality he stole for his own. Together, they created a torturous combination of base elements, a simultaneous Heaven and Hell where nothing made sense except ripping things apart. An implosion that made an explosion. A *hurt.*

"What's with you?" Nicholas said, shaking me back to earth.

"Um, I have to feed, I guess."

"You guess?" The fear of me had returned to his eyes, his very being, and he clutched the cat closer like a little boy would, for security. I hardened more.

"Yeah. I guess. I have a feeling."

His jaw tightened, the little muscle jumping near his ear. "You scare me," he said, not in the cutesy way he would say before I was a vampire, or when I showed some crazy ability as a newborn. There was no hint of love in this statement ; it was a subconscious release of anger on his part. He was angry that I'd become something so frightful. Not a trace of humanity left in me.

He said he would love me no matter what I turned into. That we were the same no matter what.

I stifled a growl.

"I'm going," I said. And I brushed out the door, leaving him behind with his cat.

Darkness became part of me as I bolted through the wet streets of New York City, searching for the depth of black blood that wanted me.

Nicholas was a distant memory as I raced, nothing more than a wind to the throng of people around me. None of them were horrid enough, angry enough, hateful enough, inhuman enough. Not for what I needed.

I needed to take in a monster and feed it to my own.

An alley. Wasn't it always an alley, where the dredges lurked? I stopped so fast that wind hit the back of my head like a brick, but it didn't faze me. The people closest to me on the street stumbled out of my way, one falling to her knees. I didn't help her. Nobody did, actually.

Panting with starved anticipation, I turned sharply, air slicing at my sides, and rushed down the alley, the dripping of the gutters pounding in my ears like thunder—or was that my own blood?

Thinking of blood, Izanagi's bubbled up in me. *He would be so ashamed,* I thought. And pushed the thought away.

I found a feral thing crouched behind a dumpster, shaking with cold. I cocked my head at it, trying to read its mind, its heart.

"What are you?" the woman croaked.

"Certain death. You?"

"Nobody. I'm nobody."

"You don't feel like nobody." Surging anger, screeching banshee blood, a need to hurt things that nestled in deep, so deeply that it was comfortable to her, protective. This was the animal I wanted. One that had been hurt and hurt others so much that she owned it and liked it. It was all she knew.

"You want to kill me?" she said, rasping. She scrambled to her feet. "Think you'll be doing someone a favor?"

"Lady, I don't care about doing favors. Do I seem like the type to do favors right now? Stalking you in an alley?"

The woman smirked. "You don't know what I was doing before you got here. Seems you might change your mind about what a favor is."

I killed her fast, not wanting to savor it in my mind, no matter what my blood screamed for. And if I was being honest, it was what my *soul* screamed for—to torture her. Ruin her more than she'd ruined herself. Take her black heart and keep it, darken it, make it mine. I was so *needful* of evil that I turned my own stomach, but the power of that need was too great to resist, even if I tried.

I was so tired, always, of trying. Always trying to be something more, something else, something better, something different… It was exhausting. And this bleak nothingness, where dark would hold me close with slippery bat wings in my heart, it felt so wrong it was right.

A lone crow cried out at me from the top of the dumpster as I dropped the woman's skinny body to the ground. I didn't feel bad. Not for her. I reached up for the crow, hoping he wouldn't try to pluck something from the body I'd left, but he backed away from me. Crows never backed away from me.

"Maybe I should start looking for bats," I said. And left the city.

Passed out cold on the sofa that had once been white, Lynch looked like a drunk who'd finally had enough to drink.

"God, you're a mess," I said, immediately huffing at the realization that I was covered in blood, still recovering, at least emotionally, from the burns I'd received on Nicholas's lawn. "If Nicholas could see us now."

I fell beside him on the couch, eyeing him as he

didn't move, thinking for a second that maybe he had found a way to end his immortal life. I nudged him with my boot. Twice. Finally, he snorted and picked his head up, a line of drool streaking his chin. Not much classier than my own streaks of blood.

"Eliza," he croaked, and turned away.

"Yeah, I came back," I said. "Happy to see me as always, huh?"

"Why do you keep coming here?" he spat.

My gut wanted me to throw some snappy comeback at him, but that wasn't what the moment called for. He was more than lost, more than in pain. He was a dead thing without direction. Chris Lynch was a mass murderer, a monster that could undo generations, and he was so *sad*. This Lynch was far more dangerous than the charmer with composure, grace, and egotism on his side. This beast was pitiful and had nothing to lose.

"Why?" he said again, voice cracking, head falling to the side.

I reached out to him. He flinched at first, but then he gave up and let me take his hand. A tear splashed onto my index finger—a human tear. Not tinged with red like all the vampire tears I'd seen and felt. A real tear. My eyes narrowed as my head snapped up to look at him. "How are these real tears?" I said, more to myself than Lynch.

"Residue," he whispered.

I zeroed in, looked harder. His aura was empty. Dried up.

He'd been feeding, but took no life from it. Even his dead heart felt shriveled to my *Shinigami* senses.

I didn't register when my body curled up on the sofa with my legs tucked under me, and faced him with rapt attention. Something was *here*, something I needed to understand. The answers pushed toward me through his skin, drifting from his pores like ash from a volcano. "Why aren't you more…?" I waved my hands around in a stupid gesture that in my head meant "animated." "It's like you haven't fed at all."

He hung his head, without answers. Without life. "Why are you here?" he said a third time, his lips twitching into a frown to hold the tears back.

"I know you don't want me here," I murmured, trying not to break him worse than he was, "but your blood called out to me, and I listened. I can see fates when I drink—"

"The Master must have loved that," Lynch muttered.

I blinked fast, making Lynch a moving picture behind my lashes in my shock. That Lynch would think of such a thing, that he would know the Master would exploit me as he had. I hadn't thought Lynch considered anyone but himself…and Kat. "Yeah, he thought it was a great old time to mess with me, mad scientist himself all over my head."

"Terrible wording, Eliza."

I laughed, wild and loud. He smirked, but the tears still fell, every one of them crystal clear and without a tinge of death in them.

No death in them.

"Holy hell. You're not killing them."

Lynch didn't move, didn't react at all.

"What are you doing with these girls, Lynch? Lynch!" I smacked his arm in a way that as a human wouldn't have done a second's worth of damage, but Lynch fell over on the couch and scrambled away, afraid of what more I could do. The fear filled me with happiness that I had to shove into a hole in my gut.

He lifted his head, looking me in the eye finally with his own flat black ones. I straightened my back at the hint of his old self, the ruthless monster who did nothing without himself in mind. I knew the answer before he said it.

"I'm making vampires."

My knees buckled with the vision that hit me—a slideshow, really—of two, then four, then six girls, all the same as his victims ever were. Young, bubbly, sweet. Kind. The usual revulsion rolled through me, and then it stopped. Right before the young ladies' hearts would stop, right before that climactic horror, the senseless murder, the disgust disappeared. Because these girls didn't die. I felt it as they did: the last beat of my heart. The hitch in my throat with the final breath. The darkness when I wondered why I was dying. So different than when I became *Shinigami;* these girls were sure death was theirs. The apologies they would never utter, the kisses they'd never give. The things they'd never learn. The dreams that turned to dust. In that split second, they were forced to accept it.

And then in the next unexpected breath, it was all in their grasp again.

Jealousy coiled in my gut like a viper, but it had no one to strike at.

These girls got a chance to not only see what they'd missed, but the chance to correct it, and to try harder. My chances looked much, much different. My chances all hinged on that moment of giving up. I hadn't had any chance until I'd died.

Like a gentle arm, the red mist embraced me on the inside, pulling me back. The time for me to lament my mortal life was over, and certainly not the problem right now. It wasn't even *one* of the problems right now.

"You turned them, and then you just let them go?" I asked, incredulous. For all I could see, I couldn't see *why* Lynch would do such a thing. "What's in it for you?"

He didn't hesitate to say, "I was lonely."

"But you left them!"

"I was lonely and I was afraid. I'm still the Abomination, am I not? I don't owe you reasons, Ellie."

His resignation turned my stomach more than the senseless killing—or not killing—of all these women. His acceptance of the monster he was…

Why can't I accept it that way? Why do I always have to try?

"No. You don't owe me reasons why you're creating vampires and leaving them to kill half the world, or die in the sun, or whatever. But you have to fix it. I can help you." *What was I saying?* As if it wasn't bad enough that I was there, spending time with this shark in shark's clothing, whether it was long past washing or not, I had this sudden compulsion to offer him my help? The Eliza who despised him before she became a vampire, before Kat was killed, wouldn't recognize me at all.

Maybe that wasn't a terrible thing.

But it was a terrible thing that I'd been cursed—or cursed myself—to connect with goddamn Lynch, of all people, when the love of my afterlife was a blink away from me with vampire speed. So much was separating us, and also nothing. And yet when I was with Nicholas, I couldn't get to the bottom of the divide between us. One thing I didn't need to question, though, was that I loved Ossipee, and all of New Hampshire. I would not let fresh vamps ravage it, and I needed to be with Lynch to stop him turning every pretty girl immortal.

"Look," Lynch was saying, inching toward me, a remarkably clear look in his soulless eyes, dirty palms turned up in supplication. "The truth is, I don't know why I'm turning them into vampires. I haven't wanted to admit it—I don't know about that either—but I've had this urge to do it, a new urge. Not like my urges before."

"Yeah, you don't need to go into detail, I've seen the remnants of your *urges.*"

"Of course. It isn't as if I've had a sudden change of morality and I can't bring myself to kill any longer. That kind of pathetic salvation is far beyond me. But a new feeling has overcome me to give them blood, to bring them across and make them immortal. As if it's my—"

"—purpose." My dead blood chilled at the thought of fate actually having a hand in the Abomination's existence. The Master made it all up: the *unmei nashi,* the alternative fates of the victims, the wasting away of the *Shinigami* who didn't feed on their intended, all of it. And yet, there was an undeniable force at work in the *Shinigami* world, and it was impossible to ignore. That fate felt very real.

I still found it hard to believe that Lynch had any greater purpose in his miserable life, and I regretted having anything to do with it. But it also felt like taking a correct turn in one of those newspaper mazes in the *Ossipee Gazette.* Like I was getting closer to the end. Completion. Everything worked together so smoothly, I wanted to race to the next turn.

If only I'd known then what was around that next corner. What terrors and atrocities I'd commit in my foolish plan to "help."

"You can sleep in here," Lynch said, pushing open a white (of course) door on the second floor.

"Your room is right over there," I snapped, not really knowing why I was snappy. I wasn't worried he would try something on me, or that he'd try to kill me in the night. It was just being *close* to him like that, able to hear his dead heart if I tried, saying "good morning" to him as we both emerged from our rooms. "This isn't a frat house, we aren't roomies. I don't want to be here."

"So why are you?"

"You keep asking me that…" I grumbled, looking away, rolling my eyes.

"And you tell me you have to be."

"Right."

He was quiet after that. I think he was waiting me to say something else, that I wanted to be there because I just *wanted to be there*. And I felt terrible that he had no one who cared to spend time with him. That for all his success, at least before Kat, and his charm and good looks and intelligence, he was alone forever. Truly alone. Even Roman hadn't wanted to be anywhere near him, and he was the one who made Lynch a vampire.

Now Roman didn't want to be near any of us. But that had to change.

"Okay," I said. "I'll stay here." *Did I imagine his shoulders relaxing?* "You can keep the east wing empty still. Unless you've got a dungeon over there or something."

Lynch did a thing then that I didn't know he was capable of. He let out a howl of nervous laughter, doubling over with shock. When he stood up his eyebrows were near his hairline, I swear, eyes wide and glistening, mouth open to show his still gleaming white shark teeth. What struck me most was the way his hair fell softly across his forehead, brushing his brows, messy like some eighties cult classic movie star. This Lynch was vulnerable and...*endearing.* I'd never seen him so human. I didn't think it was possible.

"You're smiling," he said, lips upturned.

"Don't get used to it, huh?"

"Good night, Ellie."

"Eliza, please."

His eyes darkened. He knew that only Kat called me Ellie once I'd become part of the vampire clique.

"Of course. Good night. Eliza." He smiled at me humbly, lips soft but tight, eyes dark but not quite as cruel or hurt as they'd been even a few minutes before.

"Good night," I whispered to the air. He was already gone.

~

Vampires don't need to sleep, not often. But we do get weary. Mental and emotional exhaustion follows us into immortality. Awesome, right?

So it was with great pleasure that I fell into the king-size bed with fresh sheets scented with lavender. Though things had fallen into disrepair, just like the master of the house had, the mansion was still brand spanking new; must and dust hadn't taken the place over yet. This was no ancient, abandoned castle—it was a new place without life to it. Squatted in. Soulless before, when I called it the Great White Mansion, and now it was just *vacant*. So different from Nicholas's cottage, where the fire always crackled, the teapot was always whistling, laughter was always heard. Those early days where I'd stayed in the spare room that had become mine, when Roman and Nicholas were the closest of brothers, were some of my favorite days in my life.

It never did feel quite right without Roman there.

Rolling over in the massive bed, the sheets swishing against my body, I tried to fall asleep but thoughts of Roman kept me awake. Not of Nicholas. But of Roman.

Why was he *so* adamant about keeping away from us? I wouldn't go so far as to say all was forgiven, but Nicholas, me, we'd done things we weren't proud of, too. And we loved each other still. We loved Roman still. Fate had handed us all a rotten deal, cornering us all and forcing us into solitude in more ways than we could count: Roman, his wife and child ripped away from him. Nicholas, adored and proud, but restless and ashamed underneath. Me, with death by my side—my parents, my grandmother, never even able to keep a damn dog. But when Kat became Nicholas's *unmei nashi*, fate had destroyed us all. And what fate hadn't done, Roman finished.

Death gods.

The old stories of the tortured relationships of Greek mythology sprang to mind. The *Shinigami* weren't so different. Gods indeed.

I heard the moaning first. No question who it was, of course. A short scream followed, like Jack Nicholson in *The Shining* when he has the nightmare about killing Wendy and Danny.

"Shit."

I threw off the covers like a human would, the blankets snapping. To go or not to go? If I went to Lynch—who was still making strangled screaming sounds—everything would change. We would be friends. No other way around it. A person didn't wake another person from a nightmare unless they cared. What would he do when he woke up? Would we "talk it out" and have a nice midnight—or whatever time it was—chat?

He's not my friend.

Then why was I down the hall at his door, hand raised to knock and knowing I should just go inside when I heard the sob?

"Shit," I said again, and turned the knob.

I couldn't go to him, I couldn't. "Lynch," I said loudly. He continued to thrash sporadically, kicking off blankets, revealing his nearly-nude body. Shit, again. "Lynch!" I called to him over and over, louder all the time, but finally I faced that I had to go and touch him.

His skin was slicked with icy sweat, his face ghost-white with a sickly shine. "Lynch." I shook him hard, but his own movements were more forceful, I was just white noise. *Buck up, you frigging baby.*

I gripped him by both shoulders, leaning over him

like he was an *unmei nashi* and I was saving him from his own worst ending. "Lynch, wake up."

"Dead," he said.

"Lynch—"

"Dead. Dead." He said it over and over, his jaw so tight I could hear his teeth rubbing together. The tendons in his neck looked ready to snap, I could *feel* them straining with my fresh senses, see the blood pulsing through bulging veins, not his own. I put my fingers to them without thinking, drawn to the way they stood at attention and reached out to me.

Lynch's hand shot up and grabbed my wrist with more force than I could ever have, even at my strongest, squeezing until I cried out. That sound woke him immediately—a woman's cry of anguish. Naturally. The beast.

"What are you doing?" he spat, and pushed my body away with just the force behind that one hand, sending me stumbling back with a totally human lack of grace, like the old me in a pair of heels.

"You…you were having a nightmare," I said, rubbing my wrist, rattled and afraid. God, I hated being afraid, but he took me by surprise, and being a vampire didn't change me enough to erase my fear of Lynch completely. But I had forgotten it for a while.

Never again.

"I don't remember it," he said angrily.

"Well shit, *sorry*. Next time I'll let you freak out all night. I should have slept on the third floor like I wanted…"

"No," he said, his entire demeanor changing. A trick. He wanted me near him for a reason, he had to.

"Why not? You know, I don't have to stay here—"

"And go where, Eliza? Face it, you have nowhere better to be."

He was right. Being with Nicholas and Blue felt wrong. Thinking of their names together wrenched me, even if I knew there was nothing between them. That it wasn't just always "Nicholas and Eliza" boiled me. And I had nowhere better to be, just like Lynch said. No one else who wanted me around, not even the death god who'd followed me my whole life. They were all gone, and I was alone.

As usual, I hadn't noticed the red mist that erupted in protective billows around me, slinking its way around my limbs and purring to me with a sound that only I could hear. It lifted me just off the ground, as though telling me it could take me far away from all of it. But as comforting to me as the mist was, it was a thing of nightmares to everyone else, and Lynch was no exception. I think I was worse than the nightmare I'd woken him from. He looked at me with a freshly sweat-slicked brow, more terrified than he'd been in his dream state, I felt his stomach clenching inside him.

"I won't hurt you," I said, my voice tinny through the crimson haze. Lynch didn't believe me. Why would a man so thirsty to hurt others believe such a thing?

"You couldn't," he said. And I think that hurt worse than anything else I'd heard from him. I lowered myself, the mist dissipating, replaced with a sadness I couldn't explain.

"You don't have to be this thing you are," I said. "You don't have to give in. You can change."

"I can't. And I have no reason to." When I didn't reply —because what could I say to that, when I knew all too well what it felt like to have nothing better on the horizon—he continued. "Aren't you going to tell me that it's the right thing to do, to stop killing for fun?"

"That's the reason you should fight the urge, right there. Because you're looking for someone to tell you to."

I'd found my way to sitting on the end of his bed somehow, and cursed that vampires could move so fast. I hadn't even thought about it and done it. But when I realized I had, I didn't move away. I stayed with the same creature who'd horrified me a moment before, who I'd despised from the minute we met, and who was speaking of murdering like it was simple and normal. I suppose for him, it was.

And hadn't I felt that way myself after drinking his blood? Before I'd killed that woman in New York City? Hadn't I craved to do it again?

"You're thinking about blood right now. Aren't you?" Lynch asked.

"How did you know?"

"We share the blood, remember?"

"But I can't feel…"

"Can't you?"

I did feel it before, Lynch's ache to cause terror. But what did it *mean?* I couldn't believe I was brought to Lynch's doorstep so we could bond over murder. I didn't want to share blood with him, not his own, not his victims'.

"I did feel a…rush…earlier. More savage than I ever was. I think." *Why was I sharing this with him?*

"It's not so awful, is it? You see why I go back for more?"

I shook my head wildly, bubbles of red behind my eyes. "No, this isn't the lust for blood that drives you, it's straight vicious, cruel… You kill because you hate them, you want to feel their fear. You don't think anyone can stop you. You were this way in life, and you're this way as a vampire. Now you just have the tools," I said, showing my fangs.

"Then why was I made a vampire, huh?" He rose to his feet in a heartbeat, his mood shifting from sullen and sad to brilliantly angry in the same amount of time. "We all had a purpose for being made, right?"

"Yeah, about that…"

"I know what you think. I know about the Master, and the *unmei nashi*, Nicholas told me. I never believed any of it. I don't know why the *Shinigami* are all woven together. Some higher power decided we all need to be miserable and inbred, but I do know that someone, somewhere had a plan for me." His lips were taut, eyes pleading but determined. "I was meant to be a vampire, too many events have worked together to make me this way for it to be chance. So what reason do I have to exist, Eliza? Do you know?"

In that moment, I saw that Lynch wasn't so different from me. We were both drifting, and being prepared our entire lives for a fate that had been withheld from us. I was working through my own destiny, but Lynch was just stuck. Stuck with less of a reason to live than ever, now that Kat was gone.

"I don't know, Lynch. I don't. But I know one way to find out."

With a *crack* of air, I was at his throat, pushing him back on the bed, and sinking my teeth in hard.

Drinking blood both invigorates and exhausts me, turns me inside out in such a way that I don't know if I've done something right or torn myself asunder. But drinking Lynch's blood wasn't confusing like that. His blood was a straight arrow, pointing at nothing at all. Nothing. It wasn't rich blood, metallic, like all of it. Not full of history and promise like every other. It was empty. He was empty. No potential, only nothing.

I wanted nothing. But nothing was not what I was there for.

"Aaaargghh!" I screamed, tearing at my hair and elevating off of Lynch like a ghost. I squeezed my eyes shut, hoping to see something I'd missed before, but found only a thirst for more blood. I felt Lynch's constant hunger to have more, without any reason or expectation. It was pure. So blank that it felt like falling into white cotton sheets and blocking out the world. No visions warring, no wrongs to right. I was jealous that this was a feeling he knew well.

"Why do you do this?" he cried out, hand clutching his neck, scrambling backwards across the bed, against the headboard, eyes wild and afraid. "Why did you come here to do this, is this my punishment?"

My eyes shot open, my hands still tangled in my hair. "What? You think this is *your* punishment?" I sneered, disgust rippling under my voice. "Being here with you, needing to drink your blood, and *liking* it, memories of Kat all over the place, and never knowing why? *Your* punishment... You're the most selfish monster I can think of," I hissed, still afloat, now wrapped in crimson clouds. "What the hell am I being punished for?" I cried out to no one. "Why does nothing come easy to me?"

I sank back down until my feet touched the floor. Solid ground. No white bedding to catch me, only my own two feet.

Lynch looked like he'd never stop sweating. I'd come in to relieve him of a nightmare and brought him a reality far worse, though I couldn't say if it was worse than the one he'd always lived. I walked away, with nothing more to say. Once again, his blood hadn't revealed any mysteries to me, and I was beginning to believe my own truth that fate and *unmei nashi* and everything our culture had been built upon was nonexistent.

But like everyone else, every other *Shinigami*, and

probably every human, I was too afraid of what believing in nothing would leave me with.

"You don't have to stay here," Lynch said faintly behind me, in a voice dripping with sorrow.

I kept walking, my feet touching the earth, my head under those imaginary white blankets.

CHAPTER 7

For days we avoided each other, but I couldn't bring myself to leave. Not for good. When I left to feed, I returned to that broken castle, a queen of horrors just like its master.

I'd grown into a beast with Lynch's blood in my veins, and the feeling of something more, some*one* more lingered behind it, like a shadow whispering secrets. And yet, I still knew that extra presence was not what I was looking for. God, I was so tired of searching. It was hardly fair that my prophetic ability to see alternative fates led me to the vision but then wouldn't give it to me. And in the meantime, I was just stuck. Just here.

I approached the Great White Mansion in the sunlight, the rays puncturing my skin, but warming me inside. My last victim—she'd been a good person. All the gloom and doom in me this time was my own, and the residue she'd left made the sun dance delightfully on my skin, no matter how damaging it was to me. Her residue also left an odd need to climb trees. I'd never climbed a tree in my life, and this girl hadn't looked a whole lot like a lumberjack, with her wisp of a body and heels. But this was a memory from her childhood, slipping into me like shots from a bottle, of her climbing the trees in the woods behind the school for some peace and quiet—school was so *loud* to her. The trees gave her cover from the abrasiveness of her life.

Passing Lynch's house to the backyard, past the porch where Nicholas had once come to realize that it was his "fate" to murder Kat, I stopped dead short.

The once-manicured lawn was overgrown, a forest of weeds and storm-strewn branches, long grass and dead patches. Abandoned.

Except for one very new addition.

The tree house—it could be described as nothing less —had been built so recently the lumber still had the earthy, rich and fresh scent. *Where did this come from?*

A handmade hidey-hole of a cabin, carefully crafted of seaside green, robin's egg blue, cherry blossom pink (*just like Japan!*), and nuclear family white. It abounded with rivets and reclaimed wood, barn door latches, weathered wrought iron, and was surrounded with pink roses. As if they'd been planted there for years. Smoke billowed from the smallest chimney I'd ever seen. Both beachy cottage and forest den. As if the place had been made…

For me.

The whitewashed stairs creaked in all the right places up to the wide-open barn doors. Holding my breath, I peeked inside, knowing that this had been made for me, thrilled and afraid at the same time.

It had been a long time since I'd been nervously excited about something not blood-related.

But nothing comes without some expectation.

The woodland nook sang of springtime—just what I needed after the world's longest winter. My stomach churned with the mere thought of the winter's impossible number of events. I banished the memories and took in the here and now.

A daybed beckoned, loaded with blankets to help with the shady chill from the open windows. If I wasn't cozy enough, I could plant myself on the rug in front of the tiny fireplace with a book. Empty bookshelves lined the walls, waiting for me to fill them. The fluttering in my stomach was reminiscent of all the times I went book shopping when Nicholas and I first met. I'd have read just about any piece of crap to have an excuse to go back to that simple time. But the thing that put the biggest smile on my face was the coffee pot on the windowsill, empty though it was. Tucked into a private spot, but still central.

Just like at Birch Tree Books. My place.

Our place. It became Nicholas's too.

He made this for me, even if he doesn't agree with why I'm not at the cabin.

My entire body relaxed, calm as I entered, just as gray clouds rolled overhead. A cool spring rain came in through the open windows, sudden and sweet, and I held out my fingers to feel it. Sinking onto the floor by the fireplace, I thought without guilt that Kieran could have lit it in a heartbeat for me. I smiled. I didn't stop smiling when Lynch came close, through the woods behind the house, smelling not of blood, but of flowers. He appeared at my doorstep, brow furrowed, tentative.

"I know, it showed up out of nowhere, right?" I said, grinning. Not that I should have been surprised—Nicholas had built his own cabin out of the New Hampshire trees by himself basically overnight. "He's—something," I said. Sensing Lynch's discomfort, I offered, "Come in."

He entered hesitantly, as if expecting the floor to fall out from beneath him. Even more hesitantly, he sat on the floor a foot away from me, and that was when the smell of the peonies wafted across.

Peonies. Kat.

"You like it?" Lynch asked, eyes darting around.

"What's not to like?" I asked. "It'd only be better if the coffee was already made." I elbowed him playfully, more relaxed than I'd been in forever. "Seriously, go find a coffee girl to drink so you can get barista skills for a few days."

He actually *blushed*. A hot pink tinge that didn't come from his own blood—but blood I wanted nonetheless in that instance, with the violence of springtime bursting to life.

Whipping rain gusted into the windows more fiercely, the *shush*ing of the leaves whispering across each other became a slick slapping. Tiny creature feet pounded in my ears as they scuttled into knots and burrows, a cacophony of life and destruction, and I sank my teeth into Lynch's wrist before he ever knew what happened.

Every sensation disappeared except the ocean waves of hot blood flowing through him and into me, spilling over my lips. I felt Lynch's other hand on the back of my head, still as hesitant as when he'd entered the cottage, despite the intimacy with which I'd stolen his immortal life force. Groaning, I took a long pull from his arm, the rush making me dizzy, the world turning blacker than black...

Then it snapped back, hard, fast, with a woman's scream approaching me like a train.

I don't know this woman, I thought, my anger blossoming like a bruise.

Her face approached mine, and the clarity didn't help at all. Straggly blonde hair, thinning even. Dull eyes the color of a murky lake, thin lips. Blood trickled neatly from her throat. So, another one of Lynch's playthings. My compassion dwindled more and more for these victims with every vision, seeing only another one, and another, and never what I came to see, never the things I *needed to see.*

A cry curdled from Lynch's throat—I tasted it, the flavor of raw hamburger. I'd bitten him again, a new spot inside his arm, and it was sloppy. I saw myself tear the skin, shake my head side to side to sink both fangs into the one wound—I saw it in memory, having done it so quickly, the time had passed.

And I was screaming into his skin.

Blood bubbled around my lips. Lynch shook, trying to free himself. I held down one thigh, my other hand pushing down a shoulder as I bent over him and drank in gulps so enormous they hurt my throat going down. Or maybe it was the muffled screams coming up. But it was what I needed. It worked.

Roman, finally. Roman.

And Kat. No, I didn't need to see this, I'd seen this already, watched him murder her. What pointless—

Then it was another time, another moment that I hadn't known. Roman and Kat together, without me or Nicholas nearby, and she's telling him something. What is she telling him? Why is his face twisted, but happy, and she's smiling but—

"Get off me!" Lynch screamed, finally wrestling free of me in my confusion. His shirt was drenched in blood, more in his hair, on his pants.

"I'm sorry," I whispered. But he just stared at me in horror and shock. "I didn't mean to—"

He rushed out, away from that cottage which had been so lovingly built, and was now just another place to kill things. I wanted to go after him. I felt bad, I really did… But how many people had he inflicted pain like that upon and never given it a second thought? Doing it for attention from a Master who wanted nothing to do with him.

But the fear on his face.

It had been pretty close to the fear on that roughed-up blonde woman I'd seen before Roman appeared in my vision. Another victim I had no connection to, just leftover blood from Lynch's last kill. Another puzzle that I was getting sick of trying to solve. But the one common piece, the one that kept getting lost and turning up where I least expected before disappearing again, *hiding* again…

Roman.

ethlem was…unpleasant…the first time I'd come. For my very first feeding. The smells, the bland and filthy colors, the howls and whimpers came at me like bullets, but I could see beyond them for the gleaming, screaming purpose of my visit.

My *unmei nashi*, Clara Borden.

As violent as her end was, the connection we felt, the residue of her life that ran through my dead veins after I'd killed her burst with a romantically sinister intimacy that I couldn't deny. We shared destinies.

I looked back on that first time *fondly*.

Jesus, I'm grotesque. I long for that closeness again. I'm disgusting.

Worse, after spending such little time with Lynch, I was *less* disgusted by it than I should have been, than I would have been a month ago. I understood the need more, like I'd been looking for an excuse to justify the serial killer mentality. This atrocious, crumbling, shit-soaked house of horrors was where I deserved to be.

This time, without an *unmei nashi* to guide me, my vampire eyes showed me too much. With my new strength stolen from so many victims, from Lynch, from Izanagi... Now it was an overlapping mix of timelines, one more degrading than the next, the worst of each of the hospital's eras, all assaulting me at once. Inmates in a hollow, flickering blood-red haze, brought to me by my own traitorous mist shared space with solid flesh and blood patients, ambling through and across one another never aware of the other. Ghosts and man-made ghouls, decaying together. So alone. Looking closer, I not only saw the physical anguish of the sores and wounds, but the actual medications, warring inside them, dehydrating them, crushing and weakening them, tearing their organs apart. Their thirst was my thirst, their desperation was mine to get to the wooden cistern in the overgrown courtyard, demonic watering hole that it was. A single, glorified bucket surrounded by dirt. The "lunatics" crowded around it, kicking up dust as they pushed their way in with hoarse moans. The ones who'd already overfilled as much as they could huddled mere feet away. A handful of them, unable to hold the pitiful amount of dirty water they'd gulped down too fast. Some retched, but most fell to their knees with filth trailing down their legs—the drugs I could so plainly see flushed every ounce of moisture or sustenance from their bodies. The complete *dryness* coupled with the stench of bile and shit overwhelmed me.

Shaking my head too fast, the world blurring around me, my red mist shot up from my feet to protect me, taking me away from the overload of this place. But it couldn't take away the knowledge that Roman brought himself here deliberately. This was where he felt he belonged. The man Nicholas called his brother.

And like it had with the cat, the mist reached out, extended fine tentacles all over Bethlem, quicker than even my eyes could follow.

Then *Slam! Slam! Slam!* The tentacles coiled back into me from every direction, punching me all over my body until I gasped, buckling, flinching. I coughed, struggling for air I didn't breathe, and with a great breath, the mist wound into my throat and gave me what I really needed.

"Roman."

Brushing past dumbstruck and whimpering patients and nurses, I fled to him.

He sat at the bedside of a man who spoke to him excitedly, bony hands gesturing, laughing. And Roman laughed, too.

He *laughed*.

My breath caught as I watched, having just motioned

myself through the doorway, to see Roman enjoying something, some*one*. He took the man's hand as it waved through the air, and squeezed, smiling with all the charm he ever had. Our Roman. Nicholas's Roman, who exuded goodness, community, thoughtfulness, sincerity. He was always better than the rest of us.

Even when he killed Kat. He did it with the saddest song in his heart.

Roman rose from his seat, bidding quiet farewell to the man, who finally saw me and smiled gently—though his eyes narrowed. He pursed his thin lips, bunched the blanket in his hands, and nodded to me as if we shared some great secret. One that neither of us wanted to know.

Pushing past me out the door, Roman didn't look at me. He only muttered, "Let's get this over with."

I followed him without speaking up to his same subhuman nest in the attic. "I see you did something with the place," I said. He'd swept. Cleaned and repaired the corners where before there had been rotted holes and cobwebs. The disgusting mattress was gone—replaced with a rocking chair. No bed for him to rest on now, and I supposed that was an improvement. That mattress was a haunted thing, a magnet for self-loathing. It spoke of suffering more than any piece of furniture should. He'd brought up a lamp as well, a glued-together old mess of two amber-colored glass orbs. It made me smile. I could picture it having belonged to one of the patients here, one that Roman took a liking to.

He sat in the rocker, and in the same movement, pulled up another rickety little chair to face him. I sat, and I got up the courage to look at him.

Some color had returned to his cheeks, and his eyes weren't dead anymore. The brilliant ocean-blue hadn't returned, but a shadowy sea was there, full of treasure waiting to be brought to the surface again. His hair had been brushed—golden again—taken on the color of the sun, where he'd spent some time recently, I was sure. His lips had plumped, but his neck, his arms under his button-down shirt, were still thin. He was no longer as unkempt as he'd been, worse than the patients in the beds below.

He was getting better.

"I'd offer you tea…" he said absently.

I smiled, just a little. This was far more like Roman than he'd been the last time we'd seen each other. "You aren't drinking much tea these days, are you?" I asked softly. He'd been visiting with patients, making friends, moving with a little more life, but he wasn't his old self. He would deny himself the comfort of a cup of tea or hot chocolate from the kitchens.

Actually, that was a lot like the Roman I knew. Selfless to a fault. Self-flagellating.

"You've come back," he said. "But I told you—"

"I know. You won't come back."

"No."

His voice was that gentle thing with the slightly gravelly undertone that I remembered. So warm, unlike any other voice I knew. "I don't believe that anymore, Roman. I look at you now, and I see how you want to get better. You *are* getting better."

He looked away, covering his mouth with his hand, as if afraid to agree. "I couldn't survive any longer as I'd been. I wanted so much to let the pain and the guilt consume me, but it couldn't in the end. It never really turned me into one of them downstairs. Some of them are so far gone, I can't even see remnants of who they might have been, but others…" He looked back to me, and he smiled. I couldn't help it—I let out a sob of happiness. He was still so sad, but he had hope. I felt it. "There are some patients here that aren't gone yet. Nobody visits them, though. They're left here, but I *feel* the spark in there, for some of them. Just some of them." He scooted to the edge of his seat, steepling his hands, elbows on his knees, eyes alight, as muddy as they still were. "And I started talking to a few of them in the night, when they were the most alone. I watched them get better. Then some of the ones that had been written off as little more than animals, they began to speak, too. I was doing some good, El. And it did good for me."

"You always did good, Roman, always." I took his hands in mine, squeezing as he'd done to the patient I'd found him with.

"No," he mused kindly. Still worried about how I felt, even after all he'd been through. "Nobody is good all the time, Eliza. Not me, not you, not anyone. But we show it differently. We let it show differently."

"You always let it show. So many others…"

"Don't."

"…let it goooo, let it go. They aren't nice folks anymoooore…" I sang.

He laughed. The same laugh that had warmed me more than the fireplace, the cat at my feet, the Christmas light glow on the snowy nights, the hot chocolate balanced on the tattered couch arm, the wood stove in the cabin's kitchen. All those memories and not a one of them complete without that laugh, of Nicholas's brother. My friend.

"Come home, Roman. Your blood will heal Nicholas completely. He'll be his old self again, and we miss you. We just miss you." The absence of his spirit left a void in New Hampshire. We all darkened without him.

But Roman's face hardened, not angrily, but shielding him from hurt. From rejection. I felt his fear so strongly it choked me.

"I know something that will change what you think of me, even now. Something that will make you forget that I killed Kat and hate me anew, with a greater, deeper resolve. I could never look you in the eye again."

Those words—that he could never look at me again —he'd written it in his letter to Nicholas when he left. It pained me to think he stayed away because of me, how I'd feel.

"It doesn't matter. I don't know what it is, so it can't hurt me, right?"

He opened his mouth to object, but shook his head,

dropping it to look at his lap. And he gave in to me, finally. *Finally.* "All right," he said, clear and strong.

I felt something break inside him—a barrier. An inner hatred. And I saw his acceptance take over.

But acceptance of what?

CHAPTER 8

"You're staying with *who?*"

Roman's mouth hung open, all his pointy pearlies showing, and the first thought I had was, *Wow, he kept brushing while in the insane asylum.*

"Yeah, I know," I mumbled, nervously scratching my hair as we walked casually through the center of North Conway. Perfectly normal, this, two vampires in broad daylight, touristing in a tiny tourist town. One thing that never ceased to amaze me was the way drinking blood affected us—good guy, all the sun we want. Not so good guy, and we're hiding in the darkness. "Not by choice. Not really. I'm not gonna say he's changed, but he's definitely chang*ing*. I don't know into what, but…"

We rounded the corner to Birch Tree Books, and if I'd had breath, it would have been stifled like a chihuahua in a handbag. Nicholas had no idea we were coming, that Roman was coming. It had been so long.

"It's crazy to say, but I missed Lynch some. The Abomination. I missed him."

"Well, straight outta Bethlem, I guess it's not too far-fetched. Are you ready?" My words were slow, but my dead heart pounded fast, fast, fast.

Roman glanced at me, meeting my eyes in that old Roman way—just looking at me, but always understanding me, appreciating me. It was a thing that only he could do; it changed a person. "I don't think 'ready' is a word I'd use, but let's go." His lip quirked, eyes sparkled, and the bells on the door handle rang as we entered.

His back to us, Nicholas balanced a stack of books in his arm with a steaming cup of coffee on top as he slipped one onto a high shelf. The man would do anything for attention, even when no one was around.

"Came to stalk me, like the good ol' days, El?" he said, chin on the coffee cup rim.

"I come bearing gifts," I said.

He spun around, coffee not even sloshing, and looked from me to Roman with an unreadable expression. He was so good at being indecipherable and yet wearing his heart on his sleeve at the same time. "Here to see me practice my new circus act?" He pulled another book out of the stack, coffee cup barely moving. But we were all too familiar with his vampire skills, his totally *Nicholas* skill at just about everything, including his poker face.

"How have you been, brother?" Roman asked.

Swirling eyes trained on Roman's, he paused before

saying, "Brother, huh? Brother, as in eternally connected, blood thicker than water even if it's not our own blood, that kind of brother?"

"That kind. Yes." I felt Roman tense beside me, more like a flicker of fear. Not horror movie fear, but fear that everything he ever did was wrong, and all leading to this point.

Those eyes never moved away, stared Roman down in challenge and sadness. "No. A brother doesn't run away because he's afraid of what he'd already done. Not my brother." Amazing how his words would cut to the core, but he'd say them as if they were a fly on his shoulder, merely brushing them off and it was over. He turned away, back to the bookshelves.

"I'm sorry," Roman said.

"'Bout what?" Nicholas shrugged.

"Nicholas, don't make him do this," I said quietly. "Don't make him answer for his choices. He's been doing it for so long."

A human might not have noticed, but the air chilled, a ghost of anger breezing between the musty pages of books.

"Really, Eliza? You'd know. What it's like to answer for every little decision you make until the big ones don't even matter anymore. Right? Guilt yourself long enough, and suddenly everyone has to forgive you."

I gritted my teeth, willing the red mist to stay at bay. "Can we not be an immortal Jerry Springer show right now? This isn't about Kieran, or me. Roman is home!

Roman is *home.* You've missed him all this time, been half of yourself without him, and now you're giving him a hard time for coming back. Shut up for once, Nicholas! Shut up and be happy to have your family!"

"Eliza—" Roman started.

But Nicholas cut him off, having set down the books and the coffee in one fell swoop and embraced Roman more tightly than any human could have endured. Eyes squinted shut, one hand holding his brother's head close so he could tell him all the things he needed to.

Not to toot my own horn, but I felt pretty responsible for that happy mini-ending. The Nicholas I'd met an eternity ago would have kept Roman on the wire, strutting about his business with shoulders back, dropping one-liners through an arrogant smirk until he could barely stand himself anymore. I'd had some influence in his life.

"El, you wanna flip that sign to 'closed,' please?"

"But it's the middle of the day—" Roman started.

"Like I care," Nicholas said, sinking into a dusty green armchair that I didn't recognize.

"New?" I said, gesturing to it.

"You're asking if this," he pulled a tuft of stuffing out of a hole in the arm, "is new? I took it from this guy's house. It needed a new home."

"Ah, gotcha." Reading his expression, I knew. His victim had an attachment to this chair, and the residue left Nicholas needing to hold onto it. I went to it—to him—wanting to be a part of it too, to be a part of whatever Nicholas had been doing without me. The distance between us was too great. I felt too much like we were starting over every time we saw each other. Sitting on the arm of the chair, I put my hand on his bicep. He dropped his head against me, our bodies magnetized.

If there was one thing that vampire-dom had given to me, it was this unending connection to my maker that left no questions. It wasn't only that we loved each other, as if that weren't enough. It was more than feelings. Memories, promises, fates, enigmas of a future…

Me, alone without my family

Wine, roses, death all around me

Surges of knowing I possessed a destiny, just out of reach

Nicholas, bringing it all together, and so much more

Nicholas, betraying me, called to kill Kat

Death sneaking in and taking both of them from me in different ways

The agony of denying our connection that nearly killed me before I could die...

"Eliza! *Eliza!*"

Sprawled on the floor awkwardly, one leg still hooked over the arm of the chair, I'd banged my head when I fell. It pounded, but the blood in my veins pounded harder.

"Nicholas?"

"Yeah, right here." He crouched over me, concern swimming in his hazelnut eyes, the peppermint brownie scent seeping through my red mist as it grew around me like a bed of roses.

Roman sat in the chair, leaning over to be with us both, but I still didn't know what had happened. As if reading my mind, Nicholas said, "You started telling a story, you said something about a girl who died."

But I was thinking about me, my *story, and Nicholas. Kat. There'd been no vision, only feeling...*

I couldn't stop the tears that burst forth, unable to comprehend why they'd appeared.

"This is too much like when I first started getting visions," I said gravely. "They took over—even before the Master enslaved me—I couldn't tell what was real." I choked on the words. "They interfered with who I was. It won't happen again."

I got to my feet, forcing my head clear, moving like a vampire, like *Shinigami*. Not some victim of death or blood, but the master of it. And I twisted my mist with my hands like clay, shaping it as I channeled that blackout moment on the arm of the chair, and I thrust the half-formed haze into the air. Where it did exactly what I wanted it to.

Just like the image of my *unmei nashi*, Clara Borden, my very first kill, the mist showed us a moving red picture, bloody shadows of a life that was to end. Beautiful, terrifying, a moving death omen.

"What in the hell is that?" Roman said, jumping out of the chair, either in awe or fear.

"Eliza's super freak mist? The Kit to her Hasselhoff, but with weird, bone-chilling abilities. Watch."

The mist still hadn't shown me much more than the

vague shapes of two people, a man and a girl, but it gave me no *feeling,* no knowledge. Not like with Clara, where she enveloped me and her story became my own memories.

So I pushed harder. And I *took.*

"Oh goody, she's doing the soul-suck," Nicholas said, sinking into the green chair, clutching his chest.

"Nicholas. Nicholas?" Roman was saying, backing into a bookshelf, sending it banging to the floor in a heap.

Wild-eyed, Nicholas looked at his brother and forced out, "What consumes her...makes her...stronger." He shut his eyes and composed himself, sitting up straighter, leaning forward to put his elbows on his knees as if this were a casual thing. But it made him feel more like *him.* "Emptiness, death, they drive her and destroy her, and now she uses them and it makes her stronger." He shrugged, having said it, and sat back, letting it happen.

Roman blinked hard at me. And I understood that he was giving in.

Rising into the air, the mist propelling me from underneath, I shuddered and ate up all the fear in the room and the fear that lay beneath—the fear of loss from both of them, Roman and Nicholas. Afraid of losing each other, and me, of losing their immortal lives that they hated and loved at once.

And the vision became solid.

More than shadows, but not quite real, a man and a

young lady spoke in a shroud of crimson. They stood close together, not lovers, but not far from it. He reached to her, and she took his hand. He leaned in, kissed her deeply, darkly, and the mist deepened in color to a near-purple. Then he bit her. He drank, but didn't drain her—though when she had nothing left to give him, he forcefully put his wrist to her lips, pushing until she had no choice but to clamp on to it, tear into it with her teeth. And she in turn, drank from him. She fell back, both dead and alive. And he left her.

"What am I seeing, Eliza? What are you seeing?" Roman said.

I turned my cold gaze onto him, and he shrank back more.

"Next *unmei nashi?*" Nicholas guessed.

"No," I said, my voice that hollow thing that felt like the blood pouring from the elevator in *The Shining*. I shook my head, not wanting to be that terror right now, and lowered myself to the ground, pulling the mist into me again; its job was complete. I looked to Roman, Nicholas, and smiled, trying to show them it was just me again. "It was Lynch. And that chair," I said, nodding to the mildewed green chair that Nicholas sat in like a throne, one leg thrown over the side.

Nicholas turned a suspicious eye to me, cocking his head like I was trying to pull one over on him. "Noooo, nope, no Lynch here, just me."

"Not you, and not your victim. Lynch fed on your victim's daughter. In that chair."

"Creepy," Nicholas said.

Roman said, "But why would *you* see that…this way? Why does it matter to you?" The regret showed on his face as soon as he said it. Because Roman cared about every victim, felt the pain of each one. They all mattered to him—and for him to imply that they didn't matter to me… Well, it hurt.

I debated it in my head for a split second, whether to tell them, either of them. Because I knew exactly why I'd seen it.

"Eliza?" Nicholas said quietly.

"Um, yeah, I think I saw it just because of the like, power of the chair, you know?"

"The…power…of the chair," Nicholas said in that incredibly condescending yet likeable joking tone.

"Yeah, you know. Humans carry residue through us —the chair carries a residue with me." Sounded good. "It's pretty close to home, you know? And I *am* all-powerful-like."

"I should never have told you you'd be a vampire of legend."

"Probably not."

Nicholas joked, and he didn't press me, but he knew I was lying.

I'd added another brick to the wall between us.

CHAPTER 9

"**W**here is this girl, the one you killed in the green chair?"

I'd stormed into the mansion, ready to drill Lynch.

"The girl in the green chair…" he trailed off.

"That one. Well, you didn't kill her in the green chair —you didn't kill her at all. Where is she, have you seen her since?"

I'd left Nicholas and Roman at the bookstore to catch up on the very strange events of their time apart. I didn't want to be around when Nicholas told Roman about me and Kieran, or how the Master was dead because of me. I didn't want to be there when Roman told Nicholas about Bethlem.

I didn't want to be there when Nicholas fed from him.

The idea of that much pure emotion and so much

drudging up of the past, all the *talking*, the memories, I couldn't expend that much of myself. And the warmth between Nicholas and Roman just couldn't include me right now. I didn't belong there.

You don't belong here.

I had to push the mist inside, wrap it around my heart then. Those words, being back here...coming home and realizing maybe I never had one.

The thought wrenched my heart in a way that reminded me of being human. Vulnerable, constantly searching and never finding. *How could I continually miss what I never had?*

But I had belonged once. With my parents. With my grandmother. With Kat. Missing them didn't make me any less annoyed with myself for being a baby about it. I'd spent so much of my goddamn life mourning them and fearing death.

I would not let it happen to me in my immortality. I might have eternity, but I had no more time for moping.

Being the third vampire in that room with Nicholas and Roman gave me such a sense of being *other*, especially the way I life-sucked everyone now. I couldn't let my own self-pity ruin what I had with them. But I had something else to do.

Stop thinking. Confront Lynch about the girl in the green chair, why she's important.

And she was important. She had to be for Nicholas to be called to feed on her father, the strings of fate tying her so tightly to the *Shinigami* that it bled over into her family. Even knowing what I did about the Master, our origins, I still believed in fate's ties to the *Shinigami*. I think that people can believe in something so deeply that they make it come true. And I believe that we determine our own fates—it all worked together too powerfully.

I believed in it like anyone believes in a higher power when they just have no other words to describe the eerie reality of being.

"I haven't seen her," Lynch said, setting a glass of bourbon on the table with a *clink*. So casual, so painfully disconnected. I stormed through the place right over to him, ready to Force-choke him if I had to, get him to tell me everything he knew. Snarling, I took one look in his dark eyes, and I was disheartened to find the truth.

He didn't know a goddamn thing.

I was the one who knew everything important when it came to the girl.

Lynch showed not a hint of fear. That sadness of his, it was so *sticky*, clinging to every emotion, every move and thought of his, he couldn't see past it.

"Never mind," I said calmly. No need to frighten him into doing something stupid. Stupider. "I know all I need to." I turned away to go somewhere I could figure out my next move—because the next move was completely mine. This girl…she was unfinished business that needed sorting by the only vampire who held the keys to vampire future in her hand. Lil' ol' me.

"Wait," Lynch said behind me. "Please, tell me what you're talking about."

Strange request.

I turned slowly back, hesitant to involve him in anything, but too interested in *his* sudden interest to back away.

"Well…" I started, realizing that I was telling Lynch what I wouldn't tell Nicholas or Roman just hours before. I told him about the green chair, that Nicholas had been called to the man—the man who was Lynch's victim's father. I told him how I'd created the vision-mist. "I know what happened. You turned the girl into one of us. You weren't her *shugotenshi,* she was nobody—until you turned her."

"Why would you think that?" Lynch asked, mesmerized.

"Think what?"

"That she was nobody. Why would you, of all people, think she was nobody?"

Well, that stopped me dead in my tracks.

"Um, I mean, she wasn't anything to us, like, she wasn't supposed to have anything to do with vampires."

His sneer was something I was more accustomed to than his sadness. "Still buying into fate and destiny even after you've destroyed it, are you?"

Wow, he really must have been a good lawyer when he was sane on the outside. Making me stumble across my own very opinionated nature, even now that I was all-power-ful. I gulped painfully that he saw me so easily.

I'd been nothing. Or so I thought.

Nobody was nothing.

"I do believe in fate a little. At least a little. And because Nicholas *was* called to her father. There's no other explanation for the connection. He was Nicholas's *unmei nashi.*" And a sort of pride swelled in me for Lynch, because I saw a beginning, one that I in part was orchestrating at that very moment. My voice became an urgent whisper, my senseless breathing fast. "Lynch, *you* changed fate's direction. You *forced* it to change. You created a vampire, and *then* fate decided it wanted her. That's why Nicholas fed from her father—fate wanted no ties left behind. *It wanted her alone.*"

"Like we all are."

I nodded slowly, taking his face in my hands before I could help myself, a glee filling me that I didn't recognize, the opening of a closed door that I'd just discovered. "This is your purpose, Lynch. We all have one, and this is yours. It's in my skin, I feel it." Red mist firework bursts and bubbles puffed up between us with my excitement, had me wiggling my fingers, laughing in fits.

"But," His eyes glistened with tears, a zealot looking in the face of his god, "there have been others. She's not the only vampire I've made. What makes her special?"

And so it came full circle.

"Like you said—nobody is nothing."

～

J ust like that, Lynch and I were a pair, a team, with something new between us aside from our hatred and anger and sadness over the woman we loved. We had a mystery to solve, one that *we* could determine the end of.

The Abomination was about to find out why he existed. Why he, of all murderers and narcissists and sociopaths would be chosen for immortality. I was the one who would hand the knowledge to him.

And I was racing toward the purpose that had always been waiting for me. One that stole my parents, my grandmother, my best friend, replacing it with the presence of death I'd only recently come to know as a real being—Izanagi. I was a legend. I'd been told this for as long as I'd known Nicholas, and I had powers no vampire before me had—but they weren't the reason I was different. Those powers weren't the end of my road; they were stepping stones.

One thing I'd learned in the journey toward becoming Eliza Morgan, *Shinigami*, was that the road wasn't straight with a beaming light over the finish line. No, becoming a vampire had the same path as grief. When I thought I'd finished with it, it popped back up. I'd feel better, then worse; alone, then haunted, then myself; I'd be nothing, then I'd be everything. And there was never really an end to it, not like I thought.

This girl, she held something that I needed to bring my fate to fruition.

And I was perfectly fine knowing that once I found her, my journey still wouldn't be over. There would always be something *more.* Immortality didn't come with an expiration date. Vampirism is a job with endless perks and endless responsibility.

The best part was that I could find her in a heartbeat. An instant. But for some reason, I wanted Lynch to do it for himself.

I *cared* that he was finding his reason for being.

Maybe it would stop the senseless murdering he'd committed his entire existence, before and after death.

Maybe it would help heal him from Kat's death. Because as much as I hated to admit it, I wanted him to get better. This depression that he couldn't escape, it was too terrible to watch. It wasn't him. It wasn't the man Kat fell in love with, and it hurt my memory of her to see him deteriorate so completely. Some of me wanted that shark back with the gleaming smile, the raven-black hair styled to gleaming perfection, the charm. Even the morbid ulterior motive feeling I got every time he spoke. That Chris Lynch brought me back to a time when Nicholas, Roman, Kat and I were together, a family, as dysfunctional as we were.

I never had been a fan of change.

"Lynch, she's your *unmei fumetsu.* You have a connection to her."

"I feel nothing for her," he said. I believed it.

"You've turned more than just her. Do you not feel

any of them?" In a trace of energy through the air, I'd brought him by the hand to my new tree house out back. I wondered for a split second what Nicholas would think about me sharing it with Lynch. But if I was going to pursue this new journey with him, I needed to let him in. I had to open up.

Whether it be to Lynch or anyone else, opening up, getting close, seared me inside. A challenge I'd rather not accept. It was worse than dying; the stakes were higher.

There were plenty of places to sit in my treehouse, but we sat crisscross applesauce on the braided rug, facing each other. No escape from one another.

"Uh…" He couldn't get a hold of himself with the sudden change—or maybe it was the question he didn't want to answer. "I've changed a few. More than a few."

"You don't know how many vampires you've made?"

He shook his head, eyes downcast.

I took a deep breath. "I'm not judging you. I'm not—disgusted—by you." Ellie Morgan would have been disgusted by him. Eliza *Shinigami* was not. "It was just a question."

His breath was deeper than mine. It endlessly amused Nicholas how we breathed so much when we never had to take a breath. "I don't know, Eliza," he said, voice relaxed, sad as always. "I never bothered to count. I only do it to pass the time. There's so much time with *nothing*. I just want something to happen…but then I don't care anymore just as quickly." He shot his eyes up at me. "I leave them all, I don't care what happens to them or anyone they touch. It feels *good* to do something so cruel."

Lynch never was one to mince words.

"I understand." I did. He hurt, and hurting felt good. I realized it always had been that way for him. He'd hurt when he'd killed as a human, and he hurt when he'd done it without need as a vampire. With him, it never felt tragic to me. He'd been so self-possessed, egotistical, a lawyer for crying out loud. It's not easy to feel bad for someone like that. Which is why he felt bad for himself.

"Why do you understand?"

"It's a test. How much you can hurt the world without anyone ever caring to stop you."

He *smiled*. That old Lynch smile—warm, but had once shaken me to the core. He was feeling my power, trying not to let it scare him more. "You're very astute as a vampire. Unnaturally observant."

"No, I feel it. I don't see it, I feel it." Here I was, opening up again. "I sense your greatest fears and I grow stronger with them. The more afraid you are, the more I can feel about you. I can even have visions when your fear is at the forefront."

"You'd be a fantastic lawyer," he said.

"Eliza Morgan, Vampire Lawyer."

We laughed, and he leaned back on his elbows, stretching his legs out in front of him. With the scruff and the messy hair, he reminded me of Nicholas, but he was too lithe and far too emotionally distressed.

"Lynch, I want you to stop shutting your *unmei fumetsu* out. All of them."

"I'm not."

"You're lying."

He gave an angry shake of his head and looked away from me. "I don't *want* to know them."

I dug in. I kept the mist minimal, a tinge of red underneath me, seeping out like smoke, like my pants were on fire. Lynch was mumbling to stop it, to get out of his head, but the more afraid he was, the more I wanted in, the more powerful the vampire in me became.

"Stop!" he screeched, clutching his ears as if I were needling into his brain through them.

"No," I growled without intending to. My reasons for bringing Lynch here had changed, and the death god in me was taking over when the *Shinigami* legend should have been in control. I was meant to be a leader, not a predator. "I'm sorry," I said, drawing myself back, squeezing my eyes shut. "I'm still new—"

"No you're not," Lynch said forcefully, angry now that he'd gotten his strength back. "Just because you aren't as old as the rest of us doesn't make you new. That word implies weakness, vulnerability, of which you possess neither. You're a predator, make no mistake." He swallowed hard. "But no one is safe from you. Not even the rest of us."

I chuckled. "Who's the abomination now?"

That glint returned to his eyes, that inhuman element that showed the killer he was at heart. Whatever heart he had.

Trying to reconcile that monster with the man who'd been ripped apart by my best friend's death was where I was stuck.

"I didn't mean to invade like that," I said after a shared silence between two villains. "I did mean to maybe, but I shouldn't have. I sense fear underneath this wall you've put up between your and the vampires you've created. You've done this yourself, the connection is effortless—you made this obstruction, this barrier. And it was that fear which called me to you— you're terrified of, of…" I couldn't say it, it was too close to home, same as my own nightmares, my reality.

"What is it? What do you think scares me, O Legendary One?" he spat. Aggressive like any cornered animal.

"You're afraid of caring about any of them. You know forever can end just like anything else."

The words were bitter in my throat, oozing their truth into my mouth, a blistered sore infecting everything around it.

"You would know," he said huskily.

There he was, the little boy turned monster. The tragic creature that made sure he was unloved. The one who'd lost everything. Who'd driven it away. The one who Kat saw past to the gentle heart underneath. The soul of the soulless.

"I would know," creaked out of my throat.

I embraced him, burying my face into his neck—not to feed from him.

But to love him.

CHAPTER 10

I could find her in an instant, and it killed me not to.

Lynch needed to take this new vampire under his wing, needed to open up to her and let himself get attached. I couldn't do it all myself, not if this fresh vampire was what I thought she was for me.

A new beginning. A new order of vampire.

I had to give Lynch the room he needed—or maybe I just told myself that because I missed Nicholas.

NICHOLAS.

Blood, thick, dark, pungent, curtained my eyes, turning all I saw into a sheet of pure blood.

His.

Nicholas's blood, *but he should be feeding from Roman.*

My heart clenched, stopped, and I gasped. I choked, the blood disappeared. I gagged, doubled over, head swimming.

And I was there. At Nicholas's cabin.

Not a vision. Physically there.

I fell to one knee on a stepping stone, facing the front door as my roiling stomach settled.

Deep breaths.

But all I breathed in was blood.

No deep breaths. Feel the heat on your back. Feel the dirt under your fingernails, the stone hard against your knee. The feathers against your arm.

What.

I opened my eyes to find a crow nuzzling against me, beak tilted up so I could look into his eyes. The darkness there and the *knowing* brought me back to myself. I laid my hand on his downy back. "Thanks," I said. He screeched—I winced—and he flew off.

Just as I got to my feet I was blown across the yard by a boulder, barreling into me at a speed nothing so heavy should be able to travel, the air howling in its wake.

I smashed into a tree. With a great *crack*, the tree split in two, crashing down on me like an axe, pinning me to the ground with my arms and legs splayed out on either side of its thick trunk.

Eyes glazed over, I blinked hard to see what could have done this to me. The force of the initial blow would have crippled a human, let alone what the tree would have done.

"Blue?"

My sweet friend, the impish, otherworldly beauty made of jewel tones and sugar, crouched like a feral animal. Smoke rose from her hunched shoulders where the sun pierced through holes in her ragged black shirt. Truly, her usual modern fairy tale-esque clothes, sleek with crochet black, doily-ish lace and pops of rich color, hung in tatters around her, making her wraith-like, just as her matted, overgrown hair had done. Her pale face showed through the curtain of knots, too brilliantly, too inhumanly, as she snarled at me.

She growled hearing her name and limped off into the woods, leaving me stunned.

Crimson mist rose around me like bubbles in a bathtub, lifting the tree from my body. Spots of black popped in and out of the red froth around me: crows, bobbing around like rubber duckies, to soothe me once again.

With a fair share of grunts and groans—because not even vampire strength could make *that* not hurt—I got up, brushed myself off, and came face to face with a dismayed Nicholas and horrified Roman.

"What in the holy—what the—"

"Wow, Nicholas French at a loss for words," Roman muttered, but his eyes were glued to me, assessing the damage.

"Was this Blue?" Nicholas asked, head cocked, brows furrowed, swallowing hard.

"It's okay, Nicholas," I said, seeing his struggle between shock that our little Blue could do this, and fury that *anyone* would do this to me.

"What has happened to her?" Roman said.

"She should never have left the mountain," Nicholas growled.

I couldn't help but agree. If she'd stayed in Japan, she wouldn't have been out in a world that terrified her. When I left Kieran had been in no shape to go hunting for her, but he would have taken care of her, would have healed quicker just to do it. He always found a way to make sure she was okay.

Nicholas could barely take care of himself. He was no babysitter, he wasn't the type to hold hands and do everything for a vampire who was as strong as Blue in every way.

Why on Earth did she ever leave Japan? What was she thinking?

Of all times to leave her home, she chose to go with Nicholas, to leave Kieran alone, to try to find herself in such a tumultuous time for all *Shinigami*. Why would she do it?

But I knew the truth. Her aura told me, the blankness that it had been when I first saw it had given way to a ripped and skewered, violent mass that begged me to read it.

Blue *wanted* this.

"Eliza, come back," Nicholas said, putting a hand on my arm, the only one who could snap me out of the think-hole I'd fallen into. His hand felt bonier, older.

"Did Roman feed from you?" I said, more accusingly than intended. "I smelled—"

"I just cut myself, El." He pulled up the leg of his jeans

to reveal a jagged, half-healed cut that ran the length of his shin.

"That should have healed already."

"Yeah, but it didn't. And I'm okay," he said. But we both knew that if he just drank from Roman it would be better, not just now but for good. We were pretty sure, anyway. "Besides, you're the one that just got tossed like a salad in the wind."

"I'm fine, Nicholas. I'm more worried about Blue."

"And me. And who else are you worried about?"

"Lynch," I said without thinking.

We both glanced at Roman who turned and stalked to the backyard of the cabin.

Nicholas took the moment to dip his head, force me to look into the mesmerizing eyes that I could tear myself away from even less as a vampire than I could as a human. Their motion was slower, sluggish, and the color dimmer, more like Autocrat coffee milk. I loved the color but the man was suffering—and therefore, I was too.

"El, I need you not to worry about my condition, and *don't*"—he expertly cut off my impending objection—"say you have to. You don't." His *it's that simple* face almost made me believe it. "You put the wheels in motion, you went and got Roman to come here. Right? Didn't you?"

"Yes," I answered reluctantly.

"You worry enough. And whatever you're trying to

figure out with Lynch, that's your problem. I'm not trying to solve it for you, am I?"

"Well, no, but—"

"Nope, no, uh uh. I'm not solving it for you. And you don't have to solve this one for me." A little more softly, he said, "I'm telling you that you came here to do your own thing *for us.* You didn't forget me, and I didn't forget you. Now I'm doing *this* for us. Eliza, we don't need to be joined at the hip, we're in this forever. Maybe too long, you don't know. I'm on board, babe."

"That—that's awesome," I said, and holy shit did I ever mean it. His words brought it into simple perspective. The *it's that simple* face was followed up with actual logic, at least this time. We had eternity. No way would we be able to deal with each other for every second of it, and if there weren't periods where I had to pursue something for myself, what kind of eternity would that be for me? For him? We were still ourselves.

"You get it," he said, smiling, showing me those gleaming teeth, the fangs just visible. "I think we both just want this, us, to not feel so damn fragile."

"Like everything in the world is against us just having a goddamn normal day, you mean?"

"Yep. That's what I mean. And we forgot for a minute there—well, a vampire minute—that we can *do* the apart thing and it doesn't mean we aren't together. Eliza Morgan, our love is not a fleeting thing. We don't have to treat it like it is."

Red tears clouded my eyes, and I blinked them away. Hoarsely, I said, "Yeah. I know. I love you, too. So, whatcha building?" I traced Roman's steps around the back. The smell of lumber permeated the air now that the figurative dust from the attack had settled. "You're on a streak, huh?"

"What?"

"Building. You've been building a lot."

"I don't follow."

Just walking into that backyard brought on an avalanche of emotion, the stimuli too much, the memories too much. That hill, where I'd seen Nicholas come home to me after his comatose state, fresh from a kill. When Roman and I waited for him, together in our love and need for him. The way he surrendered to me, so utterly energized and drained at once.

Nicholas turned toward me, and his eyes went to my heart. Just as they had when we first met, at Lynch's party. He was hearing and feeling my heartbeat.

"It was yours then. It is now."

Nicholas blinked and shook his head.

"You heard me," I thought.

He nodded, and let out a deep, troubled breath.

Well, that's new.

"What's the last thing you heard from me?" I asked him aloud.

"You heard me," he said.

"Not 'Well, that's new,' you didn't hear that?"

"What did I just say?"

So I can control it, too.

"Hey Nicholas. I have a new power that you don't."

"You don't know I can't do that," he said with fake nonchalance.

"I have another thing you don't," I teased.

"I can build stuff you can't," he said.

Nicholas jumped onto the new platform in the back-yard like the wild man that he was, landing with a *boom* in a superhero pose that suited him too well.

"I am Iron Man," he said.

"Yeah, I know." I grinned.

"Building a place for Blue," he told me, gesturing to the deck of a new cabin.

I looked into his head, past the place I'd read his mind from, and a red blanket of foggy knowledge bled into me.

"You didn't build the tree house, did you?" I said.

"Tree house? What, you've got a secret clubhouse now? I'm not in the club?"

"Lynch built it," I said. I'd never even entertained the idea. "Jesus, he was just trying to make me feel at home."

"Did it work? This She-Shed he made you?"

"It's not a She-Shed, and yeah, it did actually. Well, no. Yes and no. It's not easy living with Lynch, not how he is now."

"You think it would have been easy before?" Roman said from across the lawn.

"Stop eavesdropping, this is a secret club meeting."

"Nicholas, there is no secret club."

"There is too a secret club," Nicholas said to Roman,

not me. "But Eliza says there's not. Wait," he said, turning my way. "Is *Roman* in the club?"

"I love you," I blurted, laughing.

"I know."

"You did an Iron Man, you cannot do a Han Solo. Pick a theme."

He pulled my face lightning-fast to his, smothering my lips with his, stealing my breath and keeping it in his heart.

There was nothing else. Nothing to forgive. No monumental event to erase all we'd been and done. Just this one little backyard moment and the life we'd made for ourselves and together. We didn't need anything else.

"All right, take five, worker bee," Nicholas said as Roman slammed his shoulder into two tree trees, shoving them together like Lincoln Logs. "You probably should get me, I don't know. A sandwich. Not just a sandwich, a *sub.*"

Roman glared at him half-heartedly and left the two of us alone.

"There's something he doesn't want me to know," Nicholas said matter-of-factly, Sherlock Holmesy. Nothing accusing in how he said it, just a detached statement that I knew meant more to him underneath. "I tried, El," he added with a sigh, cocking his head in apology to me. "I know you wanted me to drink from him and you'd come back today to a sparkling refurbed Nicholas, but he was so twitchy, I couldn't do it. He was a mouse in a trap."

"He's just afraid, Nicholas. I don't think he's got anything to hide—I think he's done plenty on the surface to be ashamed of. We might be over it, but he's not."

"We aren't over it, Eliza."

"Yeah. No, I guess not." *Roman killed Kat.* "It won't go away. But you think there's something else?"

"I know it."

When Nicholas French *knew* something, he was never wrong. Infuriating sometimes, but handy where I could be oblivious so much of the time.

"So what happened when you tried?" I felt like one of those intrusive friends in some John Hughes movie who hounded for every detail of a date down to what his breath smelled like. "Like, did he…"

"It was a 'no means no' scenario, and I won't push him just so I can have perfect health for another few hundred years. I get it—he just came home, he needs to settle in after being in Bethlem for so long. Maybe he doesn't want that kind of responsibility." He threw his hands up. "Nope. That's not it. Roman loves responsibility. It's like, his favorite."

Nodding, I answered, "He's hiding something that his blood will reveal."

"Right, creep. You and your 'let me drink the blood and see what I will see' thing. He'll come around." Nicholas shrugged as if this were the most casual conversation. "He'll see me fading away little by little and let me drink because that guilt on top of his just-being-Roman guilt will be too much for him."

"Worst. Friend. Ever," I said, poking him in the still-muscled arm. He'd been feeding enough to keep himself burlier than the average man, but only his brother's blood would restore his vitality, bring him *back.* Everything about him was just a little slower, a little duller, a little…weaker every day. Eventually he would die like any old human would. But he deserved so much better than that.

We sat on the platform that was the unfinished floor of Blue's new cabin, the open air inviting us to stay. I'd never paid much attention to birds singing, or the springtime blooms, the difference in the forest when life returned to it. For me, the crows drowned out the tittering of sillier birds, and the darkness of winter dwelled inside me on the brightest of days. But there in the stillness with Nicholas, there was nothing between us, nothing that hated us and wanted us for its own in those woods.

"I'm glad we're all back," I said without thinking. I didn't think I'd ever get over *not* saying how I felt. Words just came out with Nicholas, in a way that they hadn't even with Kat.

"Me too. It feels right here for us."

"I don't miss Japan," I said.

"You wouldn't."

I did miss Kieran though.

It was a reversal in time, he moved so fast. Nicholas

had me on my back, kissing me as if he hadn't seen me in a year, hands in my hair, feet twined around mine. "I love you," he breathed into my hair, against my cheeks, my lips. "Never leave here again. There's nothing for you out there."

I smiled against his lips, and agreed.

Roman took a long time with those sandwiches. Subs. He went out to the place that looked like a barn, and probably was a barn, but man they could make a steak and cheese. Swinging our legs off the edge, we ate our subs in a line on the platform like a bunch of construction workers.

"You got roast beef, didn't you?" Nicholas asked him. "You know it's not real meat."

"It is too," Roman said, taking a huge bite.

"Is not."

The best part is that if Roman hadn't been there, Nicholas would have gotten roast beef, too. I laughed to myself at their ten-second arguments. This was the way home soaked into the skin, rode in on a wave of burnt-orange calm and honey. I laughed thinking of all the times Kat would tell me to "stop talking that way," and to "talk that other way I talk." I think this was exactly what she meant, but as a vampire, I couldn't know another way. Feelings take on life as a vampire, a life that keeps the undead going.

Nicholas took my hand with his free one, shoving his sub in his mouth with the other.

"Hey Roman, seen Lynch yet?" Nicholas asked, knowing goddamn well what the answer was.

"*No,*" he replied, "and you know it. I suppose you think I should go for a visit."

"You said it, not me."

Roman looked to me, and I met his eyes, unafraid of his questions, shocking myself at how willing I was to defend Chris Lynch.

"He could use your company, Roman," I said softly. Pleadingly, if I'm being honest.

"Tell me what he's been doing. Because I've neglected my duty to him."

Nicholas's head lolled back. "Ughhhhh, stop it. Your duty is only to yourself, et cetera, et cetera. Besides, Eliza murdered the Master, so there's no such thing as duty anymore."

"Holy shit!" I screeched, eyes nearly popping out of my head. Birds raced away from my booming voice. "You just throw that into casual conversation over lunch?"

"Eliza, you know I'm too good for casual conversations," he said in mock accusation. "Maybe I'm *extra* good at casual conversation because I find all subjects casual. Speaking of which, hey Roman, tell me what your not-so-little secret is. I know you've got one and I want it."

Roman didn't crack a smile, which was the thing that

Nicholas French counted on when he put someone on the spot like this; that his unique charm insured him against refusal or grudges.

"I can't," Roman whispered to his hanging feet. My heart went out to him, to have this vulnerability exploited by Nicholas in such a good-natured way. A violation for his own good. I knew the feeling all too well. But Nicholas was also the master of making anyone feel comfortable revealing their deepest, darkest secrets without feeling like they've done anything to be sorry for.

"Your secrets are our secrets," Nicholas said, leaning close to his brother. "You have nothing—*nothing*—that you need to keep from us. From me."

Blond hair too neat to truly obscure his face, Roman couldn't hide from his brother's eyes. His voice was so small, like a thoughtful child's. "I need to keep this one to myself for a while."

I wanted to yell at him that he already had, all those months in Bethlem, that keeping his secret from Nicholas meant keeping his blood, too, and his *life.*

Nicholas patted his brother on the knee and sat up straight again. "Well. I'm not building anymore until you tell me," he said lightly. "Which means you're sleeping on the floor. If you choose to sleep. Goddammit, I can't make you tell me, can I? You're so annoying."

Roman chuckled, and Nicholas didn't press any further, though he wanted to. When Roman said no, it was with a heavy heart. He never did anything to hurt a person unless necessary—and yet somehow he was always the one to do the hurting. He committed so much more deeply than the rest of us, always willing to take one for the team, to his own detriment. I'd think it would ruin him, but he always survived, overcame, went on. He was stronger than us all, probably.

I put my hand on his shoulder and sighed, wishing I could do something to make it easier in his mind.

He smiled at me, more with those kind blue eyes than his lips. "I'm going to see him now. Lynch. I owe it to both of us."

I smiled back, warmth flooding me. "He'll be so glad you did, Roman."

Roman's angelic face darkened inexplicably. But there's always an explanation for a vampire's turmoil, and I knew that better than anyone.

We let him go, Nicholas grumbling the whole time about how Lynch had a new babysitter, glaring at me but getting no reaction.

"I wish I didn't like Roman so damn much," I said. "He's being obtuse about letting you drink, when he knows how much you need it. You'll never be healthy without it, he's the only one who can help you, it's in *his* blood—" I stopped myself before saying because he murdered the woman Nicholas was supposed to murder. My friend.

Nicholas's eyes trained on me with an intensity we both felt in our blood. "I'm not his responsibility."

I shot back, "Right. You're mine."

"What the hell kind of screwed up logic—"

But I cut him off by slicing my neck open with a fingernail, sharp and fast. He went deathly still at the sight, the smell that even intoxicated me, and clutched me close to him, drinking in deep gulps, moaning, writhing against me. I actually felt his muscles thicken from the inside out, his skin tighten, his cheeks become fuller, the tender skin around his eyes puff up from their dark holes. His very ligaments grew taut and I knew the sensation was mine.

That was when he pushed.

At first it was a poke in the brain. Testing the waters, looking tentatively for a way in.

Then it was a stab.

Then a rumbling of frustration when my mind didn't give.

"What the hell are you doing?" I yelped, pushing Nicholas off me.

He didn't deny it, just ran his hands over his face, coming out from under them with the impatience of a teen delinquent's dad on prom night. "I wanted what you had for a minute, okay?" he said in that condescending and yet still charming tone. It might've been funny if it didn't make me feel like he was accusing me of catching him at something. Pure Nicholas, unlike anyone else. Endearing and aggravating as hell.

"You wanted to see what I was thinking," I barked, tapping my temple. "I'm glad you can't do what I do, you clearly wouldn't do anything nice with it."

"*Nice?* Since when do you care about nice?"

"Since you tried to not be nice to me!"

The eye roll. I think his eyeballs traveled the earth and came back.

"You can read my thoughts now if I let you, and that is enough. Stop being such a greedy baby."

"Nothing babyish about *that* statement," he muttered.

My mist tickled the soles of my feet, aching to emerge as my protector from the violation. But I didn't feel as threatened as it did. I understood. I would have done the same thing if the power to see into heads wasn't mine to wield.

Come to think of it, it wasn't as if I regularly got permission to dig into minds.

"Sorry," I said, sitting back down. "I don't need any barrier with you, I just wish you'd asked first."

"I should have. You know me and choices; the good ones aren't any fun. No excuse—I had no right. I'm sorry." His fingers twitched, and I knew he wanted to pinch the bridge of his nose, but wouldn't take his eyes from mine. This was how he punished himself, by facing the person he hurt. I loved that about him. I, on the other hand, wanted to bolt like a rabbit, and I hadn't done anything wrong. Well, not in the last few minutes.

I leaned against his shoulder. "We both just want to see more than we do. I'm getting nothing from Lynch half the time, and the other half it's like zombies piling up to push me over, all dead and grabby."

"Nice zombie analogy."

"Yeah, you know me." I shrugged.

He bit his lip, and it ran right through me like it always did. "We do this to ourselves." He turned to me, excited. I half expected him to come at me with like, "let's go to Six Flags!" But it was better. "We can just *stop it.* We can do all the other stuff later, if we feel like it. For now, you move back in here, we forget this crap with you needing to drink Lynch's blood, find out some elusive secret to change the world... Our world doesn't need changing, Eliza," he pleaded, grasping my hands. "You did enough. The *Shinigami* know the Master made it all up," he said, freeing a hand to wave it around his head. "All made up. They've got the choice of who to kill if they want it. They know Izanagi created them. They have the Irishman to lead them now—if they want a leader. You freed them. You don't have to do any more. And you and I," he said, bringing my hands up to kiss them, "we can learn about and from each other, do what's good for us for a change."

The grin spread across my face, I felt it open like a flower from the inside, unleashing life. Nicholas smiled in return, this gleaming, startlingly warm smile. *That* was my home. That was the home I deserved, that I needed.

"I could, couldn't I? Move back in," I said, looking to the towering trees. They'd always felt like a hood over me here, the roof of a cuddly nest. Now I could look down on them from a wave of red mist in seconds, freer than they'd ever be, rooted where they were for decades.

"Take my own advice, stop giving in to archaic feelings of *duty*—"

"You said—"

"Yeah, I know I said *duty*." I sighed. "But I do feel this *need* to uncover something with Lynch, and it can't wait. The difference is this isn't just some responsibility to an invisible force of fate, or even Izanagi. This is my choice. I want to know what Lynch's blood is trying to tell me. I want to follow this path, see where it leads. I do feel like it was meant to be, but I'm good with it. Good will *come* of it." My turn to plead, I guess.

"So optimistic," he said, pushing my hair out of my face. "It's unlike you."

"I am too an optimist! Tough to seem like it when you've got a goddamn flock of harbingers following you around," I said, glaring at the forever-hovering crows.

He took my cheeks in his hands in a sudden bout of seriousness. "Eliza, we need that. We need you to be optimistic. With me—dying, I guess—" I started to protest but he cut me off. "We don't *really* know Roman's blood will fix me. Right?" he said in this premature *I told you so* mode. "We've got Blue going off the deep end, you and me apart, and the worst one of all of us with some frigging secret, but probably not the same secret Roman has. We need you, Fresh Meat, to make it all better."

"No pressure then."

"Oh, all the pressure. But you've got this, El. You've got this like nobody else could."

"Please. Someone else could. You could. You could fix it all if you wanted to."

"There it is," he said, pointing at me. "You want to. I don't. I don't care about Lynch, I barely care if I fade away into nothing. I've lived long enough. It's you that keeps me here more than anything."

"That's not fair. Don't make me your reason for living."

"No, no I don't mean that. I just mean that I'd let go a hell of a lot easier if I didn't have you in my corner. I want to see what happens next with you. You're a wild card."

"I'm a sideshow for your amusement," I said, grinning.

"Yep. And I'll sneak into the big top as much as you let me."

Little did he know how fast this circus would burn down.

CHAPTER 11

"He's coming, I can feel him. What did you tell him?"

Lynch came at me like the grownups had driven up in the middle of our teenage house party.

"Roman? I didn't tell him anything." And no, I hadn't. It was our little secret that Lynch was making vampires and leaving them around like a scavenger hunt for bad choices.

"Why didn't you warn me he was coming?" Lynch whined.

"You knew faster than I could tell you; you're connected. Besides, it's good for you to see each other."

"How do you figure?" Lynch muttered.

Then Roman glided into the doorway behind me without so much as a smile. It had been so long since they'd been face to face, it almost hurt that they couldn't be happy to be together. But Roman would always see Lynch as the greatest mistake he was forced to make, and Lynch would never stop making him suffer for it.

"Lynch," he said in awful greeting.

Chris turned away and sat on his couch, the only piece of furniture not covered in dust. It pained me unexpectedly that Lynch didn't even snap a viperish comment at Roman, taunting him as he always did in his rebellious way. It shocked me even more that Roman didn't seem affected by the change in Lynch's demeanor. He was the most compassionate man I knew and the obvious state of disrepair that Lynch was in didn't bother him.

How that must feel, to be so abhorred by your maker that nothing you did would turn his heart your way.

"Tell me what you've been doing while I've been gone," Roman said robotically. I recognized that he dreaded the answer. I felt his fear in my heart, and the vampire I'd become wanted to drown in it, drink it, let it power me.

Not now, not now, not now, you monster.

"Eliza?" Lynch said, fear creeping into his voice, too.

I gulped, vision darting between the hollows under his eyes—*he's tired*—the pallor of his skin—*and weak*—the quickening of his breath—*afraid. Afraid, afraid.*

My throat went desert dry. I heard myself panting, couldn't stop it, my eyes drawn to Roman with a jerk of my head while the rest of me was paralyzed, rooted in my hunger, desperate to devour their horror which filled the space more and more with every passing second.

I dropped my jaw wide, wide, wider than humanly possible.

I'm not human.

And it made sense to me that I would do monstrous things, that I *should*.

The cold fear rose out of Lynch, an unfamiliar chill that surprised and wrenched through him as I dragged it from him. It pierced out of him, making him tremble, suck in his breath. Though the sharp green ice was only visible to me, only real to me, only meant for me. Sheer, crystalline daggers the size of small mountains tore out of him to me, and my mouth gaped, became a cavern the length of my body to engulf them.

I faintly heard Roman screaming my name, but I belonged to the fear now, and it became me, told me… It told me…

Almost there.

Spinning on Roman, I threw my arms out, willing his fear to evacuate his body and fill my own with all its wisdom. My mist gunned for him in streams, pulling him toward me, though he struggled against it. And he was afraid, yes he was, but not quite enough.

"Eliza!" he called out. Not a scream of terror, but pleading, not just with me but for me.

"No!" I screamed back. Their fear together, the two of them, could tell me all I needed to know, I was sure of it. *Imagine what Nicholas would think of me now,* I thought.

It was the one moment of clarity that allowed Roman to break free of my mist, and to stop me from sucking their souls free of fear.

The power gushed out of me, the shards of Lynch's fear I'd been devouring exploding into a thousand slivers and disappearing.

I fell to the floor, hiding my head in shame. Roman's eyes would be too kind, and too impossibly understanding. But his scent surrounded me, crisp ocean breeze and farm-fresh apples. He put his hand on the back of my head, that gentle touch of his making me shudder.

And then Lynch's cold steel scent joined Roman's. Lynch's fingers ran over my own where I clutched my hair.

"It's okay, Eliza," Lynch said. "We're all monsters here."

But the words didn't hit me in the heart the way I know he intended. Because all I could think was: *Not a monster.*

A god.

The thought struck me and stuck, sending my head spinning, and my heart reaching out for Izanagi, a better god than I could ever be. I was nothing, and he was a legend.

"You killed a legend."

I screamed, and Roman and Lynch held me harder, enveloping me in their arms as if to comfort me. But they couldn't comfort me this time.

Because those words in my head weren't mine. They

weren't Izanagi's, stretching toward me through our shared blood. Certainly not Nicholas's.

I didn't know who they belonged to.

Eerie, ethereal, pure energy, indistinguishable and utterly unique at once. The voice lit me up with a desire to learn and know that I hadn't felt for a very long time. A need to absorb as much as I could, like sitting at Birch Tree trying to figure out which books to buy because I didn't make enough to buy them all. I wanted to drink them all in, own them.

I pulled my arms out from the ball they'd been wrapped in, held tight by Roman and Lynch, and I drew the two of them close in an embrace. The red fog emerged, enveloping the three of us as we reassured one another.

"We'll figure this out, guys," I said, incredulous that *I* was comforting *them*, these two vampires who'd lived so much longer than I had, both so different. All of us killers. "We just have to trust each other to handle all the secrets we've got."

And the voice invading my mind said, *"Never."*

The voice was partly right—I couldn't say it would never happen, but our secrets stayed with us for the night. Whatever Roman was holding back remained right where it was, torturing him. Brightness colored his eyes, but his aura was diminishing. Like one dot removed from a mountain-sized Pointillist painting, it withered a speck at a time. I saw it. Withering. Slowly eating away, while Lynch's riddles ripped and mended in a flurrying madness.

My secrets—Lynch's rampage, and now the voice in my head—weren't going to be the first to come out, that was for sure. And those were just the topmost ones.

When we eventually got up from our heap on the floor, we were all too relaxed for once in our immortal lives to even try to delve into the mysteries around and within us. Instead, Lynch and I showed Roman the tree-house that wasn't in a tree.

"This is some solid woodwork, Lynch," Roman remarked, running a hand up the wall.

"Thanks. It felt good to do it, and actually be creative for once."

Creative was not a word I would ever have associated with Lynch in any respect except maybe his torture tactics.

"Do…do you have a creative side?" I asked, wishing I hadn't right away.

But he laughed, and Roman joined in. "I actually liked to paint once," Lynch said with a touch of golden energy trickling into his black, blank mess of an aura.

"I never knew that!" Roman exclaimed, making me smile but quickly hide it, afraid they'd stop being goddamn normal if they caught on to how strange it was.

"Yeah," Lynch continued, actually swooshing his foot

back and forth across the floor like a shy teenager. "Surrealist usually, but it was the Renaissance that truly fascinated me."

I wondered if Kat knew this about him. I figured I should try to learn.

"Learn," confirmed the voice in my head.

As the guys laughed over some memory, I took the moment to slide my hand over the smoky blue paint right where Lynch had. *This is so stupid,* I thought, but I tried to reach through the paint itself, to another time and place where Lynch had paint on his hands, to see what I could see, to find a memory that belonged to him.

I pictured different shades of blue.

Canvas rather than wood.

Delicate brushes rather than a roller.

Lynch, younger, before he was terrible, painting some Dali-esque weirdness.

Nothing.

So stupid. What a dumb idea.

"Not a dumb idea. An experiment."

"Oh my god, just shut up," I said, exasperated.

Obviously both Roman and Lynch looked at me like I was the biggest jerk in history.

"I didn't mean you!" I blurted out.

Lynch's eyes roamed around looking for who else I could possibly mean, while Roman's wouldn't peel away from me.

"The crows," I lied. "They never shut up."

Oh wow, is it the crows talking to me?!

"Not exactly," said the voice.

I knotted my fingers together, wishing I could rip the voice out of my damn head because if there was one thing I did not need, it was more unfamiliar shit in my brain. Never again would I be host to hordes of unknown voices and visions for everyone else's benefit and my detriment.

"I'm here for you and you alone."

"El, you don't look so good," Roman said, taking my hand off the wall. "Why don't you lie down over there, we'll make ourselves scarce, okay?"

I resisted the urge to say I was fine, because everything was blurry—something I hadn't experienced since the last party Kat dragged me to, and certainly not something I'd experienced since becoming *Shinigami.*

Something was wrong.

Trying not to trip over my own feet, I curled up under the blanket on the little sofa Lynch had managed to furnish my treehouse with and before my two friends had even left, I was asleep.

Maybe not asleep. Unconscious, more like. Taken over by lack of awareness is even more accurate.

Used for my brain activity, even.

I'd been shut down by that voice. It used me, like every vision ever had, like the Master had done when he learned what I could see. The voice knocked me the hell out, like I'd been roofied, and violated.

The "dreams," if they could be called that, inundated me. But not like a flood—no this was a carefully unfolded series of events that made little sense but were the teaser to a bigger story. The manipulative bastard in my head was setting me up to *want* to come back for more. The idea of it crushed and nauseated me in that nearly-peeing-my-pants way that happens when the whole body turns against a feeling. The utmost lack of control.

The dream began with a laugh.

A laugh that said *I got you* without saying it. I was trapped and wasn't looking for a way out.

This place it brought me reeked of hopelessness. Things moved, but nothing was visible, not even glowing eyes. Only heat. Body signatures, but nothing I wanted to drink from. Blood flowed in these beings that I wanted no part of.

A baby crying.

Then everybody crying. So many tears it washed away the darkness to reveal skittering things, running from the light. One was left. A crouching, animalistic and primitive, hurting body. Its suffering pierced me like a thousand knives.

My own voice, saying, "Blue?"

But it was Paolo who spun on his heels, his vampire teeth showing, his once-holy eyes haunted and lost.

I pleaded, "No," over and over again, and tried to get

to him but couldn't. That alone was torture. As a vampire I could move in the blink of an eye, and more recently *teleport...*

"That was a gift to you, from me," the voice boomed over everything else in my dream.

"You? You're giving me powers?"

There was no answer, only me trying again to get to Paolo, every motionless step sinking me into my own hell—because I'd left him, and he'd fallen apart. I selfishly deserted him, and he'd disappeared to—

"Yomi," I gasped.

And when I did, the darkness of Purgatory lit up in a blaze of blinding heat, and all the devils of Yomi screeched at me as one. They pointed their howling faces at me from above, below, every side. Their demon horns crashed against each other, their lionish vampire teeth jutting out of squared-off mouths, wild eyes round and ferocious, brows knitted together in sheer fury.

Paolo, in this cruel light, curled in on himself, shaking in terror of the *oni.*

"Paolo!" I cried out, aching to go to him and comfort him, protect him. No man as pure as Paolo should endure fear like he was showing.

FEAR, I thought.

Even in my dreams, my spirit breathed only to feed on the fear of anyone I could suck it from. And nowhere had I seen such unbridled, liquid horror as I did at this moment. Fear of what waits in the dark.

"Such a simple fear for a simple man," the vampire voice

inside me cooed. *"Imagine, a man of the cloth trapped in Yomi."*

But wait. Was that *my* vampire voice that had made me draw the fear from everyone I knew to gain strength from it? Or had it been *her?*

"You're Izanami," I said out loud. "Why are you coming for me?"

With a clap of thunder, Yomi blacked out again.

Izanami's face was inches from mine, hissing fetid breath on me as real as summer wind. The white paint on her face dripped in rivulets, and in their wake left maggots, wriggling down her cheeks. Black hair was piled high on her head, held in place by bloody bones. And when she spoke, spiders formed her words, running down her filthy *kimono.*

"Because we are both Izanami," she said in a voice like ice breaking.

"What? No. That makes no sense."

The cracked lips turned upward grimly. "Do you believe there is sense in this nightmare?"

She turned away with creaking bones, but as she did, I saw only the once-stunning woman she'd been. A royal goddess in shining splendor and humility and a smile like a pink crescent moon.

"Wait!"

But she kept walking in the pitch black—and then I saw what she was walking to.

A baby with flaming red hair.

CHAPTER 12

"Shut up, I think she's moving."

"I didn't say anything."

"I said shut up, what's wrong with you?"

"She's not moving, it's the mist. It's vibrating."

Nicholas, Roman, and Lynch.

I snapped my eyes open and found nothing but a crimson sheen. I could see only their shapes, the men in my afterlife, and I couldn't move, didn't want to…

"I see her eyes, she opened her eyes!" Nicholas said. "She needs to get out of there, El, get out of there!"

Out of where?

"She's struggling! Why won't it let you go, Eliza?"

Panic in Nicholas's voice made me struggle more, but I couldn't move, only moan in frustration and fear. *Where am I? Is this Yomi?*

No, there was nothing black and blinding here. Only warm, red, all-encompassing.

My mist.

I was trapped in it like a goddamn Jell-O mold.

Bursting out in a flurry of crimson fireworks, I sucked in a breath. Rubbing the red from my eyes, I concentrated on Nicholas's hands on my arms, the realness of them, the solidity of them. Nothing like Yomi.

"Cough, I feel like you should cough," Nicholas said, brushing the hair off my face.

I don't know why I listened, but I did feel like I'd been found in a river, and so I coughed.

"Nicholas. What is that?" Roman said tentatively.

"What, what's what?" Nicholas hovered over me, Roman not far behind.

"Eliza, open your mouth please," Roman said.

I opened my mouth, a vision of that gaping maw of mine eating their fears alive threatening to overpower me, but instead I coughed again. Nicholas peered in my mouth as I did, horror written all over the lines in his withered face.

He put his hand on the back of my head and I didn't ask what he was doing when he reached into my mouth.

And pulled a long black feather from my throat.

"You mean this?" Nicholas asked, handing the wet thing to Roman while Lynch gagged.

As I sat in the remnants of a red mist that had betrayed me, tried to keep me like Snow White in her glass coffin, and I watched the men look over the crow feather, I knew what was real and what wasn't.

The mist was mine; it was not from Izanami.

The crow feather, the crows themselves, no matter what Izanami wanted me to believe, were not her doing —they were her husband's.

I also knew that there was truth in what she said about us being the same. And it was one more tear in the fabric between me and Nicholas.

"What happened to you, Eliza, where did you go?" Nicholas blurted, rushing back to my side.

"I…it was just a dream. I didn't go anywhere."

"No, you flashed in and out like a goddamn disco ball in a swamp, and you came back here in a bar of glycerin soap with half a bird down your throat."

"So dramatic. It was one feather. I wasn't in a bar of soap, it was just…a Jell-O mold, and I'm weird and do weird things and we all know it. This is another one."

Again, I didn't want to tell him the particulars. It was becoming a habit.

But Nicholas French can read just about anybody, and me even more so. He wasn't buying it this time.

"El, don't hide from me. Please."

I hung my head, willed my mist to disappear completely and let me be just *me,* not Eliza Morgan, Vampire Freak. Roman asked if I wanted him and Lynch to go—but I didn't. Not only because they comforted me, and I needed to feel like they were on my side, but because I didn't want them talking too much without me.

This was not the time for Roman to find out that

Lynch was creating vampires and abandoning them in his latest psychotic break.

"Okay. Maybe you can help me figure this out. It's gonna sound total *Twilight Zone*, but I went to Yomi. Kinda."

Nobody said a word, not even Nicholas.

Japan was a sacred home for the *Shinigami*, and the Master had been a god among them. Their creator, they'd believed. But I had brought to them a real deity—Izanagi, the actual origin of the *Shinigami*. And Izanami, his wife, had become the goddess of Yomi, trapped there for eternity. To think that I once again had crossed the paths of ancient gods of myth and legend was more than a little overwhelming. To see the shock on these vampires' faces solidified that. The fact that I'd now gone to their underworld, basically… It raised a lot more questions. Not the least of which was, *How far would I go? Where did my own power end?*

Now that I'd said it out loud, I wanted to keep going.

"I saw Izanami—"

"Who?" Lynch butted in.

"Izanami. You know, just the wife of our race's creator, no big deal. Lynch, don't you know anything about the *Shinigami*?"

"You just learned it yourself, Ellie, don't get started," he retorted. "You killed the only maker we ever knew."

"You never cared about him either," Nicholas said. "So shut up and let *Eliza* tell the story we asked for, would you?"

Glaring at Lynch, I went on. "I saw Izanami there. And"—I didn't want to say it, I really didn't—"I saw Paolo too. He looks just *craven,* a shell of who he was. Nicholas," I said, red tears filling my vision, "it was just horrible. Why did he ever go there? Why would he go to a place that would do that to him?"

Without meaning to, we both looked at Roman, who met our eyes and made no apologies. Bethlem had made him even more steadfast. As strong-willed about his own choices as he was for everyone else that he loved.

"Izanami said that she and I were the same. That we were 'both Izanami.' What can she mean?"

"Nothing I want to find out," Nicholas said. And again, his eyes betrayed him.

He was genuinely afraid of me.

I didn't mention the baby. Not exactly intentionally, but it could wait for a later time. I had so little idea of what it meant, and couldn't drop that potential bombshell on top of all the other ones. I'd just add it to my list of withheld information. Also on that list: Izanami claimed to be giving me these new abilities, these gifts that other vampires didn't have.

I wasn't sure I believed her. I couldn't trust her, that was for sure. But why would she claim to have done that? She certainly didn't come across as the giving type, and Izanagi had craved freedom from her. What was she kissing my ass for? If she was giving me these gifts, what did she want me to have them for?

"We are both Izanami."

Christ, I had to figure this out.

My mind ran through a hundred scenarios and followed a thousand threads of thought in a matter of seconds. Now, I'd always been a quick thinker, but this… *Did all vampires think this way when they put their mind to it? So fast, so clear.*

Or was it another "gift" from Izanami?

Not that I had much to go on, but first impressions were everything: Izanami wanted something from me. And she was not the type to have a half-cooked plan. The woman—the *deity*—who reigned over Hell, had eternity to make things happen. Whatever she wanted, she'd have had all the time imaginable to come up with every worst-case scenario, to try and fail as much as necessary to achieve her ends.

No, whatever she wanted, it was endgame material. And I was in the middle of it. But I couldn't quite get my head to fathom what that was.

Izanami could give me powers, what else could she do to my head? Could she keep the truth from me?

Brain rushing in every direction, meeting dead ends all over, I became drained, beaten, in a matter of minutes. Weak, even. I had to feed, and I had to do it fast. My mind was becoming fuzzy, my trains of thought crashing painfully all at once.

Early morning would hurt to go hunting, but I

couldn't stop myself, I was salivating. My fingers were shaking. I needed a fix, and I'd take it from the first warm body I could pin down. The muscle memory made my teeth gnash.

I wanted to kill and drink and I didn't care from who.

I wondered if Izanami was the reason why I had so much less compassion for the victims I took. Or had I done that to myself by hanging around Lynch? Might have been nice if my cruelty wasn't my fault. But then again, was Lynch's his?

If Nicholas could come with me, keep me in check, it would be wonderful. But he couldn't know the measure of my brutality when I fed now, and besides, he was too weak to keep up with me, let alone stop me. Roman needed to just goddamn give him what he had to have. What kind of brother would withhold life's blood just to keep a secret?

Good question, Eliza. I wonder how far you'll go to keep your own.

Shaking off my philosophizing, I left the treehouse as calmly and casually as possible, trying to be somewhat civil. But the sunlight stole any civility I might have had. My skin screamed beneath my clothes, burning like a boiling lobster.

There wasn't enough goodness left in me to let me stand the sunlight. Was that it? I hadn't paid enough attention to my kills recently to read their auras, see if they were more good than bad. I'd been relentlessly fast, barely taking any pleasure from the feeding—just *doing it* was what I needed, the feeling after, the fullness and warmth that I hadn't had since I was alive.

Turns out having purpose doesn't really keep a person warm at night.

Keeping to the shadows of the trees, I bumbled through the forest, trying to escape the sun.

Grunting nearby—or vampire-nearby, which could be almost anywhere.

Blue was running alongside me, a wolf waiting for the right time to close in.

I was a predator, too.

"What do you want, Blue?" I growled under my breath.

Fleeting glimpses of black hair, black rags, running on all fours.

I don't have time for this, I thought, my throat begging me for blood. And I used my gift from Izanami to get myself the hell out of the sunlight and into a vein.

T didn't mean to end up in Japan. I sure as hell didn't want to be there.

On my knees in an unusually clean alley in Tokyo, blood pouring from my chin and all over my clothes, I could finally think clearly. Cleanly.

Three men and one woman sprawled around me, more blood shooting from their throats in geysers, all convulsing in varying stages of death and dying. I felt nothing for them. I didn't know who they were, I didn't remember their faces and couldn't see them now as they twisted and twitched on their backs.

I couldn't even be disgusted with myself, even though I wanted to be.

She'd done this to me.

Izanami. Of course, it had to be.

God, it was easy to believe it was all her fault, and that I wasn't just growing more and more inhuman.

I swaggered out of the alley into the Tokyo night, having spent the day poaching citizens and feeding on them. In Tokyo, everyone was too busy to register me, immersed in activities I couldn't understand. Nothing seemed to scare them. I barely got a second look as I strolled down the street, debating what I should do next. Where I should go. I knew, but I wanted to pretend I didn't. I wanted an excuse to wander through a crowd of prey, knowing what I'd done over and over again.

When I felt like it, I rooted my feet as firmly onto the slick black street as I could, I threw my head back and howled to the sky in that bustling square, and with more purpose than I'd put into transporting before, I let myself loose. I embraced that power from the Empress of Yomi. The air sucked me in, made me fold in on myself, then double, then expand and reach, until I was where I wanted to be.

At a long-forgotten garden bench on a mountaintop.

"What in the bloody fuck, Eliza Morgan?"

"Hi Kieran. You look really good."

Fully aware of how frightened he was that I'd burst in on him, that I was soaked in blood, that I looked more like a sadistic golem than the woman I'd once been, I waited until he could gather himself. He still sat on the bench, but loosened his shoulders up again and patted the seat beside him. We'd come here often once. He took a deep breath, finally un-rattled. No longer did I want to eat his fear like a fresh, raw steak. That was a hunger I controlled now.

This was what it must feel like.

To be Izanami.

"Woman, you look like Hell itself coughed you up."

"I look a hell of a lot better than that, come on."

He laughed, that thick Irish brogue laced with eternal cigarette smoke that set hearts to fluttering. "I suppose you'd look like a queen no matter what you'd been crawling through, love."

It softened me fast, melted me like butter on toast. Like guac on a burger.

I was human in an instant. That pudgy, fleshy, flawed and perfect woman I'd once been that fell—for just a while—in love with Kieran Coughlin.

"I've missed you," I said, in my old voice, the one Kat hated. Not at all the vampiric goddess voice that had weaseled its way in. It broke, and I sobbed suddenly. Looking down at myself, I was ashamed. Superhuman and completely apart from anything that made me *me*. I was coated in the blood of multiple strangers. Kieran was fresh and smooth in his white T-shirt, sleeve rolled up over a pack of cigarettes like some greaser. The stubble that never went away. The mussed hair, the squinting eyes, sizing me up. "I missed you so much, Kieran." The tears fell freely now, and I did nothing to stop them.

"No, no, there there, beautiful."

He didn't care about anything but helping me and making me feel better. His hands in my snarled hair, he held my face right in front of his. His eyes... I'd forgotten how flames constantly burned there, a flicker of the heat inside him. Nothing could ever give justice to that fire in him. He blazed with passion in every movement he made. When he spoke again, it was with the scent of campfire and chocolate and almonds. "Eliza, I've missed you more than you know. I didn't want to do this all alone, love, and it's safe to say that alone doesn't suit you either."

"I'm sorry I left you," I blubbered. For every second I hadn't been human, I made up for it twice in the most humanly messy way. Tears, wet lips, runny nose and all.

"You had to, you had to do that," he pleaded. "You weren't created to be a nursemaid in the immortal burn unit, Eliza dear, now were ya?"

Laughter burst out of me, ugly and wet, but I didn't sniffle it back. "I love you," I said through the gross laughter.

"Yeah, yeah, I know it."

He got me to calm down as only he could—drinking

straight from a bottle of rum and laughing at pretentious vampires who had no Master to listen to anymore.

"They look at me and all they see is… Well, I don't know what they see, but they don't like it, I'll tell ya that," he said, chuckling. "They don't exactly listen to me, right? But then again, I have nothing to tell them." He was the strongest vampire I knew. Laughing the whole time he said this, making fun of his own lack of leadership. "They're grown vampires, for chrissakes! I don't need to tell them what to do! Feed, don't kill each other, they know the drill."

He passed me the bottle again, and it was mixing really poorly with a belly full of blood. But I took it. "Kieran, there is nobody—nobody—I would want to see put in charge if I were them. They needed the exact opposite of the Master, and holy hell did you give it to them." I fell onto my side, laughing as messily as I was crying before, and it felt so powerfully loose and unplanned. I loved it as much as I loved Nicholas. I loved it the way I'd never loved being human.

"Your Golden Boy still treating you well?"

I knew that was coming.

"Of course. I mean, things are strained, but aren't they always?"

"And Blue?"

Sighing, I squished my face up, scratched my forehead, did all kinds of awkward gestures that I thought would help me avoid answering, but Kieran wasn't buying any of it.

"Eliza Morgan, tell me about Blue."

Forcing myself to meet his eyes, I told him. "Kieran…"

"Now, Eliza!"

"She's gone feral. Wild, like an animal, we don't know why, but she's not okay. She's not."

"And why am I finding this out now? How long did it take for her to become an animal? What the hell are you doing out there?"

"Calm down—"

"Like hell, woman! That's my girl." He choked. "Eliza, that's my girl, and she's in trouble, and I was stuck in this—" With a deep breath, he looked hard at me. "What am I doing here?" He threw his hands wide. "They don't need me. I don't need to be here anymore, I'm *well*. And I left her."

"No. No, Kieran, she left you. How long could you support her, feed her, hunt for her? Just like you said, they're grown vampires. So is she."

He nodded, but smoke was accumulating beneath his feet from his rage. I went on.

"She's grown, but she needs our help all the same."

The agony in his eyes when they met mine was immeasurable. Unfathomable. Blood tears danced on his lower lashes—and when they fell they became ash. "She was never meant for this world, Morgan. She's never been strong enough, and she suffers because of me," he spat, jabbing his thumb into his chest. "I stole her from life and forced her into this life of death that she cannot survive. I destroyed her and she'll never escape it."

I couldn't take my eyes off him, riveted to his suffering, aching to ease it. Black ashes cascaded in front of him, pink cherry blossoms cascading behind.

Well, if that didn't sum up Japan. Death on one side, picturesque on the other.

"Wait. I think I know what happened to her, Kieran. Not exactly how, or what…but *who*."

~

"Paolo looked, acted, just like her when I saw him in Yomi."

"In what now? How in the hell?"

"I wasn't really there, but Izanami—you know who she is." Kieran nodded. "She came to me in a dream." I told Kieran all of it, including the baby. Which raised questions, as expected.

"A baby, in that dreaded place," Kieran said, shaking his head.

"She wanted me to see the baby, I just don't know why. But that's not the point, not now. Kieran, she got to Blue somehow. Izanami got to her, drove her crazy, just like she did to Paolo. Goddammit, I won't let either of them turn into one of her devils."

Kieran always listened well. He didn't judge, and he didn't dig. He went for the solution.

"If she came to you in a dream, she's giving you these gifts… She wants you to come there."

"Well…no."

"What do you mean 'no'? We can find a way right now, Eliza."

"So, your plan is to literally go right into the trap she set. That's the strategy you're opting for?"

"I wouldn't call it a *strategy*. I would call it 'taking initiative.'"

I rubbed my eyes hard, pinched the bridge of my nose, trying to make his idea disappear. When I opened them, he had a glass of beer in each hand, the blood mixing inside a welcome sight. I didn't know where this blood came from, and I wanted it to wash away the murders I'd committed in Tokyo.

The first sip traced a line of heat down my throat that made me moan.

"Don't make noises like that, woman. Now I need a cigarette." He plucked one out of his shirt sleeve and lit it with a snap of his fingers.

"New trick?"

He winked one devilishly dark eye. "I'm full of 'em."

"You're unbelievable." I laughed. The man could always make me laugh in the direst of situations—of which we'd seen many together. So, I should have probably listened to him this time. But that wouldn't be me. "Izanami is wicked smart, right?"

"Wicked smaht," he agreed in his best Boston accent.

"And if she went after Blue and then—released her—

back to New Hampshire, she had a reason for it. Why Blue?"

Every time I mentioned her name, he stiffened. It was clearly torturous for him to hear about her. I couldn't imagine if he'd seen her, been attacked by her like I had. Hell, she'd tried to poison Nicholas. *But why?*

I answered my own question. "We all love Blue. We all want to protect her, there's no question of our loyalty to her. That makes her someone we'll fight for. We'll do anything to help her."

"Which sure gives Izanami a lot of leverage if she's the only one who can do it."

"Same for Paolo. Such a good man, it kills me to see him suffering like that. She wants me to owe her, and she wants power over all of us."

"Holy shit, Eliza, that's it. She wants power over all of us." He flicked the cigarette onto the ground, amidst others between the broken paving stones, and stomped on it, which made my teeth grit even now, but I was too enraptured by his line of thinking to yell at him. "She's a goddess. And she's trapped there, with a bunch of little ghouls—"

"And a baby," I gasped.

"Listen to me," he said, frantic. "The Master is dead, Izanagi is gone, Nicholas isn't well. I don't want to be in charge, and you're the most powerful vampire in the world now, Eliza. Don't say you're not, you know that you are."

I shut my mouth, ready to protest. I'd never put it

into words before—but he was right. I was the most powerful vampire in existence.

Of course it was me that Izanami would appeal to.

Of course it was me that she'd claim to be equal to.

"Oh my god," I choked out. "She wants to trade places with me. She wants out."

CHAPTER 13

Kieran knew I had to leave, but I don't think my going helped him worry less about Blue.

Izanami was in my head, she'd gotten into Blue's—who was far less stable than me now—and that made her a threat. The goddess hadn't just created leverage, someone we'd all fall over ourselves to save, possibly fight amongst ourselves to save. No, she'd created a secret weapon, one I'd discovered.

To destroy the life I'd died to have.

She'd taken Blue away from me, and my biggest fear was that now she'd use Blue to take away Nicholas, Roman… Blue alone could destroy all of Ossippee. My poor, sweet friend. Poisoned.

Desperate to get to Nicholas, I all but evaporated from existence to travel the distance to him. Entering his world from the one in Japan was like passing between two different planets; one rooted in ancient prophecy and responsibility, the other in comfort and the life I wanted. I didn't want to be part of both.

"El, Jesus, you ever just knock?"

"Nicholas." I fell into his arms, squeezed my eyes tight.

"Hey, hey," he said, patting my hair down. "Where'd you go? You okay?"

"Japan."

He pulled me away from him, gently, but there was a suspicion behind it. "What was in Japan?"

"We don't have time for that right now, I need to know where Blue is."

"I don't know. She doesn't punch a clock with me."

"And I do?" I said, passively aggressive because I did not like to be questioned, regardless of how important that information was. And I was more than a little embarrassed, I suppose.

Warily, eyes wide, chin down, he said, "I just wanted to know where you went. Casual question for someone who disappeared."

"I need to know where Blue is, she's not in control of her own mind, Nicholas. She's being used and she's going to do something—"

"Whoa, whoa, she's not a threat right this second, okay? If she shows up in the next five seconds, we'll deal with her."

"I don't know that we should be reactive and not proactive about this one."

"Well, I am," he said smoothly with a reassuring

smile. "If she's working for someone, if she's coming for us, then *she will come for us*, and we'll be waiting. What are we going to do if we go out there and hunt her down, El? Chain her up? Drag her back here and make her talk?"

He had a point. I had zero plan. Just confront the issue and think later, really. I nodded my concession.

"Now please, just tell me what you've been doing and why you think you need to keep it from me."

"Hunting. Nicholas, I've been hunting," I blurted. "A lot. Often and—and more than one person at a time."

I don't know why that was my leading statement. The first of many confessions I'd have to let go of.

"How do you mean?"

"You know how I mean."

He searched my face. "Like a killer," he said. Not a question. I just nodded. "How long?"

"Since we came back."

"You mean since you've been palling around with the Abomination, right?"

"Now isn't the time for...whatever that is."

"The truth?" His eyes apologized to me, and he was right. It was the truth and I didn't want to hear it.

"Yeah, I don't feel like hearing the truth. Tell me something else."

He took my hand. "Come on," he said.

Through the swinging red door into the kitchen with its cracked tile and old wood stove. He knew I needed to feel at home. Comforted. Even if I didn't deserve it. He put the tea kettle on, muscles flexing with his every move—but not as much as before. It struck me whenever I saw him how much less alive he was by the day. He turned around to lean against the counter, crossed his arms, and we just looked at each other. Happy, but troubled, but happy? For at least a minute.

"Water doesn't boil at vampire speed still," he said. "It's aggravating, really."

Silence stretched between us as we waited for the distinct whistle. Even though I kept looking over my shoulder, like Blue might jump out at me, slasher-style. The cat jumped down from the top of a high cupboard and curled up at Nicholas's feet. It wasn't even a comfy spot, it was right in the middle of the floor. But he so needed to be near the man who'd taken him in.

I knew the feeling.

When tea had been poured—that sloshing sound always made my shoulders drop and everything loosen up—Nicholas set mine in front of me. Same chipped teacup. He sat down, legs splayed in front of him, leaning back like a school delinquent. "So. Eliza goes a' huntin'. What's that like?"

I wrapped my hands around the cup, tried to channel those first moments in this kitchen when Nicholas told me—showed me—he was a vampire. I'd loved him enough even then to know that it didn't matter.

"I get this like, screaming inside me. Nothing can stop me. And the more I go out, the less satisfied I am to take just one life. Yesterday?" I couldn't look at him—but I forced myself to. "I killed four people yesterday."

"Whoa. Four. Four? In Japan?"

"Yes. I don't know—well, I didn't know why I went to Japan, but I do now."

"Kieran?"

No judgment in his eyes, no irritation in his whipped cream voice. Just looking for understanding, and to be there for me.

"I saw him, but he's not why I was there. I was there because…" *Why can't I say it?*

"Izanagi?" Nicholas guessed.

"Close." I laughed. "The wife."

I told him about the dream, and the "gifts" Izanami had bestowed upon me.

"I can't imagine you'll be sending a thank you note for her thoughtfulness."

"I actually think she'll come to collect it in person."

We drank another cup of tea while I told him our trading places theory. I wish Nicholas hadn't so readily agreed.

"Eliza, can you please explain why ancient monsters like to hang out with you so much? Are there more after this one? I think you covered them all, at least vampire-wise. Is there a boss level I should expect?"

"Well, I think the boss level is really my problem, while you'll have to be on the distract and extract front. Because Izanami will have thought this out, she's had all that time in Japanese Hell."

"Purgatory. Yomi is Purgatory."

"Uh, yeah. Okay. Anyway, Nicholas. She has Paolo. And worse, I'm pretty sure she's responsible for what's happened to Blue."

He squeezed his eyes shut. His fingers flew to the spot between his eyes that he pinched to make everything go away for a second. The thing about being *Shinigami* is that you could close your eyes to it all for decades and nothing ever went away. All those horrors waited. All we can do is try to be scarier.

Opening his eyes wide, blinking away the stars, he said, "She's in her head? That's what you're saying, right?" I didn't have to respond. His jaw set, he put his shoulders back, still stronger than any one of us. He focused on me, zeroed in. "You have to take her out."

"Whoa, what?" I mean, I thought at least it would have been a *we* have to take her out, or a plan, or *I know a guy*. But it was none of that from him. "Nicholas, she's the goddess of creation, and of Yomi. She's not... How? I can't do that. Look at what she did to Blue, look at the abilities she's given me. Think of what else she can do!"

"Think of what *you* can do!"

"This is no time for a motivational speech, Nicholas! We need a plan!"

Infuriatingly, he smiled. A big toothy one, amused by me. I could have strangled him with my mist, drawn blood and drained him—

That's not you thinking that, dammit, get control of yourself, Eliza.

Fiddling with his teaspoon, he said, "Remember at the temple, when you fought that mountain man, like, our first day there?"

"Yeah. Seems so long ago now."

"Not that long ago. You were human then. You fought—you beat—that goliath as a *human*. Zero difference from you as a death god fighting an older god. You were powerful then. You're powerful now. Not so much has changed."

A memory of Kat popped into my mind. We'd been young, just moved in together. It was a blizzard, had raged for days, and we were running out of food. Nobody with a conscience would have considered calling a restaurant for delivery on the off chance any were open. So naturally, I said I'd go out. I'd shovel as much as I could, warm up the car. If the car was frozen, I'd boil water to thaw it. If I had to walk through the storm, I'd stop any place I could go indoors along the way to warm up. There might be people who needed help I could check on as I went. There'd been no electricity for two days, and in New Hampshire that could be deadly. As I'd strung together my plan, Kat sat stunned.

"You can do anything, can't you?" she'd said without a hint of a smile.

I actually didn't think I could do much of anything. I couldn't button my jeans. I couldn't cook. I couldn't do laundry without turning something a new color. I couldn't stand anyone long enough to get a job outside of the gift shop where at least I knew the people would go away. But this? This was just survival.

"You'd do it if you could," I'd said to Kat.

"But I couldn't," she'd said. And we'd left it at that.

"She was right, you know," Nicholas said, interrupting the memory.

I shook my head. "You heard that?"

He pointed above my head to a red cloud, and the silhouetted figures fading away within it. "I saw it," he said.

"I miss her," I blurted.

"Yes. You do. Every day," Nicholas said, with a single nod. A statement as clear as my name. Like a promise.

Like the air I didn't need to breathe, like the pain I didn't need to wince from, like the food I didn't need to enjoy. Missing her became a habit that I couldn't let go because I didn't want to. But if any of those things made me sick or hurt me, I would stop them. Wouldn't I?

Wouldn't I?

If humanity had taught me anything it was that missing my parents and my grandmother could steel me into an impenetrable fortress. It ached on the inside—that fear of dying, and of losing anyone else I loved. It squeezed my heart until the *Shinigami* claimed it for their own. I kept everyone away because the inevitability of them being torn from me by that same beast, Death, was too imminent, no matter how long it gave me. Until Death was all I had left.

And so I made a choice.

I had lost Kat, yes. But missing her could not consume me any longer. I had given in to Death—and it had given me something in return. Pining for those I missed would never bring them back. And I would not endure eternity shying away from all those other lives I missed out on because I'd been eaten alive by my feelings.

Lynch had been sent to me. What he was doing now was for *me*, I could accept it now.

Turning those girls into vampires, leaving them scattered to find their own paths, he was looking for Kat every way he could and never finding her.

And he was losing *them*. As if they had nothing to offer. As if they had no purpose.

I had a mission. A plan. A path of healing.

A coven of my own.

And Nicholas would have to be a part of it.

"Nicholas, there's something I need to tell you. I probably—"

Then Roman slammed his way in, shaking the entire cabin like a leaf. When he came through the kitchen door, he wasn't even walking—pure fury held him aloft, floating him in. Any deadness behind his eyes before was purged with this anger. And I had a feeling I knew why.

"Eliza Morgan, what have you done?"

"Oh hey Roman, whatcha been doin'?" Nicholas didn't even raise an eyebrow as he threw an arm over the back of his chair.

"You have no idea what she knows," Roman said, still hovering in the air. I'd never seen him so viciously angry, and *accusing*.

"Well, I don't know, I'm learning some stuff," Nicholas said, nodding at me as if to say that we were really getting somewhere.

"Roman, calm down," I said, which is the stupidest advice for anyone having a serious meltdown. "I mean, please let's talk."

"Let's talk?" he screeched. "You're no better than Lynch!"

"Whoa," Nicholas said, getting to his feet in a move faster than light. "Back off her, right now, or it will get ugly." He put his hand on Roman's chest, and Roman blinked long and hard before lowering himself to the ground.

"You don't know what she's done, Nicholas," Roman said in little more than a whisper.

"Why don't you tell me, hmm? Come on, sit down. This is Eliza we're talking about. We've probably seen worse together."

But Roman's glare said he disagreed.

While Roman and I sat down as if we were facing off over a chess board, Nicholas made his brother a cup of tea. And he brought a pie out of the fridge.

"This is my favorite *Golden Girls* episode," he said as he sat with us. "Where the ladies talk about life and death and morality over banana cream pie. Okay Roman, go. What happened at Lynch's?"

Roman, to his credit, picked up one of the forks Nicholas tossed on the table, and took a bite straight from the pie. "Lynch is turning women," he said simply. "And Eliza knew. She's been letting him. Encouraging him."

"Turning women? What women? Where?"

So this was it. I'd kept it secret for what, ten minutes? This was what I got for not being totally up front. Since when did I keep secrets and not, often stupidly, face the uncomfortable stuff head-on?

"Everywhere," I told Nicholas, drawing his attention from Roman. "He's not..." I almost said Lynch wasn't right in the head, but that would be a poor argument. He never had been.

"He's pollinating the world with vampires," Nicholas said, lips turned down, raising his eyebrows in a familiar unsuitably-impressed look. "I mean, when you're a serial killer and you want to step up your game, I guess you make more killers."

Again, I had to stop myself from defending him.

Roman gave me reason to throw fuel on the fire though.

"Eliza knew he was doing this, Nicholas," he barked, pointing a finger at me. "She was there with him the whole time, and she let it happen!"

Fury filled me, right or not. "What would you have me do, Roman? Huh? What, should I talk some sense into him? Is that how you reform a next-level serial killer? Maybe you're the wrong guy to ask, seeing as you not only knew he was a murderer, you made him one for eternity."

Nicholas sucked in a breath and looked away.

Roman had the cleanest, clearest blue eyes I'd ever seen. When I said this to him, they muddied, not in anger, but like a pure thing turned forever wrong, a violated beauty.

"I know," he said, all his anger gone, along with his spirit, his love of life.

But not his fear.

His aura still held onto it, a gray-brown, focused mass like a disease around him. And I knew then that while Roman wore his shame on the outside, almost saintly in his humbleness and compassion, he also harbored a secret. A terrible secret that he'd never let go of.

And being me, I was certain I wouldn't stop until I uncovered it.

The somber air around us was thick, and we had nothing to do but acknowledge it and move on.

"Okay," I said. "We're all clear that none of us is mistake-free and error-proof, yeah?"

"*Yeah?*" Nicholas mocked me. "Channeling your inner Irishman?"

"YEAH," I said more loudly at him. "We aren't error-proof, *as I was saying*. But we have forever to fix things."

"I suggest we don't take that long," Roman said with a sad laugh. "We have to stop him."

I nearly said that stopping Blue was a far bigger

problem, but I just could not get into that with Roman now, not when he was so upset with me. He was good at rationalizing evidence against whoever he was angry with.

"What do you suggest?" Nicholas asked Roman, but I didn't hear much after that. I was busy in my own head, reasoning out that I wasn't so gung-ho about stopping him.

I wanted to make a coven of my own. It was there, in front of me, waiting.

"No," I said, more to myself than either of them.

"This'll be good," Nicholas said.

"Just listen for a minute. A Stop-the-Abomination plan focuses our attention on the wrong issue."

"What other issue could there possibly be?" Roman asked, incredulous.

"That there's already a bunch of newborn vampires out there, flailing around in the world, maybe so many that we can't get to them all before they're lost forever. And I mean, *really* forever. If we don't focus on contacting those women and helping them, we could truly be creating serial killers all over the globe."

"She's right," Nicholas said.

"But we have to do both," Roman said, shaking his head. "Stop him and start with them."

"Our Stop-the-Abomination plans *suck*, though," Nicholas said. "They never work. For as heartless a beast as she was to say it, Eliza's right—we can't just talk the serial killer out of being a serial killer. We don't run a rehab. But we *can* run an Avengers-style Vampire Camp."

"I am *not* a heartless beast, but I like your idea. We gather them up. Bring them here. Lynch has room for some… I don't know how many there are, guys. But I'm like…well, I have a fine ability to sorta teleport these days," I said. Roman raised his eyebrows. "We keep them close."

We make a coven, I thought. It was all working out.

"Okay," Roman said. Which shocked both Nicholas and me.

"I'm sorry, did you say 'okay'?"

"Yes. I think it's a good idea."

I ran with it. "We give them a purpose." Before either of them could butt in with the *Shinigami*-esqueness feel of that, I bowled them over with logic. "One thing that has worked all these centuries is that the *Shinigami* had a common place to feel grounded in Japan. A home made for them. We can do that."

"Yeah, but El, giving them a purpose sounds sorta culty, don't you think? Like we're starting a religion," Roman said.

"It could be, sure, but it won't be. We'll be organized. And we need to give them *some* direction or they'll fall back on the one thing that always feels good—blood."

Nicholas cleared his throat, which meant he was actually going to be completely serious. "And what *will* we tell them about blood? We've got no Master to manipulate us into… Whoa, *we* were a cult!"

There it was. An entire species following the teachings of one man who turned out to be lying all along.

While we were all dumbstruck, Nicholas said, "I need to write a tell-all. *Vampire Cult* by The Golden Boy."

"I can't believe you haven't written a book yet, Lestat. It was a matter of time," I said, getting a hearty laugh from Roman while Nicholas struggled to argue that he wasn't self-aggrandizing. Then everything lightened up.

Because yes, there were going to be challenges, and problems, and we were rounding up killers before they knew what they'd become, but we were doing a good thing, and together. Starting as a family.

A family with one extremely unstable son named Chris Lynch.

CHAPTER 14

I was getting what I wanted.

Difficult to say, how often I actually got what I wanted completely, let alone handed to me with little struggle. But here we were. I thought I'd need to drag Nicholas kicking and screaming into the idea of starting my own coven. I hadn't thought of Roman's role in it at all. I never considered that they'd actually listen to me and think I was right.

Was there actually a chance of this turning out *well*? It seemed impossible. It was a winning lottery ticket that multiplied.

Chris was a wild card, there was no getting around it. I never saw where the problem really routed from, but goddammit, I should have. It's something I'll never let myself live down.

We planned, we *created*, made all the trappings of an organized mess until we were exhausted. Three tired vampires was the sign of a job well done, Nicholas said. And so we all went to bed, though there wasn't much rest in it for the two of us.

Even though we were in this together, even though it was obvious to me that he was excited, I couldn't tell Nicholas how much I wanted to do this. The words wouldn't come. We showed each other instead.

I'll never be like the Master, I thought when I could think, but I didn't want to think, only feel, and be there with Nicholas.

It's not a myth that vampires have heightened senses. Supernatural abilities. Well, they could be natural for *us* —we're a different species. Some can see every minute detail of every little thing in existence. Some become flooded by the minutiae, and get washed away in the tides of emotion, reality, imagination, fear.

That night with Nicholas, I was that flood. I was possibility incarnate.

We were part of each other and something bigger.

When I could breathe, I tasted him. When I floated away, I saw Lynch, creating. When my eyes fluttered open, vision came to me like the sun rising.

I had drunk the blood of a god and become one myself.

This. This was what it felt like to be beyond understanding.

When dawn broke and Nicholas was asleep on the low bed, Zen-like, I stood at the glass doors in his room and looked out at the woods the way I did as a human.

Seeing just what was before me. I needed to slow down, and not let the power of who I was and what I was about to do become who I was. *Shinigami* love their myths and destinies and prophecies, and I was *Shinigami* in my heart.

Izanagi's *Shinigami.* Not the Master's.

Izanagi was as much man as he was god, and I wouldn't take for granted that he'd become one with me. He was there throughout my life, that wine and roses headiness that meant the consistency of funerals to me. He was the connection between what I was and what I became. I had learned through him that vampires are not perfect. They make their purpose, using the gifts given them through the blood.

The forest beyond the tree line was visible to me but I shut it out.

I would not let the grand vision of defining a new race of vampires blind me to everything in front of me. And it wasn't lost on me that Izanami could be in my head at any time, knowing what I knew, shaping what I did.

Like I'd watched Nicholas do so many times, I opened the doors to his little porch, its grass mat crunching under my feet. I used the breath I didn't need to take to ground me. *In through the nose. Out through the mouth.* I focused my every movement, forming blocks, strikes, kicks in slow motion, never leaving the imme-diate space. *Use what you have.* Learning martial arts in Japan leaves...an impression. A vitality all its own. I would channel it now to remind me that everything done well is done in steps.

I don't know how long I was out there, but a sheen of sweat touched every inch of me when Nicholas put a hand on my waist, bringing me to a halt.

"Eliza," he said dreamily, kissing my neck.

"You're awake." *Obviously.*

He spun me around, his skin glowing through its ashiness, like a pearl covered in dust. "You know you've been out here for hours."

"Oh." I looked around the woods, the signs every-where. "You were asleep for longer."

"You win." He kissed me hard, making me giggle like I wasn't a vampire god. "So, you got a god in your head right now?"

"I don't know. Can't tell." I knew what he was think-ing: Was that all me last night? "It was all me last night," I said.

"That's not what I asked."

"And you know what I'm going to say to that."

His laugh rumbled down through me, pooled in my belly, right back up and out in my own voice. I threw my arms around him, joy filling my aura for me to see. I wished he could see it too, hoped that he could in a way.

"Nicholas, we're really doing this. Aren't we?" I said it reverently, like we were a couple that decided to have a baby. This wasn't so different. The closest we could come.

I squinted against the image of the red-haired baby

in my head, living in Yomi. What kind of a childhood was that? How was he…she…there?

And suddenly I felt such a kinship with this anonymous baby that was probably a tiny monster too, because we'd both been born to live among death.

As if called to the mere thought of it, Blue whipped by us in a midnight slash through the daylight, a haunt among the trees.

"Nicholas," I whispered. "What can we do for her?"

"An in-law cottage in the backyard hardly seems the answer, huh?"

We stared into the woods for a sign of her again. "Blue!" I called out. "Blue!"

But I don't think either of us really wanted her to come. I was terrified of what might happen when she did.

Little difference that made when Blue fell upon us from above, having found her way to the roof. Snarling and gnashing her teeth, she tore at my hair and clothes while Nicholas yelled her name, pulling her off with great effort. He threw her to the ground off the porch, eliciting a wild yelp from her. I wiped at the tears pouring from my face, leaving watery pink stains on my hands. Why, why did this have to happen to that sweet soul?

I had an answer for that. Because she could be used against me.

As Blue scuttled like a crab into the woods, whining

and whimpering, I steeled myself against what I must do.

"I have to go to Yomi."

Nicholas more fell than sat on the porch, exhausted once again. *Dammit, Roman, feed him already!* My mind was reeling in so many directions, I had to remind myself of my original resolve: One step at a time. Focus.

"El, sending you into Purgatory now would be—and I can't stand myself for this not-quite pun—a death sentence." His voice was raspy, his breath short. "You—" he had to stop to take a breath, his chest heaving with the effort. "You can't be everywhere at once." He coughed, doubling over.

Once again, my priority shifted. From getting ready for Izanami, to stopping Lynch, to building a vampire coven, to going to Yomi itself, and now to Nicholas. Because if I did all those other things and couldn't manage to get Roman to heal the man he calls his brother in a way that only he could, then what was it for? What would my eternity be if I couldn't make that happen for the person closest in all the world to me?

I helped Nicholas back to bed. I don't know if I was seeing time move ultra-fast, or if it was a vision of the future coming to pass, but with every step Nicholas looked more and more frail. His health drained out of him with each breath that rattled through him. I shook from the waking vision, finally struggling not to sob as I laid him down—and he was little more than a corpse. *It's not real,* I told myself.

But it would be. I knew that.

He was skin and a skeleton in that bed. His T-shirt hung against his body, every rib visible, a death rattle in his breath. His upper arms were as thin as my forearm, his cheeks hollow and hugging his teeth. The only reminder of who he'd been were the fangs dimpling his cracked, colorless lips, and the slow swirling of his cocoa eyes before they went dark and still.

"Nicholas, no," I moaned, running my hands through his hair. I expected that hair to come off in my hands, but it felt healthy enough that I could convince myself I was seeing things. It wasn't real.

A trick to keep me here. A vision given to me by Izanami.

It wasn't real, but it would be. It was coming. Once again, I remembered first things first.

I was done waiting for Roman to come to terms with the secrets he held. No secret shame was worth Nicholas's life. Roman's time was up. He would feed Nicholas if it killed all three of us.

CHAPTER 15

I needed him when he was alone. I wouldn't use Nicholas as a tool to make Roman do what he needed to do. It hadn't worked so far.

We may not be any good at Stop-the-Abomination plans, but the Abomination was good for something.

Back at the mansion, I found Lynch in his usual spot on the couch, staring idly, this time with a glass of whiskey in his hand. Apparently he did have a taste for something again.

"Can I have one of those?" I said, making him jump from the thoughts he'd been lost in.

He turned his cold eyes on me. Unreadable. Intent but directionless. Dangerous. "You don't like whiskey," he said flatly.

Amusing. "You know that?"

"I never liked you. It doesn't mean I didn't notice

you," he said, and got up, like a human, returning in a vampire second with a cold beer.

"You…keep beer here?"

"No. I have beer here. I don't know how old it is."

"It's not dusty, anyway. Let's go outside."

"Why?"

"You built me a treehouse. I can sit on the steps of it and have a beer with you, can't I?"

There was no twitch on his lips when he turned his eyes on me this time. Black eyes. "Like a doll's eyes," I remembered from Jaws, and smirked. *You don't scare me, Chris Lynch.*

The shocking thing even after all this time was that it was still jarring how quickly he changed from sadness to ambivalence to psychotic to depressed to charming.

"You want something," he said.

"Don't we all?"

He followed me—*he* followed *me*—to the spot I wanted. This was how it would have to be. I would establish dominance in little ways, but he'd know I was doing it. He was keen to tactics. I would have to let him know that we were playing this silent game together and that there could be only one winner.

I cracked the beer, sitting on the short steps to my little home.

There wasn't fear exactly in his aura—just hesitation. Fight or flight. But he sat beside me on the step, our legs touching in the narrow area, and that contact made him relax.

That was a shock I wasn't prepared for. I comforted him, even when he was unsure of me. Maybe *because* he was unsure of me. We were more alike than I thought.

"We have problems to solve, you and I," I said.

"What did you do, Eliza?" he asked me.

"What? Nothing, I'm not talking about anything *I've* done."

"You don't think we should talk about the things you're doing?"

"What?" I said again, aggravated that this conversation was being taken away from me. "No, it's about the things you're doing, so listen." But he was shaking his head, lifted his eyebrows in a *can you believe this* way, like I was crazy. It was impossible to go on without addressing it. "What, Lynch? What's bothering you?"

"You are!" he burst out. "You've been killing, like I do." And his face softened, took on a dark warmth. "Like me. Like you're sick with it."

"Sick?" I breathed out. "Lynch, I'm just not holding back now. That's all. I do not kill like you do," I growled. "You stalk, choose, get close to them, *you're* sick, I'm not…not addicted to it like you are." The disgust oozed from my voice like a sickness itself, and I remembered who I was talking to.

"And yet you're not trying to cure me, are you?" he said.

I shuddered as he penetrated me with that vicious gaze I remembered him having when we first met, and before Kat died. Like he was playing a one-sided game of chess and was just waiting to flip the board on me.

"No," I said. "I'm not. There's no curing you, we all know it. What I can do though is put you to use. You're the most conniving person I know."

"Gee, thanks."

"You're welcome. You want to redeem yourself in some way?"

"Never said that."

"I'm telling you that you do. Help me get Nicholas back on his feet."

"And how do you propose I do that? He despises me."

"What he needs is Roman's blood. Only Roman's blood will restore him because he drank…" I didn't need to say it; we both knew. "Here's the thing. Roman won't feed Nicholas because he's hiding something and he's afraid that his blood will betray him. Either to Nicholas through residue or to me if I drink from him… I don't know yet. But I do know that whatever I'm here to learn from your blood, it's a puzzle, and Nicholas feeding is the first piece I have to place. Do you want to know why I was brought back here?"

"Not especially."

Something rose up between us like the tension in a funeral home. An understanding.

"Lynch… I won't just leave you alone here when I figure it all out, you know."

He glared at me the way a hurt child does when a

parent apologizes. Reluctant and wary. "You want me to get Roman to feed Nicholas?" he said slowly.

"Inadvertently. Roman did that horrible… He killed Kat just to save Nicholas from having to do it. And now he's willing to let him wither away when he could so easily prevent it? Whatever he's hiding, it's powerful, and he can't be given a choice to tell us or not. You're the only person I know who can back him up against a wall. Corner him. I need you to do it now."

I was asking for an energy level from him that I wasn't sure he had anymore, and I didn't even know how he'd do it—which is why I had to ask him. He knew how to get under Roman's skin in a way I never could, and I didn't know what other options I could find.

Quietly, soothingly, I appealed to him. "Don't you think Kat would want you to know why we've been drawn together?" He snapped his head around at me in defiance. "She would want you to do this."

Rubbing a hand over his face, he sighed. "I'll find a way," he mumbled into his hands. "You might not like how I do it."

"Oh, I thought that was pretty much a guarantee. But I like the alternative even less. And Lynch, there's something else." I almost didn't tell him, but he knew how to use every bit of knowledge as a weapon, and he needed a lot of ammo. "Nicholas and I calmed Roman down about the vampires you've been creating. He almost murdered me for knowing and not telling him. But we've got a plan."

I told him that we were rounding up the vampires he'd left and creating our own coven, and the delight in his eyes was wildly malicious. He'd always loved to watch the world burn.

"I know what to do," he said.

The three of us had agreed that I should be the one to tell Lynch about the new coven. He could hardly stand Nicholas, and Roman was too much of an angry father for him to listen. Lynch could find those girls through his connection to them, if he wanted to. He could just plain tell us where to go, for the ones he remembered. But not only did he want nothing to do with the vampires he'd abandoned, he was, as expected, using all the information he had to his advantage.

He would refuse to help Roman locate the women. Nicholas could scare him into doing whatever he wanted—but not in the weakened condition he was currently in. It had to be me who approached him. So we'd play them. It was the only way I could get everyone to work together.

My heart stank like rotten meat with the deception of it all. It churned in me, aching to be wiped clean. But secrets beget secrets, and vampires accumulated them in hordes. My own intentions changed with every passing minute, it seemed.

While the clock ticked, I pretended to be holed up with Lynch, convincing him to help me find the women. In actuality, we were simply *being*, and it felt pretty good. We played cards, I got him to drink tea, we listened to the rain fall on the roof of the treehouse. Two days passed while Nicholas wasted away and hungry vampires roamed without direction or help.

"You go, and you tell them I won't help you no matter what," he said when we thought enough time had passed.

"No way, you have to do it. They'll see me lying a mile away."

"You think I should go over there and tell them to leave me alone?"

"Yeah, sort of. Tell them you'll leave and never reveal the locations of these vampires if they don't get me off your back."

"Eliza, what if I told you I don't know where they are? That I don't feel them at all?"

"Well. I have a plan for that, too," I said quietly. The level of deviousness I'd reached was just staggering to me. *It's all for a good cause, Eliza. They're just lies. They can be forgiven. They're a means to an end.* I told myself that a lot.

"Let me guess," Lynch said with a sneer, "you're going to drink from me until you see them all."

It wasn't a stretch, after all. But I'd be doing it against his will—at least it would seem that way to Roman and Nicholas. And maybe it would be true. Lynch really didn't want anything to do with the new vampires. Whatever his purpose was, it wasn't being the leader of a fresh coven. Those kills had been a coping mechanism for him. Having them around would be a constant reminder of what he'd been trying to escape, or trying to bring back in a Frankenstein-like way: Kat.

I was apologetic, pitying, when I said, "There's no other choice for me than to get him well. You see that, right?"

He chuckled under his breath. "You have to win. That's what I see. You need this all to go exactly as you want."

"It's far from going the way I want." I laughed. We were about six degrees from the problem, but I refused to let Chris think he had the upper hand here. "Go, before I change my mind. Stick to the plan."

Daylight, and Lynch strode outside into the sunshine without so much as a flinch. He'd been drinking from good people, with clean auras. And yet it did nothing to lighten him, left no residue to make him any happier.

I had not been feeding on the best quality folks. The light seemed to reach for me with hot fingers, scrambling for me when Lynch opened the door. Amusement was all over his face, but he left without a word. I would wait until the sun was low, and go to them. If all went well, hopefully Roman would see that the only way to make Lynch do what they wanted was for him to feel threatened by Nicholas. And then Nicholas would feed from Roman. Wildly convoluted plan, but then again, vampires aren't known for their simplicity of spirit.

But when darkness descended, I was trembling with the desire for blood.

Just a quick hunt.

I hadn't hunted since the men in Japan, my appetite all but gone. With the encroaching hunger came the lingering in the darkness. And then the desire for dark blood. It didn't matter that there wasn't time.

Lynch called it a sickness. I *wanted* to fall into it, for just a few minutes, let myself drift away in the lowliness of a kill and be gone, for just a little while. Then I could face all the lies, the responsibility, the haunting and the evil.

There was enough time for me to be a little evil myself.

Singing Pines Park was where I ended up, sitting on a bench. The place where I'd first seen Lynch lose control so much that he dropped the veil that hides us from mortals. I, just a girl then, saw him drink deeply from that young lady, her blood spotting the snow beautifully. Horrifying then—beautiful now. A romantically stunning scene of black, white, and red with the frozen pond and the trees singing in the cold wind, Christmas lights dotting the duskiness. Life meant something different to me then.

The ground was muddy—not the best place for a walk, but that never stopped the starry-eyed nature lovers from dawdling.

Did I really want to kill one of them?

I did. I really did. But could I coach a bunch of newbies to do the same thing?

I dropped my head into my hands. "What in the holy hell have I committed to?"

No, the question was, what choice did I have? The vampires existed—I was only going to help them find their way, make good choices. I thought.

She walked by, alone, leggings and some fancy hoodie-thing but the kind that hugs every curve and shows off just how much time the yoga mat has seen. Her hair gleamed, up in an artful messy bun with strands straying flawlessly here and there. I could see darkness in her eyes. She was smiling ever-so-faintly, was certainly the head of the PTA, and a valued member of her community. Her aura floated airily about her as if to say "namaste." But other words were scrawled throughout. Vicious words that immortality made even more ghastly for how commonplace they were among so many. Words attached to skin color, to where someone grew up, to sex. The kinds of words that for so many became who they were, and to think that such an idea, a falseness, could follow a person for *eternity...* It certainly changed my idea of what a "good" person could look like, act like. If they were the type of person who should be made immortal. Or should it be the damaged ones, the recipients of that often silent abuse? Who *was* worthy of immortality?

Who deserved death at an immortal's hand? Or teeth.

Leggings Lady came upon me, and I made no attempt to cloak myself from her. Her aura was…forgiving…when she met my eyes. Apparently I was good-looking enough for her. And I was white, so I guess that worked, too.

If I killed her, she would be missed by many. The other PTA moms, the clerks at the grocery store where she was always so kind. Her family. Both kids. But her thoughts smelled like sulfur and no wildly expensive facial cream could hide it on her skin. Not from me.

I guess the final question was, would the world be better without her?

"Hello," she said coldly but with a tight-lipped smile.

"Hi."

I was no longer hungry.

~

"You're going to leave me alone."

Lynch had gotten to the cottage before me, as planned. I was still several yards away myself, approaching on foot, but of course heard everything.

"Ugh, why did you let him in?" Nicholas groaned. I laughed out loud, slowing once I reached the yard. Might as well enjoy the banter before it all went ugly.

"This idea is ridiculous, and I won't have any part of it," Lynch said.

Then Roman started. This was where it would begin.

"Chris," he said. Immediately, I pulled forth the red

mist, creating a miniaturized version of the whole scene inside. The three men were clear to me. But I didn't need to see anything at all to know Lynch caught the one word, *Chris*, and knew he was being worked.

And poorly.

I thought of how he always called Nicholas "Nick," and how Nicholas fumed about it. And here Lynch was, not mentioning at all that Roman never called him "Chris."

Roman continued, "We have an opportunity, Chris, to do some good. You have a chance to do the right thing here." His words were loaded, the tone of his voice off, but I couldn't see beneath it.

"There have been plenty of opportunities for me to do 'good' before this. This time isn't different," Lynch said, some of that old shark sneaking into his words.

Roman's silhouette in the mist flickered and darkened, sharpened, narrowed and stretched like a thing finding its way into the world.

His aura was shifting.

The voice in my head—Izanami—burst into my mind. *"Focus harder, foolish girl. You've been given gifts."* And of course, she was right.

The *telling* was there. All I had to do was pull it along.

"Wouldn't you want to...to...create something," Roman choked up, "if you could?"

His words bled into his aura, blobs of pain and deterioration of his heart. *What is getting to you, Roman?*

"I did create something. Quite a few of them. Not

much of a creator, it turns out. I feel nothing for them. Nothing you can do will make me be a part of your backwoods family, Roman. What will you do, bring them all here? Show them how to hunt, as if they have no idea what they want, like they're completely imbecilic and can't follow their own craving for blood? You going to show them how to hide themselves while they drink, as if that will do anything to protect them? You are no Master, and this isn't some mountain in Japan."

"No," Nicholas interjected, "it's a mountain in the U.S. and we can update what we've been taught, make it mean something. We can start the right way."

"The right way?" Lynch laughed. "You presume there's a right way to murder people. That's what you're saying."

"Goddammit, Lynch!" Nicholas exploded, shocking all of us. "We have to contend with who we are! I won't go through this for the millionth time. We are who we are and we do what we can do. But listen to me, you have to stop making new vampires until we get these ones under control." The argument was taking so much energy out of him, gray lines were forming around his eyes, miniscule to a human but like open veins to me. "No more vampires, Lynch."

In an instant, those condescending final words tipped Lynch over the edge into the voraciously cruel creature I'd first met. I had to stop myself from rushing into the cabin to protect Nicholas, stop Lynch. This was what we needed.

"And who's going to stop me?" Chris spelled out menacingly.

Only one of us could. A cascade of delight crashed over me—Nicholas back to himself, and knowing what Roman was hiding—I needed this like blood. Willing the mist to stay focused on the scene before me rather than give in to its own sentient excitement, I trained my eyes on the Lynch figure. Until the little silhouette glanced my way.

"Keep pushing them," I thought at him.

Lynch's image faltered as he tried to understand where my voice was coming from. I'd broken his concentration.

"Lynch," Roman choked out. The emotion there, the guilt and fear ate at me, itching for me to drag it out of my friend. "You don't have to help us guide them, but you have to stop creating vampires."

"Didn't you just tell me it would feel *good* to create something?"

"Something good! But more than that, to take responsibility for an existence you brought..." But Roman couldn't finish. His words hung in the air, traced like a shadowy finger through the scene in the mist, and I felt the stab in his heart—though I could never truly *feel* it.

Because I'd never had a child, and I'd never lost one.

I finally dropped the mist and entered the cabin, straight past Nicholas and Lynch to wrap Roman in my arms, hoping that he could feel how sorry I was, while both trying to relay and hide my guilt at pushing him the way I had. Lynch may have said the words, but it was only because of me. Roman didn't embrace me back, though—a move entirely unlike this man made of compassion. Pulling back, I blinked hard, trying to see what I was missing in his aura, but nothing happened.

"Eliza..." he began.

That one word sounded like an apology.

I cocked my head, as if it could help un-confuse me. "What's going on, Roman?"

It was Nicholas who answered. "He's not going to let me drink," he said with a casual shrug.

Roman's eyes told a different story, though. He didn't plan to let Nicholas drink, no, but that wasn't what he was hiding. Why he needed to apologize to me.

Backing away, I shoved him off with a mere thought, and he stumbled backwards. "Whatever *betrayal*," I snarled, "you're smothering? It can't be worse than leaving your brother to wither away. You came back here, for what? Because you were too weak to say no to me?" Fury fueled my words, my hurt. "You just love this self-flagellation. The martyr. Right? You said you would bring Nicholas back."

"Did it ever occur to you that we aren't supposed to live forever, Eliza?" Roman muttered, and immediately dropped his head, remorseful.

But I'd already propelled myself across the space and slapped him hard. He hit the ground, me standing over him while Nicholas begged me to leave him alone. "No.

It never occurred to me that Nicholas should die. And if you can look at him and think that, well then the wrong brother is dying."

"El," Nicholas whispered, defeated, hand on my shoulder. "No."

I stifled a scream that rumbled up from inside me, boiling the mist in my body, exploding my soul. Because all I wanted to do at that moment was rip Roman limb from limb and gorge myself on his blood.

Then the voice of the demon goddess in my head cackled. She wanted this, this chaos.

She's doing this, I thought. And of course, she heard.

CHAPTER 16

"Stop!" I yelled—but I was the only one doing anything to stop. They all turned to me, waiting for my next move, whatever latent crazy would show itself.

I had to wonder how far back Izanami had been messing with me. How much of this new vampire was actually *me*, not some extension of *her*?

And I shoved the crippling betrayal away from me at a thought that had no basis in reality: Did Izanagi somehow let her in?

"This fighting, the secrets, it's all orchestrated by her," I murmured.

"Her?" Lynch said.

"Izanami."

Lots of questions about that were to follow, but I could only shake my head, confusion rattling my brain as the voices came one after the other in an onslaught and I tried my hardest to work through the nagging thought that Izanagi had set me up. Could have been recently, could have been part of his escaping the mountain, could have been when I lost my parents and death hung around me. Waiting. Was this what fate really was? Betrayal by gods who befriended you, attached themselves to your soul and turned it inside out, made it unrecognizable? Ones you didn't know, manipulating you from a hellscape?

Goddammit, I only ever wanted peace and quiet.

"Eliza, what the hell are you talking about?" Nicholas barked, his chest heaving with the energy it stole. "Why is he here?" he said, raising a hand in Lynch's direction. "And what the hell does it have to do with Izanami or…" Flabbergasted, he fell into his favorite chair by the unlit fireplace.

Our plan to get Roman to feed Nicholas had fallen apart almost instantly.

I pulled myself out of the thoughts of Izanami for the moment, determined to stay on track, to get Lynch back into character. I snarled at him, angry that he'd failed to show his recklessness, what it *could* be, if he'd cared.

"I won't stop," Lynch said, unconvincingly. "I'll make as many vampires as I want to. It feels good to me now, better than killing. Like laying waste to a lovely hotel room." He grew more convincing by the second.

"We'll stop you," Roman said solidly.

"No," Lynch laughed, "you won't. When will you learn? After all these years, you still fight this ridiculous battle of controlling me, but you can't even control yourself. She was the kindest…" Lynch faltered. "You ground the sweetness right out of her. *Killed* her. She was your friend."

It was the healthiest way I'd seen him deal with Kat's death yet. *To think that I spurned him into it, forcing him to be a conniving jackass.*

What would Kat have said?

I stopped that right away. Kat would have said to do what was necessary to get what I wanted. She wasn't innocent. She was kind, yes, but she was sly, determined, seductive. All those things made me love her more—she was no angel, but she could act like one.

Lynch didn't need to act to get what he wanted right now, what *we* wanted. He was finally letting it all go.

"You killed her, the only person who mattered to me, and now you think I'll do what you want? Do the *right thing*? Tell me about what's right, Roman. Letting Nicholas die? That's right? You killed Eliza's dearest friend, you want to take him from her too? Who's the brutal one now? Hmm?" His teeth were bared. His eyes glinted with sorrow and the madness it brought along. "She was innocent," Lynch said at last.

I could see Roman's knees buckle ever-so-slightly when he heard "innocent," saw it hang around him like an aura in itself.

"If you only knew…" Roman said, trailing off.

"Knew what?" I butted in, grasping at the straw that might lead him to finally release his secret. If this was the way to get him to feed Nicholas, I'd take it. "Stop hiding, Roman," I growled. "What don't we know?"

But Roman was silent.

"Enough of this," Lynch spat. "I'll never help you. I'm not your brother and I never will be. We won't ever work together, Roman, do you hear me? If it's a coven of vampires you want, a coven you'll get. I'll make as many as I can, more than you can handle, more than you'll ever find. And rest assured, it's because of *you* that I'll tear their lives from them and make them eternal killers."

This was going too far. I'd seen Lynch start to deal with his feelings, and I liked it, wanted to see more of it. Instead I'd sent him spiraling into killing again. I'd only wanted it to be an act, and here I'd done…

My god, what had I done?

Lynch pounded out of the cabin like a man who needed to hear every footstep to remind him of what solid ground felt like. A man who had a god complex that could get away from him if he let it. And he most likely would.

This was the kind of chaos that Izanami wanted, and I'd handed it to her, just handed it right over like a goddamn moron.

Roman still stood there, dumbstruck, lost in thought, and Nicholas was trying to pretend nothing weird had happened. Though many terrible things had happened, actually. He sat in his favorite chair by the unlit fire, crossed his leg with a grunt, and put his head back to stare at the log ceiling.

"Don't walk out on this, Roman," I said quietly, hoping Nicholas wasn't paying attention. "You have to face it."

I couldn't care anymore about the defeat on his face that meant he was giving up on his brother. Roman had put a barrier between us that I had no energy to repair.

Speaking of no energy, I went to Nicholas's side, sitting on the arm of the chair, running my fingers through those thinner-than-usual curls that still framed his face like an angel's. "You'll be okay, no matter what," I said, more to myself than him.

But there wasn't a whisper or grunt of response. Not his usual lean-in to my hand in his hair.

There was no sign of life at all.

"Nicholas," I said, shaking him hard. Harder than a human would have been able to, rocking the chair on its legs—but Nicholas, eyes open, just stared straight ahead, a dead man, looking above for someone to bring him home.

"Roman," I choked out. Not even a vampire could have heard it. "Ro—Roman," I tried again, voice a strangled scream at the end as I shook the man we loved to no avail. His head lolled to the side, and I hastily lifted it back up, propped it, his eyes staring the same direction as nausea roiled in my gut. The salt of my tears stung my tongue as they slid into my mouth, dripped down my chin. Roman was a blurry ghost of movement on

Nicholas's other side, but not moving fast enough for me, there was no glint of blood being poured into my lover's mouth, nothing to save him, nothing different than the bullshit I was doing, shaking him like I could rattle the sense to survive into him.

"Feed him!" rumbled out of me in a violent, spittle-infused roar.

Everything stopped when Roman's eyes met mine and I was the one who drank.

Drank his terror, its faces as many as a rough-cut diamond. Grief for his brother washed over fear of his secrets revealed, flooded disgust over his selfishness, drowned out revulsion over his actions. Fear was the crest of them all and I imagined myself bathed in it until I lost myself in it. I felt my jaw unhinge, my chin brush my sternum as my mouth grew longer, wider, drinking in the multi-colors of fear that raced around Roman, crippling him.

NO. NO. STOP, I told myself. *Not now, this isn't* you, *this isn't you this isn't you not now...*

Roman fell, a marionette with his strings clipped but so much less alive.

Nicholas.

Now, with my every nerve on fire, having fed on fear and glowing with electric power, I could sense Nicholas —not dead, then.

Comatose.

I remembered those long hours before, me merely human, Nicholas the only god I knew, and how he snapped out of it, called to a victim that restored him completely. I remembered watching him emerge over the hillside, the snow a blank canvas with the white-trimmed dark forest framing him. My heartbeat when I'd see him…a feeling I would never forget and never feel again.

Could he come back this time? And here, the blood he needed should have been served up to him on a silver platter.

Roman was stirring, groaning. And it was totally me, not any god's intervention, that wanted to knock him out again, slit his wrist and pour his blood into Nicholas's waiting mouth.

And I wondered again, if Izanami played a part in all the events that had transpired, and Izanagi had been a presence in my life for decades…did he play a part in Nicholas's demise too? Would he betray me this way? He'd taken everything from me for so long, he would *not*—

That's when the birds came.

Like black lightning bolts, they tore through the front door, crashed through my favorite window by the fireplace, screaming and surrounding me, a black storm of motion in stark contrast to Nicholas's unmoving body. Hundreds of them, on the floor, perched on the chairs and the mantle, the exposed beams in the ceiling. They all looked to me—not just at me, but *to* me, waiting for a response.

This was Izanagi, reassuring me. The crows were

always a part of him.

I kneeled down and looked closer. I noticed that their eyes… I'd never actually looked deeply into them before. I hadn't needed to. With a deep breath, I reached out my hand to one bird. He didn't move away or squawk in fear as I rested it upon his broad back.

Once again, I was overcome by yet another force—a vision.

I saw a green chair, occupied by a young man. A smiling little girl sat in his lap as he read her a book. The vision shifted, and the man was older, the little girl in his lap still, this time talking animatedly. Next, the man was old and the little girl was gone.

This was the green chair. That was the man Nicholas had been called to, meaning that little girl was the one Lynch had turned into a vampire.

I bent further down, to truly see into his eyes, and they told me the story.

This bird and that man were the same.

Slow motion as I looked around at all the crows, all these souls that came for me.

Getting to my feet like a mortal, like clumsy Ellie who had to adjust her shirt and pants every time she moved, I tried to make sense of quivering Roman, motionless Nicholas, the horde of birds, of Lynch taking off, of Blue out there somewhere, waiting for a weak moment to attack.

"Roman," I breathed. "Stay with him. Do you understand me? Stay by his side and if Blue comes, you get her out of here any way you must. Any. Way. She's not herself. I'm going to get—"

What, answers? Help?

But Roman nodded solemnly without me having to finish. With one final promise to Nicholas to fix him, I let the crows lead the way.

CHAPTER 17

I raced through the woods, as I had so many times before, now with the murder of crows ahead of me in a midnight swarm. With giant leaps and bounds that cleared the trees, I furthered myself from Ossipee, but never from the problems there or my responsibility to them.

I was running right into a trouble I never could have imagined before.

Having gotten the mortal need to *do* out of the way, like I could outrun my own mind, the horror that my world had become, I pictured myself in the Yomi from my dream. Still running, leaping, I felt my body become less real. Less solid. But I didn't do anything except nearly fall from the air into the trees below. I tried to envision Yomi again, to no avail. But the surge of willpower made me jump higher, until I was brushing clouds.

Despite the circumstances, I was laughing hysterically, even as I came down to the ground to push off again. I knew that it was a matter of moments before I came to the ocean.

No way can I cross the damn ocean.

But what would hold me back?

I ran again through the trees, the black birds a shroud around me, a blur in front of me, and the ocean was close, the sea salt stinging my nose. Before I could think twice, talk myself out of it, I took the final leap over open water.

Exhilarating. The only word that could describe it.

Clouds tickling my head, waves lapping in tune with the flapping of bird wings, and just as black.

Until the plummet began. Panic overtook me and I flailed, screaming until I would have done anything at all for blood to soothe my throat. The crows screeched along with me, diving at the water in a massive streak. The time passed so slowly—maybe just regular time, but for me, it was an eternity—every vampire sense popping like fireworks in the darkness. My heart was paralyzed in my throat while my body couldn't stop moving.

And then I hit the water.

No crows to guide me under here.

In a heart-stopping millisecond, silence enveloped me. The darkness, velvety before, became impenetrable, thicker than gods' blood. Suddenly, time fast-forwarded and the still ocean I'd invaded sprang to life. Every speck of life within those waters swirled into a dance that my presence interrupted, an unnatural thing in an ancient environment. I hovered there, hair spread out around me, limbs weightless, my mind anything but. Tentacles whipped fathoms below me, scales gleamed, teeth glinted, and I was no longer the prime predator.

For the first time in a long time, *I* was the one afraid.

I swam hard for the surface but it wasn't anything like it was in mortal dreams, where you can't move no matter how desperately you flail. No, vampire strength still fueled me, and I torpedoed to the top, and I swear the beasts of the deep howled with rage.

"What a trophy you would be," the voice in my head said.

"Izanami?" I thought as I broke the surface, where I was met by the hovering gang of crows.

They grabbed me as I shot up, lifting me higher with claws and beaks clinging to every part of me, bringing me back up as close to the clouds as their strength would allow them.

And I clung to that feeling for as long as I could. Not the dreaminess of it, not the surrealness of realizing I wasn't the greatest power in my world—because that was how I had felt all the time since becoming *Shinigami* —but the feeling of not being in charge. For this time I was at the mercy of birds and sea creatures.

God, I was so tired.

The birds called out to me as they carried me, and I let myself reach out to them in my heart, even though I was just too drained of life and will to *interact* at all. I longed for Birch Tree Books, for the icy New England air and shaking snow off my boots, the *quiet* of being nobody but Ellie.

I curled my fingers around the claws of the crows holding my hands. I trained my eyes on them to see their auras. I felt so close to them, so invited *not* to speak.

Their auras didn't glow as one as I thought they might. No, these were human, complicated colors of a lifetime of memories, held behind a flourish of blue-gray that was the reinvigorated life of a creature with only nature to answer to.

No, not only nature.

I breathed in, encouraged by their simplicity and peace. The scent that greeted me wasn't the salt of the ocean below, but of wine. And roses.

I gasped, "Izanagi?" and whipped my head around. My hair pulled as it hung from the beaks of the—

"Tengu."

A sob broke free, and I rolled my eyes at myself for how goddamn exhausting it was, at how often I did that, how weak I felt. But Izanagi was here, somehow, and I'd needed him so much. I strained to find a way to see him, but he couldn't be seen—I knew that. So I let myself be carried still, and listened.

"Tengu. Spirits of the dead not pure enough for Heaven, and not terrible enough for Hell. They live between worlds, where neither matters."

Crows had followed me my entire life. And now they were bringing me to Yomi.

"Yomi is a place for others, *too, Eliza. The ones who don't belong. They may be called demons but there is no such thing as merely evil, there is only reason and belief. The demons of Yomi are the heroes of their own tale, as any hero is. Can you fault them for that?"*

"No…"

"Would you consider that to be abominable?"

"No…" What was he getting at?

"Do you not live between worlds yourself?"

My brain skidded to a stop at the thought, a clue, the *point* I'd always searched for. It was in those—

The *tengu* dove, eliciting a scream from me as we plunged toward the water. And even though I knew Izanagi had sent them and that he was on my side, terror of those monsters below strangled me and I struggled again. "Yomi is on a mountaintop, for chrissakes!" I yelped.

Seconds before we'd have smashed into the water fast enough to obliterate bones, they pulled back, and let me gently glide into the depths.

CHAPTER 18

My own fear gripped me again.

That which consumes me makes me stronger.

Long ago words from Kieran that rang so true they almost drowned out the sub-aquatic screams of the marine predators that descended upon me.

I swear, they'd had time to gather their friends while the crows flew with me and Izanagi gave me riddles to unpack, but these ancient creatures had nothing but time. The further I sank, the thicker the swarm of tentacles, fins, teeth. I swung out an arm when a razor-sharp fin whipped my back, just in time for a blue streak of a shark to latch on and sink his massive teeth right in.

Pain, physical pain, is something I hadn't felt since being human and falling down the stairs in our crappy old apartment.

This far exceeded that.

Every nerve leaped to life as the shark snapped me

back and forth, bones cracking so loudly in my own ears that I wanted to scream. But a flood of ocean water invaded my mouth, and I went limp for a second, just a second, because it would be really easy to give up.

The shark let go.

Taking my arm with it.

Agony came first in the form of nausea but my stomach was thankfully empty. Delirium hit me when my thought was, *Kat would laugh so hard if I was swimming in my own puke and limbs.*

The shark thrashed, sliced across my face with its tail. *That's what sharks do,* I thought, serene and without a hint of anger. *They're predators.*

Izanagi's words: *"Would you consider that to be abominable?"*

I laughed, swallowed more water. Did *everything* in my life have to mean something? Seriously, at some point it would be nice if I didn't live in a goddamn tapestry of Big Picture threads.

Of course, I wasn't going to live through it much longer.

This was it, then? This was how it all ended, torn limb from limb after *all that*? That...that...*ridiculous* life and the deaths and vampires and battling and winning and losing and now this was the end?

I watched the wide river of blood stretch between the shark and my shoulder. The pain came next, searing under the water, disconcerting. The trail of red never dissipated, just flowed thick and dark.

Because it wasn't my blood. Not all of it anyway.

My crimson mist extended from the gaping wound in my arm that had other sharks swimming closer and closer, faster and faster. But when they came too near, the mist lashed out, frightening them off in a rush of whitewater. Or was that my blurred vision? Fish darted this way and that, carefully avoiding the mist as it twisted in and around itself, thickening and strengthening.

The pain dwindled to a tingling.

The tentacles that had pulled at my ankles disappeared. And the sound of the deep overcame the noises of predators that only a vampire might hear. Never heard anything about those terrifying sounds on Nat Geo.

I was sounding more like myself in my brain.

The mist had reached the shark holding what was left of my arm and lunged at it. My mist exploded like fireworks, obliterating the shark in a flurry of actual blood, simultaneously stitching itself to my arm.

Slowly, magically, the mist slinked itself back to me in a cascade of winding tendrils. I dared not flinch when it approached the raw socket where my arm had been torn away, the bleeding stopped now. I didn't have my own blood to flow, not really. The mist-veins knit themselves together, braided and overlapped, stitched themselves around the two pieces of me, and with an odd sizzle underwater, re-attached my lost arm. A jagged red welt was all that remained of the nightmare.

"There is loneliness burrowed in the strength we have," Izanami said in my mind. *Christ,* did I hate having someone rattling around in my head, and here I had both Izanagi and Izanami sending me messages.

I'd been dragged so deep into the ocean I could scarcely see the surface. The sea still offered resistance to my body, vampire or not, as I swam upward to a place I never thought I'd reach.

"You aren't unmatched. That should frighten you, and give you peace."

What the hell was she talking about now?

The surface had only been a reflection of a shimmer of a wave before, a detection of another place, and now glimmered like stardust.

I would not be taken down.

I powered up harder, my injured arm now moving with greater and greater mobility.

My heart was not invincible, but my spirit would be. *Strength is more than constant bravery, constant vigilance,* I told myself. I'd told Nicholas the same thing, over and over against all our odds.

Nicholas.

The thought of him bristled Izanami, I could feel it like an aggressive tickle.

"Imagine the loneliness in my strength," she growled.

I rocketed higher until I exploded out of the water, met by the hundreds of crows again. Suspended in the sky by the red mist that had saved me over and over, I wondered for the briefest time if the mist was a gift from Izanami, too—but it didn't matter. It was mine. I had power in so many ways, and I would bring Nicholas back to life with it one way or another.

"Worth another try," I said to the birds, and they agreed in their silence, their knowing eyes all the encouragement I needed.

I closed my eyes, felt the soaked canvas of my Chucks. Somewhat invincible or not, Chucks were the only shoes for me. I felt my Overlook Hotel T-shirt clinging to me, and remembered always pulling it out from my waist, always sucking in my stomach. I didn't have to do that now, but I still did sometimes. Muscles pulsed in my back, ones I'd never had or used when I was human. They made my bra straps uncomfortable occasionally.

Because I was still Eliza and I'd survived so much. And dead, I was still surviving. Nicholas would, too.

The great purpose that constantly hovered over me could pound sand right now. I had to get to Yomi and save Nicholas first.

I said the word in my head, knew Izanami would hear it, knew it was the equivalent of wishing myself to Oz, but I pictured myself in Yomi anyway. Because if I didn't know the way, the mist certainly did.

At once, the crows screeched with human voices, making my stomach twist—or was that the way the air and sea seemed to create a vacuum with me in the center, sucking and pushing me apart at once? The demons of Yomi added their howls to the human crow screeches, and nothing made sense, nothing was real and everything was new but impossibly ancient. The smell morphed from briny to sulfurous and strangely sweet, the atmosphere nothing but a million auras melding into one. Screams and peace.

This was Yomi.

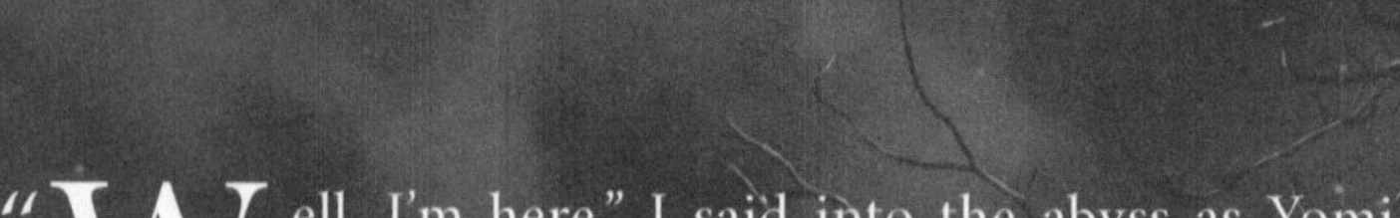

CHAPTER 19

"Well, I'm here," I said into the abyss as Yomi slowly came into view like human eyes going from Christmas lights to sunlight.

Izanami glided out of the tunnel of blackness, trailing red light behind her along with the bustle of an angelic white kimono trimmed in the colors of the sun. It was easy to see how Izanagi fell in love with her. Her seeming purity, her demure magnetism. She was a princess in this empty, overflowing place where the dark was so monstrous it was impossible. Unidentifiable moans or animal noises emanated from the dark, more in shockwaves than sound. There was no ground below, no sky above, only dark.

Until she cast her eyes upon it.

One glance upwards with her pearly, glistening face, from her deep liquid eyes, the slightest smile on her dainty ruby lips, and the sky appeared, the deathly film wiped away. A blissful, baby-blanket shade of blue tried to peek out, but even this princess couldn't bring it forth entirely. Instead she revealed a dusky blue-gray riddled with slow-roaming thunderclouds, eerie and beautiful. A flash of lightning shocked the sky, creating a menagerie of gigantic creatures of the clouds, parading through the evening like carousel animals.

A second flash had them all turning their heads toward me. And they were not just animals at all. They were eyeless shadows in the shapes of all kinds of beasts that leered down at me—but in the next illumination they'd pulled back, their blurry holes of mouths down-turned, their vacant eyes wide Os.

"They recognize the *tengu*," Izanami's sing-song voice said as she approached. "They are not so different from one another."

"Wha—what are they?" I asked, looking up to the monstrous clouds as they morphed from demons to common creatures.

Izanami smiled at me, her dark eyes meeting mine with only a hint of malice. "My souls," she said.

My throat sucked in on itself, frozen. *I have to get out of here.* "You know why I've come," I choked out.

She laughed, coming closer. "Yes! But do you?"

"I know exactly why I'm here."

"Liar!" she screamed, sending answering howls up from the darkness, the demons or souls or monsters hiding even from vampire eyes. "You think you're here to save him, the Golden Boy. But it was never about him."

More wailing from the shadows. "For me it is."

Her smile opened so wide I thought it would swallow me whole. *Like your own when you swallow fear, you freak.* But it was she who'd point out the monster that I was. "There!" She waggled a long, elegant finger at me. *"For me it is,"* she said, perfectly repeating my own words in my own voice. My stomach clenched. "Even though your friend Blue is drifting into madness, and Roman is being consumed by a secret, and Paolo—"

"Where is Paolo?" I demanded. But it was half-hearted. Because I hadn't thought of him once since I got here, focused as I was on getting what I came for.

Her blood. Heal Nicholas. Bring him back.

Her power.

She'd drawn me here with her lovely "gifts" and I'd fallen for it.

"It's not about Nicholas, huh?" I said, cold reality sinking in. "You knew saving him would get me here. It's about me. Isn't it?" Fury quaked in my bones, my body shook with anger, at her, at myself for being lured in. *"This* is my great purpose?" I spat, sweeping my arms around me.

In a flash she was before me, her face inches from mine, and it was no longer the face of a princess or a god.

Decay poured from her like a fountain, stinking and rotten. Her skin slid from her cheeks, leaving gaping, meaty holes, bits clinging to the bare bone underneath. A tangle of black stringy hair hung over the yellow flares burning deep in her eye sockets. Teeth became daggers, lips became bloodless lines.

"DO YOU THINK IT WAS MINE?" she boomed, and all of Yomi shook with fear. It tasted like ancient blood and ashes and it all pooled around her. I licked my lips without thinking.

The dead thing that was Izanami calmed herself inhumanly fast, replaced her smooth smile, now on broken lips. It gave me a second to think, a second I needed because my mind didn't move the way it should here. Not in this place. But I thought: *She's right.*

When she gave birth to deities, when she and Izanagi were happy, was this the fate she was bound for? It wasn't fair. Fair may not matter, but still, it wasn't fair.

"You don't want to be alone anymore," I said quietly. Because she'd been alone for so long, with remnants of her former life clinging to her like the skin that fell from her skull.

Her smile was genuine, if not macabre. She turned away from me in a gentle swoop of light, and when she turned back, she was beautiful again. "But I'm not alone anymore."

"Where is Paolo?" Everything was so jumbled here, confused, it was hard to keep track of even a sentence with the demon shadows looming overhead, coursing around me.

"I didn't mean Paolo," Izanami said.

She fed me images of the baby, dreamlike again. "She's real?" I said with a gasp.

"As real as anything can be in this place," Izanami said mournfully. Yomi groaned. "But hers is not the life I long for." When I gave her the pause she was obviously looking for, she continued. "Did you know my children were taken from me? We were *gods*. The goddess of creation is nothing more than a vessel, not to be worshipped but *used*. My children, stolen from me to create Japan itself, and I will never have them back. Except for the imperfect ones. They call this one 'leech child.' Can you imagine? *Fumeiyo*." Disgrace. She gestured down at a slug-like, bald toddler, with no arms or legs and slippery, wet skin that wiggled at her feet. I couldn't help it—I jumped back, grimacing. She leered at me. "Easy enough to see why they've been deemed the Devils of Yomi."

"I—I'm sorry," I choked out.

She came closer, slowly, each step terrifying me into paralysis.

"Of course you are," she sneered. "How dare you pity me? You. You who has my husband's blood running through her veins."

The slug baby wrapped itself around my feet like a boa constrictor and Izanami's eyes blazed.

"I—it's not my fault!" I cried out, hating myself for the weakness of it. I despised when people shirked blame, and if she blamed me for having Izanagi's affections, who was I to turn that around on her? When she was trapped here like a zoo animal in Hell? "But you have the baby now…"

Her voice boomed, sending up wails of agony from the devils of Yomi, every one of them feeling her pain as their own. "I created the islands of Japan! Born of my very womb!" she screamed, clutching her stomach as it morphed into one of a disgusting corpse again, maggots falling between her fingers to the ground. "One child is an insult, a consolation prize, a *travesty*! That child is nothing more than a sign that I am meant to mother once more."

Leech-child slithered around my feet.

"I don't understand what you want," I said, measuring every word so as not to spark her anger again.

"Your monster has begun a new race of vampires," she cooed to me, kimono stitching itself back together, recreating her pristine form. "One without a meddling old man to control them, thanks to you."

It began to come together.

"You want to be the master of the new vampires?" I asked, and was answered with a sinister smile.

"He creates them, satisfies his need, and I mother them. It satisfies my needs and theirs," she answered.

I dug through the words in my head, nothing coming together as smoothly as it should. Did she want to walk the earth again to be with Lynch's vampires?

"Izanami, you can't be released into the world, you must know that. You're not…" What could I say that wouldn't condemn me to death with her rage? "You aren't the woman you used to be."

Her eyes went dark, dead. "You are so much better than I? A murderer, consorting with a murderer, the pair of you digging your heels into the ground and poisoning it. Your Golden One would be fully restored to watch over me on Earth. Nicholas could be healed beyond your imagination with my gifts! This is where *you* belong, both you and the Abomination. With her."

The baby appeared in her arms, swathed in a pink silk blanket, a tuft of red hair peeking out the top.

It can't be.

I stumbled, my body turning against me in a way it hadn't since I'd been human, in those last throes of life. The ghouls and devils whirled around me in a sickening twister.

How foolish I'd been to not see it before. To have ignored what was too clear.

The baby.

She was Kat's.

"How is this possible?" The noxious, cavernous blackness spun.

"Ah, you've woven it together at last," Izanami said with a grin that was too wide, the thing of a demon, not of a goddess. "It is simple. Your friend was with child when she became *unmei nashi.*"

No, it couldn't be. Lynch was a vampire. How could he create life?

And yet, didn't he? With countless girls across the world, turning them into death gods.

"*Gods do not play by human guidelines,* musume," Izanami said into my whirling mind.

"I am not your daughter. Get out of my head."

"As you wish." But she was laughing at me. "You believe that all things were created for a purpose, do you not? And that the *Shinigami* had the greatest purpose of all—to keep that balance, and put a finite line where lives end. This Abomination has done truly godly things, in his own life, in his immortality. He has taken life and given it, created rules of creation himself. He has renewed the world of *Shinigami.* It is his reason. His purpose. His *mokuteki.* He has redesigned what forever can be."

My head buzzed with all that this meant, gurgled under the oceans of meaning. The Abomination that was Chris Lynch, the man was suffering personified. This race he'd made—was making—could be a new breed of predator forces that worked within the laws of the *Shinigami.* They could join the food chain, keep the balance as they always had with more choices and more independence, with more conscience than they'd have been allowed under the Master.

· · ·

But they could become monsters like Lynch, who slayed people at random, without ever quenching their thirst. No balance. No humanity. They could become earth-bound devils of Yomi, themselves.

If I wasn't there to lead them, if Nicholas was in a coma, if Roman wasn't there to keep Lynch on the straight and narrow—as much as such a wraith could be —what would happen to those countless vampires?

But I could just make out Izanami's angle.

"If I take your place here," I said, unable to focus my eyes, my voice a tinny thing, "you'll save Nicholas. And if I don't…"

"Do you need to ask?" Izanami said. I didn't, really. I knew the answer. She would let Nicholas suffer forever, or until he couldn't handle it anymore.

The bigger question that I couldn't ask myself because she'd have seen the answer in my mind, was this:

Could I take the blood from her by force?

"Neverrrrr," she hissed, her face suddenly enormous, blocking all else from my eyes, her breath reeking of rotten meat. And just as suddenly she was back to the false beauty. Because there was nothing beautiful about her.

I had seen into her then; it had been impossible not to.

Not only would she refuse to give Nicholas the blood

he needed if I didn't stay in Yomi, she'd turn him into a mad thing, like Paolo, like Blue. A creature whose greatest strengths attacked their minds, crippling them into subservient beasts. We'd said she was using them as weapons to get to us. But she was using them as examples.

"I don't need you," I croaked, not believing a word I said. "Roman will feed—"

Her laugh was startling, sending the crows that had been my companions into flight. "Roman? He allowed you to venture *here* instead of helping the Golden One! Watching as his *brother* withers into nothingness! At one time Roman was willing to betray you all in order to save Nicholas and what you had with him. Now the prospect of Nicholas's death is completely acceptable to him! Tell me, what do you think would change him so? What do you think he knows that would make his brother expendable in his mind?"

"I don't know what you're implying," I growled, "but Nicholas is the most honorable person I've ever known. He's done nothing to make Roman think less of him."

That laugh again. "What is it then? What changed, Eliza?"

"Nothing I can't change back." I felt blood drip down my wrists, I was digging my nails into my palms so powerfully. "Roman came back here to help Nicholas, I can still—"

"And even if you do have this persuasive power that

you think you have, Roman's blood isn't enough now. *Kat's* blood isn't enough now."

She had me and she knew it. Because she'd caused this coma Nicholas fell under the spell of, and only she could restore him. Everything inside me deflated. My mist didn't even attempt to coil around me and comfort me, weakened by what we knew to be true.

"Did you poison Lynch's mind, too? Are you responsible for what he is?"

"You speak as if choice played no role in his life."

"But you did instill the seed of his…of the Abomination. Didn't you?"

That slash of a smile again, bright red lips against a chasm of teeth. "If only I could claim such extensive depravity."

Lynch acted on his own, then. He'd always been this.

"Imagine what I could do with the strength of the Golden One's mind," she said in my head and I couldn't help it, I sobbed, cried out. I'd never been backed into such a corner in my life or my death.

"I can't let it happen, Izanami. Even if you take Nicholas away, and restore Blue and Paolo. You and Lynch turning girls into vampires forever will be hell on earth. I can't ever trade the *world* for them. They would never let me, even if I could make myself do it."

"But it's not just about letting Nicholas die," she reminded me. "I would twist him into the most vengeful monster the world has ever known, with an army of the Abomination's creations to do his bidding. I would plunge him into a darkness of the mind with no escape, a golem of my own bidding, and if you dared to oppose him he would smite you down with the conviction only betrayed love can give him."

He'd always told me he'd love me no matter what I became. But would he love me no matter what *he* became?

All I had to do was stay.

Nicholas, Roman, Blue and Paolo, even Kieran would make sure Izanami was controlled.

Hell, maybe I would have the power to control her, just like she's been messing with me.

"Yes," she piped in, reading my thoughts. "My power would be what you have now, and you…you would have mine. We are the same, Eliza. We are both Izanami. You would rule Yomi, and I would be your anchor upon Earth. And when your Abomination discovers who I have here?"

Izanami inclined her head toward the baby, who became visible out of the darkness. That night-blooming jasmine whose petals had been stolen away.

Like my future had been, like all of the Shinigami *had been. But before she could ever begin to breathe a breath. Before she knew who she was, or how loved she would be. Trapped here, in this death place with devils and gods.*

"This child could turn his heart to light. The promise, and the memory, all in one. His beloved in all ways. His truest and greatest creation, the one that could undo all he has done."

The stipulation hung in the dank blackness like a cloud of devils.

"Or," I started for her.

"Or she could become more vicious than he's ever been, slighted before she ever knew what goodness or life was. A Master unlike any other vampire before her."

"She's a vampire?" I breathed out.

"Not yet," Izanami hissed.

The idea of Kat's baby—*Kat's* baby…

"But, the baby's not alive," I said, gulping back a sob.

"But could she be?" Izanami said, and then in my head, "*Gods create their own rules. Creation is ever-changing.*"

"Are you saying…are you trying to tell me that you could give her life again?" I said. "Wouldn't that be wrapped up with a shiny red bow, you could just *change* the rules, bring life and death together. Nope. If you had that power, you'd be out there yourself."

Izanami held the cooing baby out to me, her arms creaking like old doors with the gesture, her face alternating between ghastly and gorgeous each second, wielding the baby like a weapon, like she did with Blue and Paolo. And yet, I was drawn in. "Touch her," Izanami said, her voice hissing steam.

But terror gripped me as I relived touching the things all around Lynch's mansion, the connections to Kat that were everywhere. I backed away. The baby whimpered, but I couldn't, I couldn't. This was a trick. I was here to save Nicholas, not be lured into…into what?

Taking care of a baby? Freeing a demon goddess? Trapping myself in a hellscape?

Could the soft pink beauty with sweet strawberry curls framing her delicate face answer all my questions?

Trap or not, I wouldn't be put down by my fears. *That which consumes me makes me stronger.*

Not humanly at all, I took the baby from Izanami in a flicker of vampiric swiftness and wrapped the little creature in red mist in my arms, careful not to contact her skin just yet. Her eyes—the softest doe brown with long, fluttering lashes. I blinked pink tears from my own, but one fell onto her peachy cheek, and she giggled. I brushed the drop away with the tip of my finger.

And that one drop became a flood the likes of which I could never survive.

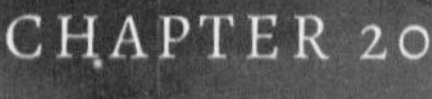

CHAPTER 20

I thought I was screaming. Maybe I was laughing. I was no one.

I'd vowed to never let myself be swept into that ceaseless void of pasts, presents and indeterminable futures that the Master had subjected me to in Japan, stealing my consciousness, turning it into a tool, a monstrosity. But this time, I'd walked into it willingly and I wouldn't have had it any other way.

A culmination of the blood of the gods that flowed through me, of my love for my best friend reemerged into this tiny beloved soul. The prophecy that I would be the one to change the world of the *Shinigami* in ways no one else could, the desperation with which I would save everyone I loved, and the battle with fate that I forever fought.

This child. This was what purpose meant.

I let the mist fall away and pulled the baby as close as

I could, terrified to feel any more. The idea that I could ever give up this feeling was reprehensible. I took a deep breath, closed my eyes to her perfection, and reached my mind out to force the images and feelings into order.

Because this was it. This was the moment it all came down to, and I needed to rise to a place I'd never been, where no one had ever been, to comprehend it.

The groaning shadow monsters hushed. Izanami's presence evaporated like everything else. Black light exploded from my body, death and stars and forever, and in the midst of it came Kat.

My red mist surrounding her face, brilliant smile bright, leaning in, conspiring happily with Roman over two cups of coffee. Black Bear Café, his brotherly love for her alight in his eyes. Then shock in his eyes. Then a smile. Then a hug.

She'd told him she was pregnant. She knew. She didn't tell me.

She told him.

And he killed her anyway.

Bile, human bile burst into my mouth. I struggled to hold the baby while the strange black light swirled around us. *Not from me,* I realized, *from* her. The black light bled into crimson mist. Everything bled into everything else: betrayal, *she'd told Roman and not me*; desperation to have changed it all; fury that he'd taken her life, *this* little life, *the baby is so cold, she's really not alive in my arms and yet she is.* And memories of Roman, the wound of losing his own child fresh, forever fresh in his heart leaked into sadness for him, for Kat, for us all. *And so this is what he'd kept from us. His much-deserved shame. The dirtiest secret any of us could ever have.*

Disgusting that he wouldn't risk Nicholas seeing it through the blood that would flow between them, would let Nicholas *die* instead. Even though it was for him that he'd committed the atrocity to begin with!

"All for nothing?!" I cried out, but it was silent in the chasm of energy the baby and I emitted.

The baby gurgled, brought me back to the thick of visions and understanding. Now of Roman, countless times arguing with Lynch, flickers of fear, anger, guilt as he tried to reconcile having created the Abomination, struggling to understand what purpose in it there could ever be.

Roman, vomiting bile like the burning in my own mouth and throat that kept coming and going. Him exploding into the woods behind the cabin, leaning defeated, sobbing against a tree, sliding down its trunk.

I didn't need a vision to tell me what horrendous turmoil my friend was suffering.

The baby screamed. I wanted to scream but I was paralyzed.

Poor Roman, I thought, despite my rage. Losing his own baby, losing the love of his life, his own life. The possibility of losing Nicholas, Kat, watching our happiness die as *Shinigami purpose* replaced us. Knowing he'd created Lynch, a serial killer, and then the girl we loved carried the Abomination's child…

If he could stop a new Abomination from entering the world, saving his brother's life in the process, would he?

Yes. He would. At the cost of his own sanity, his own soul.

"Did he know?" I cried out into the thick void of black and red that whirled like the cocoa and cream of Nicholas's eyes. "Did he know that—" I couldn't say the words out loud.

Did he know that the baby's soul would be trapped in Yomi?

Of course not. Had he even thought of it, he'd never have been able to take its life. He'd have spent another eternity trying to save the world from a father-child team of mass murderers rather than condemn a baby to this Hell.

For a split second, I wanted nothing more than to tell him what he'd done, but instantly sucked the idea into my subconscious. As hurt as I would forever be, I could never hurt Roman more than he was already. Never.

I was even a little relieved that he hadn't killed my best friend *only* for Nicholas, and for what we had.

Jesus Christ, is nothing simple or clean?

The baby shuddered, I cooed to her, as if we were the only two beings in this cyclone of power and horror. But I shuddered too as a cold chill inched up and down my body, slowly and all at once, and squeezed. Paolo had managed to find his way through the storm of crackling, screeching energy, and though madness was in his eyes, when he touched me I felt his intent. To tell me that there was more to know.

Trying to focus on him for just a moment, I covered his hand with mine, and memories of the days I spent immobilized in Japan by the Master, riddled with blood and visions, swept me away from the present.

"There was purpose then and there is purpose now."

That wasn't Izanami in my head—that was Paolo. Clear and cool like his eyes had once been, as if touched by the heavens. He was still in there.

I had to free him.

"Focus, Eliza," he said, his body buckling like a tortured animal's. *"There was purpose then, and there is purpose now,"* he repeated. And fell to the ground. I felt seconds tick by and knew it was too long, I had so many lives depending on me.

Purpose, purpose, purpose...

I pictured Nicholas—healthy Nicholas—his bare, muscular back to me through the French doors of his bedroom (*"They named these after me,"* he said), meditating on the moss mat on the little porch.

Purpose, purpose, purpose.

Breathe in...

The answer was in my arms.

I leaned down and kissed the baby's forehead, cold, but sweet-smelling. A mix of life and death. Balanced. She was the perfect balance.

Kat's bright sweetness and Lynch's cold monstrosity.

Living forever and killing forever.

Eternal life through death.

Monster and human.

Fate and choice.

Every one of us tipped the scales over and over, always questioning if our purpose was real, if we were more horrible than good, if there was hope for us. This little creature never had that conflict and yet she was the apex of it all.

Because when my lips touched her skin, it was all laid bare.

In a silent cacophony of images, my own purpose came to life—to reveal hers. Her alternate fates descended upon me as my murder of crows descended upon Yomi to protect me while I endured the throes of visions. *Show me.*

Kat holding this child, both their faces alight with smiles. Lynch coming to sit beside them, and he's human…he's *human.*

I shook my head as if flipping the channel, because had they even met while Lynch lived, Lynch wouldn't be the man he is now, this would never have happened. *Lynch was meant to be this way.*

Page two of the book of her fates showed me a flame-haired teenager, blood pouring from her mouth as she hunched over a nameless girl.

The next, the same except Lynch was behind her, ready to turn the ended girl into an eternal vampire. *Creation and death together.*

Then Kat, streaks of gray racing through her hair,

laugh lines around her mouth and eyes, but she was not laughing now. For her daughter, only an infant, was draining the blood from her breast, a puddle of it surrounding them both as Kat cried, unable to stop herself from feeding her baby the only way she could imagine. I sobbed, bringing me back to Yomi, to the child in my arms. *That couldn't be her.*

The crows screeched, urging me onward.

A young woman, the picture of Kat. It came to me in a tunnel, expanding outward like a camera lens. She sat upon a throne, for lack of a better word. *The Master's throne.* A black kimono wrapped around her lithe, strong body. Kieran standing at her side, guarding her. But this woman didn't need guarding. She was the new Master. And as the camera panned out, hordes of vampires grew into the frame, on their knees, heads bowed to her. And she sneered.

"No," I said aloud. The baby stirred, pulled a strand of my hair, but I couldn't see her, could see nothing except the image that replaced it.

The same young lady. Kat's life in her cheeks and eyes, Lynch's strength in her shoulders and jaw. The same kimono, pitch black but with white threading that sang of birch trees in the snow, and a smile played upon her cherry lips. She emanated life—but she was not alive. She was here, in Yomi still, which sent pangs of sadness through my body, even as I was unaware of myself. I would feel them later. Forever. But Yomi was… different. The monsters remained, but the horror did not. The shadow monsters surrounding us held no malice in their forms, and the crippled creatures, limping, crawling, mad, were no longer mad but at peace. Of sorts. As much as they could be, knowing what—who—they had. Having been part of Izanami's world. And now...

Now cared for by this beauty from both worlds.

Then a torrent of visions: a laughing group of vampires in the cabin kitchen, female and male, listening to...me. And Nicholas, healthy, telling some story that only he could tell filled with sarcasm and good intention; Roman—in Yomi—sharing a smile with a fully restored Paolo; Lynch holding his baby daughter, a shining look in his eyes that spoke of rebirth; me again, this time with Kieran, crouching in snow-topped mountains, such joy between us, blood on our lips and peace in our hearts; me, my arms around the child, now grown. Holding each other as if meeting for coffee, but in Yomi. A gray and pink Yomi, with fewer shadows and more faces.

With a gasp, I came to, and Yomi returned in a rush, along with Izanami. I hadn't seen her in any of those visions. For as much as I knew this baby was my responsibility to care for, because she was more important than any of us, I refused to forget what I came there for.

"Bring Nicholas back to us, and I'll take the baby off your hands."

Izanami burst out laughing, a raucous thing that

didn't fit her now-tiny body. "You're clever, and funny. I've not known humor for a very long time."

"Thanks, I pride myself on maintaining a sense of humor when faced with a manipulative demon goddess. Look, I came here for one thing, and you're trying to keep me here by preying on my loyalty to my dead best friend. A solidly unexpected twist—but not one I'm falling for. I'll take the baby—"

"You cannot!"

"—I'll take the baby, and if you want me to come back, then take Nicholas out of the coma. That's it. That's the deal."

"She cannot leave this place. She was born into it."

I held my chin high when I said, "We don't have to live what we were born into."

"I won't do it," she blurted. "Take her and I will take him."

Ice ran down my limbs, spread from my heart, made me think of Nicholas's cold, the way he could become it, release it. I couldn't take not having him in the world.

Take.

"I'll have to do some taking of my own."

CHAPTER 21

S he was in my head, even without me knowing, and so I had to act faster than I could think.

I dropped the baby.

I rode on the truth that my mist had caught me a million times in a million ways, and I let it carry me in a blink to Izanami.

She is only Shinigami.

As she shifted back to a six-story Amazon, I grabbed her, was carried up into the shadow clouds with my fangs buried in her neck. She cried out, and Yomi cried out with her. The ground shook beneath her feet, reminding me that no matter how much of a *nothing* place Yomi felt like, it was just a cave. Just a cave on a mountaintop.

Everything feels so small if you use the word "just." Especially me, clinging to this vampire goddess, and she would never allow me to leave here, not with her blood in my body. All these thoughts in a fraction of a second, because it was then that she plucked me off like a piece of lint and held me in front of her face.

She's going to swallow me whole.

I wrenched around and sank my teeth into her thumb, and she dropped me. Grabbing the sleeve of her kimono, I bit down onto her wrist and sucked up as much as I could in the second I had.

Black licorice and the briny smell of Cape Cod low tide. Evil, pure evil squeezed my veins as Izanami's blood ran through them. But not her evil—the evil of this place, and of the world that stole her children from her. Of a system that wasn't a system but a way of life, and the goodness born of it, and her stuck in the middle of it, forever giving and never receiving. And such hatred.

That part was all hers. I bit harder, to taste it deeper because I could absorb it and I could *handle* it. I didn't have any hate of my own.

Like the rush of blood, the realization that I only knew love reeled through me. Tears clouded my vision with red as Izanami's arm waved, me waving with it.

Only love. Any hate I had—for Lynch, for Death— had been transformed before long. I could never be as vengeful as Izanami was. I could never take her place. We were not the same. I had much, much more.

I'd drunk more than I thought, because she wavered. Flickering like an old TV, she faded in and out, and every time she stabilized she was smaller. Or I was bigger. At her weakest, finally her normal size, I curled around her like a crab, dragged her to the ground, punctured her skin with my short nails, bit as many places as I could in rapid succession. Moving so fast I generated heat, my teeth a high-powered stapler, drawing like a needle, my skin leaving burns on her where I touched. She wasn't crying out anymore. Yomi no longer howled. And I was FILLED. Full to bursting, like nothing I'd felt before. A sedentary power, without moral compass or fear or pain, just a sense of existing, waiting, but *dark*. And without promise.

But I did have promise. And so did the baby.

Heaving and exalted, I rose off of Izanami motionlessly, lifted by the mist. The same mist that cradled the baby, and held the shadow monsters and demons of Yomi at bay. They watched, stupefied, lost. Paolo stood at his full height, head held high as it normally was, a faint smile upon his pale, chapped lips. He had known me at my most lost, enslaved by the Master. He had felt it himself, now. I gave him a knowing nod.

"Give her to me," he said in that soft, lilting voice of his. I sobbed, relieved to hear him as he was meant to be. Taking the baby in my hands, I passed her to him, and it was heavenly to look upon. This man of God wrapped around this little enigma, made of promise and power and hope.

"I have to go," I blurted out, frantic with this blood roaring into my limbs and heart, my eyes and brain.

"I know," he said.

~

Yomi was just a place. A cave. A mystical one, yes, one human eyes could never behold, but for a *thing* like me, it was just a place now. And so I left it, without the aid of the crows, though they followed close by. All of their eyes, when they met mine as we passed through time and space like feathers on the wind, were cocoa and cream swirls.

Hurry. He needs you, they told me.

Teleporting didn't come to me, I just had to get there, had to feel myself get there.

The wind doused the fire of my skin, the steam in my blood, and I screamed wild as I flew without wings, desperate to go faster, faster, faster. My mind was an overflowing dam, a geyser that needed *more* even as it exploded. My senses were an army, both defending and attacking me. *Faster.*

I burst through the cabin wall like a bulldozer, ripping it wide open. Logs coursed through the air end over end but I didn't falter as I stalked to Nicholas, slumped in the chair by the still-standing fireplace. With my own teeth—sharper now, colder somehow, different with her blood fresh on them—I punctured my wrist. *Too hard.* Izanami's blood rang through me like a wild animal, weakened by endless captivity, making up for it with ferocious longing for vengeance. My hand hung by a few tendons, snapped bones, viscous not-blood flowing out of it, pungent and brighter, but darker than any blood I'd ever seen, fluffy like Roman's omelets. The ripe, flowery, hypnotic smell of it made Nicholas's nose twitch, even as his eyes, dead-still, never blinked, sunken into a body that was as still and as thin as a corpse.

I held my dangling hand over him, let the blood pour onto him in a life-giving shower. It had a vitality of its own, frothing out of me as a scarlet whipped cream, my mist infusing it.

Nicholas twitched under the rush, but his tongue didn't reach for it, his throat didn't bob.

"Come on, Nicholas," I pleaded, my voice hollow and tinny.

Gently, I pulled his chin down, massaged his throat like I was giving medicine to a puppy, but the blood just bubbled around him. I grabbed his arms, *so frail, so cold,* and sat him up straighter. But there was nothing.

And I was becoming nothing. The blood was looking more like my own blood now, normal. I was running dry. Powerful as it was, Izanami's un-life force hit hard and fast. But not hard enough.

I collapsed, the wind from the gaping hole of the wall slapping my hair into my face, and I willed the cradling mist away in order to feel the hard, splintered floor. Maybe knock myself out, maybe impale myself like vampires from stories and be *done* with this joke of an existence, this misery. Nicholas's foot was within reach —Roman had put his old plaid slippers on him. I held it, felt the bones beneath the fabric, the sedentary blood under his skin that wasn't strong enough to propel him, had nothing left.

Blinking, regrettably still conscious, I saw the rubble of the cabin in the yard shuffle. *Roman.* I couldn't face him, not knowing what he knew, not having let Nicholas die, not ever again. He emerged from the logs, shards of wood sticking through him all over, blood pouring from the punctures. A moan escaped me when I saw the one that went clean through his eye. I tried to push myself up, but one-handed now, I failed. Again. Roman toddled over, a monster Tom Savini would have been proud of, pulling the stick out of his eye—it had gone through the back of his head. Yanking more daggers out with every step, he waved me off as I tried to get up and go to him, desperate to help remove the debris I'd destroyed him with, *God, I destroyed another person I love.* He went straight to his brother's body.

I couldn't look. I turned to the disaster I'd created of our home, their home, knowing I should never have been there to begin with. I never should have met Nicholas, never should have gone to that party. Never should have gone to the bookstore over and over. Now, he was gone. I'd killed the one they all called the Golden One. This was my destiny after all. To be a harbinger of death, befriended by it and despising myself for it. Izanami had been right—I *was* meant to replace her in Yomi. Maybe I could make existence more livable for those beasts. I could raise Kat's baby—isn't that what I should be doing? Didn't I owe her that? Had I really thought I could escape Kat's memory, let time heal the wound? That wasn't the Eliza I was. No, I clung to memories, let them drown me. That kind of life was what thrived in Yomi.

Barely able to see through my pathetic, red-tinged tears, I wiped them away with my single hand, *forever losing a damn limb now,* sick to death of feeling sorry for myself, and turned back to Roman at his brother's side.

But he wasn't mourning. He was *doing.*

Roman's throat was pressed against Nicholas's lips, covering his face.

"Roman, it's—" I tried to say it was over, to stop torturing himself, but I couldn't get the words out. I couldn't say that Nicholas was…

I swore I saw Nicholas's leg move. My eyes, clouded as they were, could detect movement before it happened, but I couldn't let myself believe that we'd been saved from the fate I'd brought us. Roman shifted, and it happened again, this time a finger. I sobbed, wanted to retch, wanted to sing, wanted to punch and jump and drink and beg forgiveness, but couldn't believe it. Not yet.

CHAPTER 22

Roman stood, and I saw Nicholas, the foamy blood I'd given him spitting from the sides of his mouth and growing like suds when I'd overflowed the washing machine. It multiplied, pink and red and thick, and Nicholas attempted to roll over in the chair, to curl up, but the blood came from him in waves.

"Eliza, do something!" Roman cried out.

Do something? The blood I'd brought him had done nothing, and now erupted from him in a geyser.

There'd been too much. Roman's blood, what he should have had to begin with, was too much. Too much, too late. What could I—

In a black flash, Blue was cutting through the foam of Izanami's blood as she made her way to Nicholas. Terror-stricken, I rushed her, toppled her over into the pink and red clouds of gelatinous, yet bubbly blood, and it soaked into her.

"Blue, no!" I cried, but she was frenzied, jaws gnashing, eyes wild, staring past me at Nicholas. She bit me so hard I screamed, then kicked me off of her with the force I'd seen her fight with, this little woman who'd been such a powerful enigma. She descended upon Nicholas in that second, forced him down again in the chair, clung to him, and before I could move, with speed that wasn't hers, she buried her fangs into his neck. Nicholas didn't struggle.

Roman got to them first, tried to tear Blue off Nicholas, calling to me for help, and I rushed there, but she was done. Blue stood—straight up, not like she'd been, a humpbacked, feral thing. For a second, I was only grateful that she was back. But when she looked at me, she wasn't just Blue.

Izanami was there, too.

Blue's petite body, but held more regally. Blue's supple lips, but pursed thoughtfully. Blue's dancing eyes —thankfully, Blue's playful expression—but behind it, another presence, darker, stronger. She smiled at me.

Nicholas rolled over without as much effort as before, and I cried out his name. I could only see his back past her, but his spine wasn't prominent through his shirt.

"I'm sorry," Blue said, in Blue's voice.

"Is that you?" Roman said, coming up beside me. "Blue, you're okay?"

She reached out to him, took his hand. "I was never in as much pain as you were, darling," she said. With a wave of her hand, all the knives of tree bark tore out of his body. He gasped, doubled over. I didn't know what to do—didn't know if she'd done him a favor or put the final nail in his coffin.

"You couldn't kill me," Izanami said to me, a different voice from Blue's.

"I didn't want to," I said.

"I'm out now," she said.

"Not completely," Blue said. Their voices were distinguishable, like talking to two different people from the same face. But a *peace* emanated from them, a gentle melding together of two incredible souls. Souls beyond death.

Nicholas got to his feet behind them, and everything else faded. He unfolded, it seemed, like a paper doll coming to life, and I lingered on every fold.

His arms were robust, the muscles straining against his shirt sleeves. His chest swelled up in a way I'd nearly forgotten, he'd been wasting away so long. The aging of his neck had reversed with pulsing, thick veins beneath. His jawline no longer sagged, but stood strong, his cheeks full, wrinkles returning to laugh lines, his lips pink, and his eyes…

His eyes danced, the cocoa and cream of my dreams, the warmth in them radiating toward me, long black lashes thick, and a new knowing behind them, a tinge of gold that hadn't been there before.

"God, I missed having good hair," he said, running his hands through the tousled locks that needed a good wash. "You count on having something your whole life, you know? Then *fwoosh,* first thing to go."

"Your *hair.*" Roman had recovered, hands on his knees, and I thought I might pass out from all the goodness around me happening all at once.

"I know, it was probably nice to have the best hair for a while, but those days are over now. Sorry, brother."

As hard as it was to tear my eyes from Nicholas, his presence alone was enough for me to do what I needed to do, which was to observe Blue. Izanami. Whoever this new being was, observing us. What thoughts were going through their heads?

"Love what you've done with the place," Nicholas said. Roman and I looked at each other, both of us too shocked to know what to say, how to react, where to go from here. "So," he continued, stepping through some remaining globs of bloody stuff, and kicking aside debris. "Who might *you* be?"

Blue-Izanami raised their chin to him. "I think you know."

"Do I?" Nicholas said, stopping to wink at me. My knees buckled. "Pretty sure you were one person when I saw you last. Sure doesn't seem like that now."

"I fed you Izanami's blood," I butted in. "It came back out." I waved a hand, gesturing at Blue, and realized it was my not-so-there hand. It just flopped against my forearm.

"Gross," Nicholas said. "We'll get that fixed up." He went closer to Blue. "A new god, goddess, somebody in there?" Silence answered him. Nicholas squinted, twisting his lip up in thought, and he crooned to her. "Tell me, are you a good witch, or a bad witch?"

"Good and bad are figments of the imagination," Blue replied. And it was definitely Blue that time.

He put a hand on her cheek. "Atta girl," he said.

Nicholas's willingness to just sorta let this new being *be,* at least for now, was enough for Roman and me. There was plenty more to do, to fix, to care for, to become.

"And how is our Abomination?" Nicholas said.

Roman winced. "Shit."

CHAPTER 23

I zanami's eyes lit up at the mention of Lynch, and the start of our encounter in Yomi rushed back in a flood of dread. What would she do when she met him? We couldn't find out.

But lo and behold, here was Lynch coming back to the scene of the crime. "Nice to not have any footwork, I guess," I muttered to Nicholas. He took my hand, for the first time in a million years, and the bird wing beating of my heart slowed. The ever-present fear that had become my way of life recently, diminished. I closed my eyes, breathed in the scent that was buried in him but *was* him to me: peppermint brownies on a cold day; pine trees and fresh snow; coffee and cookies.

When I opened my eyes, there Lynch was, covered in fresh blood. The way he strutted through the tree line and across the yard revealed how proud of himself he was. The thought of starting a new coven still thrilled me, and now that I'd seen who we'd be answering to…

Oh my God. I have to tell Lynch about his baby. Before Izanami does.

"Hi Nick, you're looking better than ever," Lynch said silkily. "Eliza," he said, turning to me. But his eyes stopped, his smooth smile became a happy grin, his self-involved bravado softened into a happy stance that radiated *enjoyment* of someone else. I don't think I'd seen him enjoy anyone, or anything, since Kat.

He was looking at Blue.

"Hi there," Blue said, no Izanami behind it.

"You're…different," he replied, eyelashes fluttering with an odd shyness. Odd for him. "I mean, I know we've…we haven't really gotten to talk much, but you've changed. Haven't you?"

Izanami's eyes appeared over Blue's, a double exposure where the shape and color and intensity of Izanami's eyes slipped over my friend's. "We are more," they both said in a symphony.

"Wow. You," Nicholas said, poking a finger into Blue's shoulder, "just took top billing on the freak scale. El, you're a silver medalist."

"Is it top billing like a concert, or silver medal like the Olympics? Can't have both," I said.

The whole time Lynch was mesmerized by Blue, and I just wanted to know what he was doing back here. And I was terrified of telling him about the baby. *Maybe time can just stop here, in this post-apocalyptic camp setting.*

"Whatcha doing, Lynch?" Nicholas asked. "Last we saw you, you were going to kill a bunch of girls, right?"

"The *Shinigami* has met its new leader," Blue/Izanami said breathlessly, eyes shining at Chris.

"Um, no it hasn't," I said.

"I second that," Roman said. "Lynch answers to us." He nodded at Nicholas and me.

"And we—" I couldn't breathe. "We answer to someone else. Someone *more.*" I locked eyes with Nicholas, afraid to look at anyone else, excitement and anticipation swelling in my stomach like Izanami's blood across the cabin.

"Maybe we should, uh—" Nicholas looked toward the kitchen, still standing, visible beyond the swinging-turned-dangling red door. "Have some tea."

Roman pushed the door aside, and it fell off. "Oh."

Nicholas strode past him. "Maybe we need French doors."

The kitchen was fairly untouched and I breathed a sigh of relief just to enter it. This was the time stop I was looking for. I plunked into an upright chair to examine my hand. While the others picked up the mismatched chairs and Nicholas put on the kettle, I created a little burst of red mist that wrapped itself around the wound like a bandage, holding it on. It didn't trouble me that it hadn't healed yet—I was exhausted, depleted, every part of me. And there was some comfort in not being 100 percent, if I was being my basest self. A predetermined excuse to not be the foreman solving all the problems.

Roman busied himself sweeping while Lynch and Blue/Izanami huddled together, murmuring at one side of the table. *Is she telling him the truth about his baby right now?* No, he'd have been wild, inconsolable and over-joyed at the same time. But boy, did they seem cozy. It warmed my heart. And it gave me a little hope.

The few minutes of quiet soon ended with the kettle whistling, and I steeled myself to give the news of the baby. The reactions were going to be...memorable. Nicholas poured tea, human speed, relishing the moment before the next storm. The ridiculous thing was, it didn't *feel* like a storm. Here we were. My friend Blue, possessed by a demon goddess who had manipu-lated us all for...who knows how long. Nicholas, who'd blown up into health like a bouncy house. Roman, who had no idea still about the baby or the fact that I knew *he* had known Kat was pregnant. A serial killer turned vampire serial killer.

And we were all putting a new coven together, *together*. Plus the house was falling apart because I had destroyed it.

Yet it was calm. As if maybe the storm had been there all along. The epitome of the fight or flight syndrome I'd been working through for most of my existence—

always waiting for the next tragedy, seeking them out half the time.

"Okay, El," Nicholas said, leaning against the counter with his cup of tea. "We're listening."

"I don't know where to start."

"You came to me in Yomi," Izanami said in a layered voice that creeped me the hell out.

With a glance at Roman, I began. "Roman, you wouldn't help Nicholas, even after coming home, but when the coma happened I realized who would. It was her," I said, nodding at Izanami/Blue. "She's been in our heads," I spat, "working us. She's the one who immobilized you, Nicholas. And she was damn well going to fix it." I spoke through teeth gritted so hard I thought they might crack, nostrils flaring as I stared at the possessed Blue. "Then I went to her, which is exactly what she wanted me to do. Right?"

The woman smiled knowingly.

"And I...I saw why Roman wouldn't feed you, Nicholas. What he was afraid you would learn through the residue." I trained my eyes on Nicholas. The thought of seeing Roman's face when I revealed his secret, if he knew at all that the baby was alive, or in Yomi, or Lynch's reaction, too overwhelming. "In Yomi, there's a —" The words choked me. "I can only show you."

The mist, an extension of myself, recreated the scene for all to see in a haze the color of blood. When the baby came into view, for the first time ever, the mist cleared of hue and showed her to us like a clear picture, a still.

The room choked as I had. What could anyone say?

"Whose baby is that?" Nicholas said. Of course. "Where the hell did a baby come from? El?"

But Lynch was up silently, slowly, approaching the image of the wiggling child.

"No," Roman whispered.

"She's mine," Lynch said in a voice sure and strong. It made me smile.

Nicholas was watching Roman, whose hands were shaking so hard the cup of tea clattered against the table. Sharp as a tack, Nicholas got it. "Kat was pregnant," my love murmured.

"I never thought I could…" Lynch trailed off. "I need to see her," he said, whipping around to Izanami. "Bring her to me, please."

"She can't leave Yomi," I managed to say.

"That's my child," Lynch snapped. "And she will be with me."

"Chris," Izanami said, "she was never a child of this mortal plane. She cannot leave Yomi."

I think we all expected him to fly into a rage like only he could, barely sane yet in complete control, a calculated, venomous anger that he directed like the weapon he was. He was a monster, and I'd managed to forget it.

"Chris—" I started.

"Then I go to her," he said coolly.

"It's not a vacation spot," I said. "You can't just walk in and out of there." *Paolo*, I remembered, my heart sinking. "Izanami. Did you bring Paolo there or did he go on his own?" Kieran said he'd gone to Yomi, a pilgrimage of sorts as only a holy man could, looking for a renewal of faith. I think he got something else. "He went to you," I answered for myself. "You turned him into that thing he became to use against me—but he's not that now. Can he leave?"

Izanami's demure smile crossed Blue's lips. "It is not a vacation spot," she said in my own words.

"If I choose to go there, I can't leave," Lynch said. No one had to answer. And no one begged him to stay with us either. What argument could we give, even if we'd wanted to? He'd never felt at home with any of us. He was a monster among us, his brutality unforgiveable, and he'd despised us all at one time or another; a sting that never left him. Even now, his future was wildly uncertain. He created vampires out of spite, and to satisfy a need that had driven him for longer than we could know. But when I drank from him, I understood one thing—that he created these new vampires and left them, hoping they would hate him the way he hated himself.

It only became clear to me now that he had been hoping they would end him for it.

"No, that's not right," Nicholas said, shaking his head. "A baby, bound to Hell with a damn serial killer and *you*?" He pointed at Izanami.

"She can change that place," I said before I knew what I was doing. "I've seen that she can." All eyes turned to me. I stood up, like I was preaching or something, like I couldn't deliver such news sitting comfortably. Like I was a prophet, and I suppose that I was. "It's not Hell to her. It's not really Hell at all."

Izanami, nodded emphatically in agreement, her body tensing with excitement. "Yomi is a place *between*—and she is a child between. She's not out of place in Yomi. She isn't trapped. The child is beyond your created rules of good and evil, and can become so much more."

"She's right," I said, breathlessly as the vision of the baby shifted in the mist. "All of the *Shinigami*, every coven will emulate her. She will lead us without having to lead us. She is…everything." One would think all my years of reading would have taught me to say things powerfully, but there was no grasping the promise of that child. There was no way to say what I knew, and it was for me to understand alone.

Because I was her messenger.

"I want to go back with you," Lynch said, taking Izanami's hand in his. "I don't belong here," he said with a sad laugh. "I need to be where Eliza said, where good and evil aren't different. I knew it as soon as you and I met, Izanami, that you were here for *me*. An angel of death—to deliver me to a new life."

His words, so heartfelt, so *right*, and necessary, were true—he couldn't stay in our world forever, making vampires and pining away, resisting his murderous urges. He wasn't a good man, but he also wasn't always bad. He had a conscience, as much as he fought it. And the baby—his baby—could do so much for the man I'd briefly glimpsed, the one that Kat fell head over heels for. She could breathe new life into him. With Paolo there to soothe his tortured mind, the way only Paolo could, Lynch could finally have peace. Closure with himself.

"Izanami?" I ventured. Blue looked at me, the Blueness of her fading behind the goddess. "What about you, and what you've been doing, trying to break free of Yomi?"

She was soft, sweet when she answered. "I only ever wanted to feel free and feel love again."

"Oh, that doesn't seem true," Nicholas said.

She snapped her attention to him. "Yomi does not care for its inhabitants. It has worn upon me. Twisted me. *Honjitsu,*" she said, clenching a fist against her sternum, darkness welling in her eyes. "Changed forever. But you, Eliza, have changed me forever as well."

"Yeah, she makes a habit of that," Nicholas said.

Why me? was right there, wiggling behind my teeth to be said, but I held it back. I wanted to ask why me of all the vampires, of all the eons of undead. Why had she finally only tried to escape when I showed up? But the two-word question had weaseled its way into most of my existence. Why did death—or Izanagi—attach to me? Why me for Nicholas? Why me to lose Kat, why could I see alternate fates, why did I have the mist, why had I been victimized by the Master, why had Izanami chosen me? Why me, why now?

I'd spent much of my life feeling like I was meant for something *different*, but with nothing to back the feeling up. No special skills, no important lineage, nothing outstanding about me, and when the different things began to happen, I asked myself why plenty of times. But the real question was why *not* me? Why should I question what everyone else seemed to know? That I was a thing of prophecy waiting to fall into place? Maybe nothing had *made* me special, but that didn't mean I couldn't be special.

I was a creature of change, both reluctant and willing, and there was no reason it couldn't be me. There was no why. There didn't have to be.

Izanami watched me, and a moment of understanding came between us. She'd heard my thoughts, probably, I don't know. But between us was a presence of *more*, and I was done asking why.

"Uh, what exact weird thing is going on here?" Nicholas said, eyebrows raised, waving a hand between Izanami and me.

I snapped out of my mini-trance. "There's a baby in a cloud in the kitchen and you're questioning why I'm quiet for a minute?"

"Fair. Proceed."

"Thank you," I said to Izanami, surprising myself. "I don't even know exactly why, but thanks. I guess, thanks for saying I'm important enough to give you strength?"

"It was not you alone," she said with a smile. "Your friend, Blue, is extraordinary."

I felt Roman stiffen from across the room. I had to speak for Blue.

"What you did to Blue is unforgivable. Hijacking her mind like that, you made her an animal. You can't take Blue's body to move forever between worlds, she's in there. She's a person without you."

Her features shifted ever-so-slightly, and Blue's playful eyes dominated them. "Here I am," she said with a smile. "I'm not like, *possessed*, I'm right here." Her fangs poked out when she grinned. God, I loved to see her this bubbly. "And it's not like I haven't sequestered myself to a remote Japanese mountaintop before. I guess..." she said more seriously, "I guess this way we both get what we really want. I can hide away, and Izanami can leave, both of us together. I think we're both stronger now. This is what I want to do, go to Yomi, and you know what? If I hate it? You know I'll find a way to get out of there."

She would. She got her way all the time without hurting a soul to do it. Always managed to make everyone feel at home, loved.

Love.

"Blue, have you spoken with Kieran?" I asked.

"In the last hour, no. I'll tell him something, put his fears to rest. He's got his hands full with the *Shinigami*, and I wouldn't be insulted if he was happy to be done with me for a while. I'm kind of a lot, you know?"

Nicholas and Roman had been murmuring to each other for a while now, and I'd been blocking out their words. An irrational fear that Nicholas would want to go to Yomi too pecked at my brain. If any of us was a god, it was him. I didn't *really* think he could pocket himself into a cave forever—nobody there would appreciate him, his sense of humor, his tea, his strength and confidence, his determination. He was a man who needed people. A home that he created himself.

But Roman was another matter.

"Roman?" I interrupted. "Are you okay?"

He'd avoided speaking to me directly this entire time, and now it had to be done. "El, Lynch, I didn't know—"

"But you did," I cut him off. "You did know she was pregnant, I saw that she told you."

His eyes watered, his mouth drooped. "I did know. But it didn't change what Nicholas needed, and it was a choice I had to make."

"You did *not*!" Lynch boomed, heat generating from him. "You killed my child! You murdered the woman I loved, murdered our *baby* before I even knew she existed!" His entire body shook violently, like a human earthquake, but nothing around him moved. He was a contained disaster, but he would explode. I had to do something.

"I didn't know that the baby would make it! Kat didn't know you were a vampire, Lynch! What kind of creature might you have…" Roman couldn't finish, though. I'm sure we'd all thought it, as much as we hated to admit it. What kind of monster might the Abomination bring to life that way? Would Kat have even lived through it?

"Don't you dare pretend that what you did was for anyone but yourself. How you need the Golden Child. How you didn't want to see me happy. How you couldn't bear to see me with a child when yours is gone."

Ice raced across the floor, swallowed Lynch up in a tomb.

Nicholas, apparently more powerful than ever, was rooted to the floor in ice himself from sending it Lynch's way. Silvery icicles darted up his arms, under his shirt sleeves and up the sides of his neck, licking at his chin and ears. And his eyes had turned to a disarming shade of cold blue-white that chilled me as much as the frost coating the room.

"I've had enough of our friendly neighborhood Abomination," Nicholas said with a sarcastic downturn of his lips and a nod to Izanami. "How's about you pack him up and take him home now?" He joked but the fury under that layer of ice was as plain as day.

"No way," I scoffed, eyes darting between Izanami and Nicholas. "She's done all this to get out of Yomi. Not a chance."

"It feels...unlike me here," the goddess said, but I still didn't believe she'd go back to Yomi that easily. "Eliza, I see your doubt, but circumstances have changed. I have a reason to stay in Yomi now, don't I? And I can leave when I choose."

I supposed prison didn't feel so much like prison if you had a get out of jail free card.

"Well, you don't have to go home but you can't stay here," Nicholas said to her.

Blue straightened up with that flirty smile of hers, and turned her teacup upside down. "My tea was getting cold anyway," she said, as a solid block of ice fell out. She stood up, graceful as the Blue I always knew but with a regality that was all Izanami's. She held out her hands, examining the backs of them, turning them over, coming to terms with this new form of hers. She clenched her fists, closed her eyes, and took a deep breath.

Terror heated up my body, melting away the ice, and suddenly I was well aware that she was only beginning to realize what power she held now. What abilities she might have.

With a way in and out of Yomi, a baby to care for, a strange little family, a lifeline in Blue and Lynch, Izanami had what she wanted. She'd always had power; that didn't mean she had to flex it.

Except a new race of vampires all to herself.

Izanami was on our side for now. I couldn't think of what might happen if she weren't, but I was the one who needed to ensure our safety. I had to put the case closed stamp on this one if we were ever to just relax. Izanagi had kept her in his sights and in Yomi for so unimaginably long, he would be able to tell me. He had to.

With a gleeful smile, she swung her arms up high and

clapped her hands together over her head. Living shadows slipped from the ceiling, down the walls like molasses, consuming the ice. I'd have known they were alive even without the lidless eyeball here and there showing itself, studying us as they covered Lynch in his cold cocoon.

"See you 'round," Blue said to me, then winked at Nicholas and was gone.

CHAPTER 24

And just like that, Nicholas and I were alone. For a moment, I could be still, forget that there was anything else to be done, anyone else to be responsible for.

"Where's Roman?" I always managed to ruin it for myself.

Nicholas didn't look surprised that Roman wasn't in the room.

"Nicholas," I said, "where is Roman?"

"He just needs a little time—"

"Oh, again? For a guy who'll live until the end of time, he never seems to have enough of it. Where did he go? He can't just go moping off whenever he doesn't want to face—"

"Could you face what he's done, if it were you?" he interrupted, head tilted, eyes pleading.

More gently, I said, "You know that I could."

He nodded, head dropping. If I was good for anything, it was owning up to my bad decisions. Nicholas was at my side in a flash, had gathered me into his arms. His strong arms, the Nicholas I first met at Lynch's stupid mansion, knowing and mysterious and yet so forward at the same time. Once again, we were where we belonged, no matter what ruin surrounded us.

But would it ever not surround us? When would *we* have time?

With effort, I released myself from him, kissed him until I couldn't think, and we tumbled to the kitchen floor, to take the time we deserved and desperately needed. My heart pounded, needing nothing but him. Not blood, not resolution, nothing but his body and mine. The standing walls shook with our bodies, the floor cracking beneath us. The preoccupying pain in my hand forgotten now.

"Stop destroying my house," he gasped into my ear. I answered him with harder kisses, squeezing closer, pulling him nearer and deeper, sweat smelling of ice and blood, black stars bursting in my eyes, his animal sounds reverberating through me like thunder.

"I think we've successfully melted all the frost you made in here," I said, spread on my back, my chest rising and falling as if I were human. It felt beyond good.

He rolled over onto me, kissed me gently. Not joking when he said, "Please don't leave me again. Not ever."

The thought of it was a car crash in my head. "I won't. I don't want to be away from you, from home...

My purpose is mine. I've done what I needed to do, a million times over. Fate is coming to us now, everything we do next, we are the epicenter of it. And I don't care if it ever comes," I said, curling his hair in my fingers, relishing in the health of it. Of him. And of us.

His eyes drew me in again, as usual, mesmerizing, magnetic even as powerful as I was. It felt *good* to not be powerful in that stare. "You're *so you* right now," he said, kissing my lips with the taste of sugar and chill of winter. "Like you're here, and not obligated anywhere else. I've never known you this way, you realize."

"I've been searching and searching for so long, and running from what I really wanted for even longer… I've always been afraid. I'm sick of being afraid, nothing can hurt me now."

"But it's not about being strong."

"No, no, I mean everything has fallen—no, I've *put* everything in place. I've exhausted myself leaving behind the only thing I've ever wanted. A home. It's a terrible thing to long for something so much and still be so scared to get comfortable in it. Everything always goes away, is taken from me. But not you, and not this place, I'll always make it back here if I have to crawl. I deserve home. And it won't be taken from me."

He pulled me to him and whispered, "I love you," with such ferocity, I knew this home wouldn't leave me without a fight.

"I love you," I said back.

We didn't have to ignore our obligations for days after that. The things we wanted to do were ours to do. There was no axe held over my head, no prophecy that said I had to hurry, no ultimatums, no impending doom. We were fate's vampires, but fate didn't ride on us alone, not on me alone. Not anymore.

Once we'd finished with each other for a while, we did rebuild the cabin. The satisfaction of *building* something like that was one I'd never experienced. Simple creation, by my own hands. And it was fast. Nicholas may have built the cabin and most of its furniture the first time, but to do it together filled me with such pride and comfort, ownership. It was *mine*, this whole world we were making together, ours and mine. I carved our initials with my fingernail into our new coffee table—once I'd finally made it right. Putting things together came quickly, but doing it well sure didn't.

"Hey! Nice job," Nicholas said, knocking on the simple tabletop. "Could use some sanding."

"Yeah, that's your job."

"You carved our initials into it?" he said with a mischievous glint in his eye.

"Yeah, with this," I said, grinning, holding up my index finger.

"Pretty cool, El, pretty cool. Super strong fingernails."

"That's why I got into this whole vampire business. Kat could never make me get another manicure again."

"Can I say something…" Nicholas asked.

"Don't you always?" I said, sitting on the table.

"Since Yomi, after you came back, you don't seem as broken over her as you've been. You're Eliza, without the pain all the time."

I just nodded. It was true. I think when the events of my life, and my afterlife, fell into place, even if they didn't all click together smoothly, I could breathe with the thought of having lost her. And to have brought knowledge of the baby to all of us, to have put Lynch and her together in whatever way they were in Yomi—I didn't know—was as much as I could do. Quite honestly, the world was a safer place without Chris Lynch roaming around in it, and no matter what he was and the damage he'd done, I was happy to have given him some peace and someone to love.

I hope that's what's happening in Yomi, I thought, but dismissed it right away. That wasn't my problem to solve. Just like Roman wasn't, wherever he'd gone. He'd come back to us this time, and so would news from Yomi.

Nicholas did leave for a while; he'd gotten a calling. An *unmei nashi,* he said. It certainly looked like it always did when he had a calling, and now as a vampire I could sense more changes. His blood slowed down. His body went cold, as if the ice he could use had turned inward. Saliva flooded his mouth, the swirl of his eyes chugged to a stop.

When Nicholas went to feed, I went to feed as well. There was no blood calling, nothing special about this victim to me. The guy was in the wrong place at the wrong time. I'd gone to Singing Pines Park but it felt dirty there this time, like I was following in some of Lynch's worst footsteps—and some of my own. I hadn't realized how long, and how deeply entrenched in my head Izanami had been, the bloodlust she'd instilled there. She wasn't entirely to blame. Tired of being told who and what I was, of being thrust into an immortal society built on this puritanical righteousness, I loved making that choice for myself. I loved not guilting myself over my choice of prey. I didn't regret my more brutal kills now, but I didn't want that anymore. At least for the time being.

We both arrived home in the dead of night, sated and ready to be together, wrap ourselves in each other.

But we found we were not alone.

CHAPTER 25

"Um, hi?" I recognized her, this girl on our worse-for-wear sofa, but man did she take me by surprise. Nicholas peered at her warily.

The one we'd only ever called the Girl in the Green Chair.

"Hi," she snapped, uncrossing her skinny-jeaned legs and standing up proudly. She wore cat-eye liner and bright red lipstick, a shade darker than the red peach fuzz of her shaved head. "Mind telling me what the hell I'm doing here?"

"Delivery girl?" Nicholas asked. "Sorry, delivery woman? We didn't order anything. We already ate."

She shifted feet in her probably fifteen-inch black stilettos. "Look, some lady dug into my brain," she said through gritted teeth, jabbing a long black fingernail into her temple, "and wouldn't let go. She told me to come here," waving her arms around. *So animated, I* thought, ridiculously. "I wouldn't, so she *made* me." A hard swallow. This girl was not accustomed to being out of control. This one gave the orders, didn't take them.

"I know you," I said, voice cracking.

"Yeah, well, I don't know you."

"What's your name?" I asked, approaching her until she snarled at me.

"Sierra. Tell me why I'm here." She didn't ask our names. Didn't care.

Glancing at Nicholas, I began hesitantly, "You're a vampire."

"No kidding."

"We're the ones who will take you in and help you."

She laughed, so boisterously it sent chills down my spine. Emotionally tainted. Cold. "I was dragged here against my will so you could *help* me?" she said with narrowed green eyes. "I don't need your help."

"If I may," Nicholas butted in. "We are quite a bit older than you. Well, I am, anyway, and I know our history. Our world. Others like you. We can guide you, so you won't be alone."

"What makes you think I'm alone?"

Hadn't expected that.

Nicholas looked at me, shook his head with wide eyes. "I've got nothing."

"We know who your maker was, and that he left you without any reasoning, or telling you what to do—"

Wrong thing to say.

"I figured out what I am, I don't need a man to tell me. Instinct showed me plenty."

"You've been feeding then?" I asked.

She snickered, "Well, yeah."

I wanted to ask who, when, how often, but she didn't invite questions in any way.

Nicholas asked, splayed out on the couch, "Did you feel anything that made you pick those people to drink from?"

"Feel anything but hunger? No. And drink from? Not exactly."

"What do you mean by that?" he asked. But my blood had already run cold.

"Why only drink from them?"

"You…you ate…" I couldn't say the words.

She smiled. "You never have?"

Nicholas's eyebrows nearly crossed over each other they were so furrowed. Neither of us, for once, had anything to say. What on earth *could* we say?

"Suffice it to say, no, we haven't considered cannibalism," he finally said.

With a fingernail between her teeth, she smirked. "You're missing out."

~

"I just wanted to go to the grocery store. Get a cheesecake. Maybe like, half a dozen pizzas, watch a possession movie or six. I'm feeling possession movies today." I was rambling, leaving Sierra in the living room and storming my way into the kitchen with Nicholas on my heels.

"Eliza, why did your friend send a cannibal to my house?"

"Our house, and she's not my friend."

We plopped into the kitchen chairs, the bewilderment palpable between us. "Izanami sent this weird lady here for a reason," Nicholas said.

"Yeah, because she's twisted and likes playing games."

"Well, Izanami's got Lynch. And Lynch created Sierra, has a connection to her—"

"—even if he wants to deny it," I muttered.

"It's got to be strong enough that Izanami was able to use it. Use her. Jesus, do they ever stop *using* us? Why *her* and not the other newbies? Don't get me wrong, she's nice scenery, but she's a cannibal."

I rolled my eyes at him. "Maybe that's why Izanami sent her here. Because she needs help even if she doesn't think she does."

The kitchen door—a swinging door again, now that we'd fixed it—slammed against the kitchen wall as Sierra busted through it. "I can hear you. I'd rather be part of the conversation than the subject of it. And no, I don't need your help. Maybe this lady sent me here to help *you*. Thought of that?"

Amusement danced in Nicholas's eyes. "If eating people isn't a cry for help, I don't know what is. And we definitely don't need your help."

"We have to talk to Izanami, there's no other way to get to the bottom of this," I said.

"Can you just walk in and out of Yomi, though? I feel like it won't go over well."

"I've bested Izanami. I can go back to Yomi if I want, and nobody will stop me from leaving. I need to make an agreement with her, and Blue, about what role they're going to play in the *Shinigami* coven now. What they're doing for the baby. I mean, it was the *baby* I saw that grows up and leads the *Shinigami*, not Izanami—but we have a while before the baby grows into that role. I don't want Izanami interfering with us down here in the meantime. She can't be puppet-mastering our recruits whenever the mood suits."

"*Recruits?*" Sierra said, arms crossed. "I'm not joining whatever thing you have here. And whatever this shinny-hey-hey is, I don't need it. I have my own people."

Sierra's porcelain cheeks lit up a happy pink as she described the Blue Hole in New Jersey to us—a mysterious but beautiful pool of frigid cerulean water that unnerves the locals. Unexplained currents pull swimmers under; quicksand grabs ahold of people on the ground around it; disappearances; the infamous Jersey

Devil is known to frequently pop his head up from the seemingly bottomless depths. When we asked why she'd gone to the Blue Hole to begin with, she said she'd followed the smell of organs there. Closing her eyes drowsily, she took a deep whiff of the air. "The Blue Hole Devils reek of flesh and human parts. Stronger than anything I've ever smelled."

"I'm sorry," Nicholas said, and I anticipated his smartass comment, "but the Blue Hole Devils? Did you join a swimming hole biker gang?"

Sierra smiled wickedly. "There is no Jersey Devil," she said, eyes glinting. "Vampires live under the Blue Hole."

"Under a pond? They live under a pond? You live with pond people?" Nicholas prodded.

"It's *not* a pond," Sierra snapped. "It's an anomaly from the Ice Age, buried ice that burst like a bomb, creating the Blue Hole and leaving ice caverns below."

"Wow," I said in a whisper, fascinated. I wanted to know everything—what they looked like, living under the ice, like a cross between Nosferatu and Marvel's Ice Man. My mind conjured up images of them digging under the icy ground, sleeping beneath it. "Obviously the currents you say that pull swimmers under—"

"Right," she said. "And the quicksand. It's the Devils."

"Jesus Christ," Nicholas said, squeezing his eyes shut. "They must be absolute beasts, pulling people down, feeding off them—" He stopped himself.

"Nicholas?" I asked, fear leaking into my voice. "What's going on?"

"Picture it, Eliza," he said fervently. "The bastards suck people down and keep them there, eating them. Don't they?" He snapped at Sierra.

She shrugged, totally cool with it. "They can't live on the blood of one swimmer here and there alone, now can they? And the Devils learn from those swimmers! It's how they know about the world at all! Without those people the vampires would be trapped in a time cap—"

"Yeah, stop it, it's gross," I said. "And you could smell them all the way from here?"

"Sure. You can't smell that far?"

Clearly, she had some gifts of her own. And I was beginning to believe that she really didn't need our help at all.

"El, we'll find another way to contact Izanami. She'll find us first, actually, like she sent this one here," Nicholas said.

"Sierra, let me touch you," I said, suddenly able to think of nothing else.

She moaned, smiling at me.

"Not like that." I twined my fingers through hers.

I did see some of her past. I felt her heart break when she saw her father dead. I heard her anguish as Lynch made her. I saw the green chair. Forever with the green chair. But it wasn't enough, and she saw it.

I flipped our hands over, exposing our wrists. It only took a second for her to understand my hard swallow, the quickening of my breath and what it meant I wanted. She said, "Do it."

I pinned her hand to the table and bit.

First I saw the horrified faces of those people abducted from the narrow, scrub-brush trails around the Blue Hole. Saw nearly translucent vampires in the night, with bat-like webbed arms, dragging a screaming girl up into the trees. Through her blood I walked the glittering crystalline caves—and the stacks of stripped bones. And then I tasted past her skin to all the skin she'd eaten. Their lives before, how fast they ended, and how fragrant their flesh. Some bitter, others sweet and dense… An entirely different taste than blood. A different world of flavor.

But it was over in a heartbeat, and I watched an invisible force drag Sierra up through the Blue Hole, spit her onto the quicksand shore, then drag her through all manner of terrain and drop her here, in our cabin. Then Izanami's face filled my vision, her smile a thing between elation and mania. She shed her face in a wave, like removing a mask, to show me Blue.

"Blue, are you okay?" I thought. She smiled and simply nodded. I wasn't sure whether or not to believe her, but I'd learned not to underestimate Blue before.

"Can you hear me?" she asked.

"Yes," as I continued to drink.

"You're draining Sierra."

"She likes it."

"I'll be quick all the same. Sierra is different, independent and vicious. She doesn't want to be *Shinigami,* and she isn't meant to be. The Devils adore her. She's the only vampire they've accepted into their ranks in centuries because she came *looking* for them, these invisible monsters. Who knew that some of the most hidden vampires ever wanted to be found? Thousands of years, changed by this one woman. She's powerful, like you, but in a different way. What I'm saying is she's got her own coven now; she isn't your problem. You don't have to police who she kills, and you don't have to *do* anything for her. This isn't the *Shinigami* you know, and because of you, that's possible. Lynch…Chris…" She smiled when she said his name. "Wanted to show you that he's connected to her."

"Yeah, they're both psychotic."

She rolled her eyes. "That's not what he means. Like you and Nicholas, me and Kieran. Creator and created. He can watch her now, while you do what you must with the other new vampires."

Sierra moaned, and the wrist under my mouth twitched. I didn't have much time.

"I'll come down from this mountain again, Izanami and me. We will watch with Lynch, make sure no one goes too far astray. There's so much possibility now for me, Eliza, I can *breathe* it." Her eyes went wild for a moment, but I tried to tell myself, *not my problem.* "You're draining her," she said. "Time to go. But someone has something to show you."

With a great gulp of breath, drowning in the taste of

knowledge, I let go of Sierra, a rush of savory skin taste going with her as she fell back. She waved Nicholas off when he tried to go to her. *Strong.* I was occupied watching a sheet of red mist taking over the wall behind her.

"What the hell is that, El?" Nicholas said. I could only shake my head.

Out of the mist emerged the maroon silhouette of Chris Lynch, then Izanami as herself, kimono, hair flowing freely like a veil down the middle of her back.

She handed Chris the baby.

The stillness in the kitchen was palpable, pained and expectant as Chris came nearer and nearer Sierra, who we didn't trust, who was so strange to us. It was stranger when I realized she'd taken the same sort of strides toward Lynch as he had toward her, sure and long, head held at a pompous angle. Stranger still when she held her arms out before her, cradling the empty air, just as Lynch cradled his child.

"Why is she mimicking him?' Nicholas choked out.

"She's not. Not exactly," I said. This was the connection between them coming to life, in a way we'd never seen, bridging two worlds. Sierra had become both part of the vision in the mist and the vampire in this world. Both ends essential, different and visceral.

Sierra's blood stopped pounding through me like a million hammers and settled into the lazy lapping of a river, an untapped peace. "She's perfect," Sierra let out in a sob, and I watched Lynch's shadowed lips say the same words.

Then the image of Lynch shifted. The presence of pure love, untainted by grief or murder became an actual golden glow from Sierra's body. The baby was suddenly in *her* arms, until milliseconds later the golden glow flashed again, revealing Sierra emptyhanded. But the not-quite-real silhouette of the baby had become a young lady, lithe and fresh, vibrant, hair bouncing around her with a life more than life.

"It's her," Nicholas whispered.

The child—no longer a child—grew larger as she came closer to the edge of the vision. But now, with every step, a black inkiness filtered into the mist, muddying it.

"This okay?" Nicholas murmured. But I couldn't answer, unable to reconcile that this darkness could exist in the same space as the sweet purity of that baby. But it was undeniably the same girl.

As the darkness overtook the red, she remained untouched, golden and pristine. Rather, she blossomed out of the darkness like night-blooming jasmine, growing faster with the love that poured from Lynch, through Sierra. Her heart, soul, flourished—a human, beautiful soul, just like our Kat's. Just like hers.

She lifted a wrist and sliced it open with a long fingernail.

"No!" I screamed. She could *not* hurt herself, she could never—

But rather than blood, blackness pinpricked with stars, like a universe in itself flowed from her veins in a perfect mix of darkness and light. A dark so deep I would lose myself in it if Nicholas hadn't pulled me back out.

I jumped when a grimace of cruelty slapped across her face as if assaulting her, unwelcome, unbelonging. *What's happening to her?* I wondered desperately.

Still so beautiful, but now with a greed that leaked into her heart, and that soul of Kat's didn't so much drift away as run. Behind her, an image of the New Hampshire woods, our woods. And littering the forest floor were limbs. Human limbs in a pile, others strewn recklessly, all with chunks the size of a human mouth taken from them.

"What in the holy hell is happening? Eliza?" Panic overtook Nicholas and that scared me just as much as the monster in the mist. A human being, not a vampire, a *person* that looked a little like Kat and a little like Lynch, and a lot like something horrible. And without fangs, without immortal speed, without fate's calling and without a purpose but for her own lust, she had taken these lives.

Images of her with an array of knives, cross-legged and covered in blood on the forest floor, sawing slowly and steadily at human arms, tearing chunks from them and chewing as she went to her work.

A hand wrapped around my ankle, and for one horrific second I was sure it was *her,* come to take me, to tear me limb from limb with nothing but revolting, purely human determination. But a second was all it took for me to know it was Sierra—because through her I felt it, what Lynch, what the child, what Izanami and even the Master and Izanagi wanted me to feel. The reason why I'd been given the damned ability to see futures through blood.

When Sierra touched me, the victims' gory ends in the nightmarescape rewound, until I saw their lives. Straight through their deaths and into the future. All the promise that they'd held, the children left behind, the terrible choices those children would make because of all the *hurt* they had suffered. The missing parts of the world that would never repair. The thousands, *millions* of lives affected by the loss of one of these victims' ideas, until finally—

"The end of everything," Kat's child said in a gentle voice, beyond mortal and yet entirely human. It actually reminded me of Izanagi.

In my peripheral vision, Nicholas stumbled, his swirling, wide eyes glued to the girl, mouth agape. He reached for a chair but fell unceremoniously to the floor. The emotions cascaded from him in frost and reverence, demanding my attention, and I knew that look on him, I knew that humbleness. He'd been floating without an anchor since the Master had fallen, the core of his beliefs torn away by storm. Everything he'd come to see himself as, what the *Shinigami* meant, had been shaken and exposed, but her... Kat's child was undeniable proof that there was a bigger picture, no matter who had molded it to fit their own story.

Clean, clear tears rolled down Nicholas's face. While I saw the reason why Kat's child had never been born, he recognized the birth of a goddess.

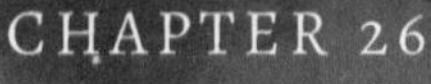

CHAPTER 26

Without so much as a goodbye, Izanami had taken Lynch and the baby back through the mist and disappeared. Though Nicholas was too stunned to move, and Roman was…

Where was Roman?

I couldn't stop to think of the possibility that he'd gone to Yomi as well, but accepted that Roman was great at taking leave of emotional situations. He'd just flap right out of there like Dracula.

Sierra wasn't as tough as she seemed—okay, she was tougher, but she still let me help her up and get situated on the couch where she could rest. She'd need to feed, quickly.

Once Nicholas got his wits about him he joined me. "Don't suppose you'd eat pizza, huh?" Nicholas asked Sierra as he tucked a blanket under her feet. She was too dazed to answer. "What do you think we should do? Can you feed her? I mean, you *did* take all her blood."

"I didn't take all her blood," I huffed. I leaned over her, offering her my neck. She moaned but rolled her head away, wincing, which I tried not to take personally. Her residue clung to my insides, to the basest part of me, the memory of the taste of flesh. I took a long whiff of her, from her abdomen to the top of her head to *read* her, know what she wanted.

"You never stop getting creepier. When does it end, Eliza?" Nicholas joked, and I grinned, my heart pounding at how happy he was and how alive.

"She wants meat," I said through a smile. Overjoyed, no matter how confused I was by what we'd just witnessed.

"Ooookay, well, I'll make her a burger."

"No. She wants fresh meat."

"Gross."

I heard a feral hiss, and bristled—until I realized it was coming from me. "Sorry, got a little cannibal residue in there, I guess," I said. "She needs flesh, like we need blood. I'll take care of it."

"And we'll talk about what *that* just was later," he said, waving a hand at the kitchen like he was swatting a fly.

"Later." Kissing Nicholas goodbye, long and lingering until the transferred need for meat pulled me away, I left through the back door in the kitchen to head for the woods. For a second, I stood looking across the vast green field that was the backyard, ignoring the abandoned construction project, and remembered watching Nicholas come home in the snow-coated darkness, the trees great black golems behind him, the glow of his skin a halo. My heart leapt.

We'd be together now. I could watch him come home time after time, fresh senses awaiting his arrival, the hot chocolate ready. I could be at this back door to wrap him in my arms, smell the woods on him musky and mossy, and know that we had forever to be this way. For as much as had changed, for as much loss as we'd seen, in the trauma of *meeting* my best friend's undead daughter, seeing fate unfold and tell all in a flash, I was happy. We would be happy.

But for now, I had flesh to find.

I dashed for the woods, the scent of a thousand animals above ground and below sweeping through my senses, and I worked to ignore the scent of humanity in the town on the other side. It was one thing for a person or two to go missing in North Conway here and there, normal even—but to be dismembered wouldn't work out in our hometown. Sierra would have to save that for the Blue Hole. For now, I wanted to feed her and send her home. But I didn't want to kill an animal.

Funny how that works. I'll kill people, but taking down a fox is out of the question.

Growling with frustration, snarling at my predicament, I reached out with my mind for an answer where I wouldn't have to compromise. Red billowed around my feet as my gears turned, and black flocked overhead in the wings of a thousand crows. They circled above, the mist churning the opposite way below, until I was the center of the greater machine. Steady crow eyes looked down upon me as they swirled, humanoid and beastly, telling me something through the air. Then they took off toward the cabin. I followed as if on wings of my own.

The door opened with the rushing wind of their wings, much to Nicholas's annoyance. "Now what?" he grumbled.

A collection of the birds flew in, landing gently on the weakened Sierra. The first one trotted up her chest, nuzzling into her neck. When she didn't awaken from her semi-consciousness it pecked her, drawing blood. The scent of her own blood woke her, red-ringed eyes focusing on the creature, and she turned her head to bite into it.

The bird didn't even struggle.

"No!" I cried out. The spirit guides had done enough, had always been with me. I wouldn't watch them do this.

"Eliza," Nicholas said softly, and took my hand. That was what sent me sobbing.

One by one the silky black birds went to her, peacefully, purposefully, and let the vampire drain them. These creatures, these souls, knew their reason for being and went to it willingly, took part in it.

As have you, I heard in my head.

"Izanagi?" I blubbered. I only needed to see beyond

the cabin wall for my answer, to the trees beyond, to see a giant crow the height of moose antlers bending the branches where it perched. The sun blazed behind him, mist-red, filtering into my mind as wildly and completely as my dream had once of a moon sheathed in blood. The creature had the eyes of the god I loved—and three legs.

"Heaven, Earth, and life itself, all components of creation. Feeding each other, branching and recreating, reforming."

"I've never seen you like this before."

"You see me as Yatagarasu *now as you have now witnessed those three elements and absorbed them within."*

"Heaven, Earth, life…"

"Heaven and Yomi are one in this cycle, my dear," he said, forging a path through my overwhelming clarity, the bursting of ideas and understanding. *"You have accepted them into yourself. As you have death."*

He didn't need to explain that to me.

Death—wine and roses—drinking Izanagi's blood— becoming *Shinigami*—losing everyone, gaining immortality…

Death is who I am.

And life is what I give and take.

Izanagi said, *"And life is what you have given me again."*

"Meaning?"

"I am Yatagarasu *now only. You have, in a sense, replaced me."*

"No! I won't replace you! I need you!" I cried out, and Izanagi listened.

"Eliza Morgan," he said, love pouring from every syllable, *"you have replaced me, allowed me to ascend to this form forevermore. And with that you have relieved me of my duty to Yomi. Do you see?"*

His plea for me to understand rang true in my heart. He was no longer beholden to Yomi, or to guarding his wife.

That was something I could do now in his place.

"I won't let you down," I said. I was answered by a warm breeze of wine and roses.

Nicholas tightened his grip as the ever-present residue of the creation god's blood blossomed into my mind. Izanagi had always been there, and he always would be, the closing of the back cover of my book. And the birds' peace became mine.

When I could see beyond the red glaze of my tears and the pulsing burn of the sun behind the great crow, Sierra was sitting up, pink flushing her cheeks, eyes glistening, the shadows gone. She cradled the remains of the *tengu*, murmuring to them. I did all I could to push the devastation away, knowing that they weren't really gone. They'd be back, they always were. *Kat would have laughed forever at me for buying into this circle of life crap,* I thought. But I realized I was wrong, because one second with her daughter would have told her that life and death were so much bigger than we were.

But the daughter she'd have known would have brought about the end of the world. Fate wasn't set in stone. We chose it, we created it like we did everything else. I knew what Izanagi was telling me. That the vampire race lived, too. It should thrive, as all life should. Izanami and I were one, after all—we were both creators of terrible, wonderful things.

And while one terrible, wonderful creation would rule us all, it couldn't be done without me.

CHAPTER 27

It was two weeks before I was able to be seen among people again. I might have handled the...everything...pretty well in the moment, aside from several instances where I absolutely did not, but when the dust settled, I broke. My insides felt totally clawed up, and I just wanted to be away from them. I told Nicholas we needed to go looking for Lynch's girls, and brilliant jerk that he was he saw right through it. He lit up with triumph when he figured out I was too weak mentally to just *find* the new vampires—until he realized that it meant I'd been depleted. Then it was all worry. And cringing from my now-overpowering voice.

Physically, I had cannibal blood running through my veins, mixed with the ever-present traces of Izanagi and short-circuiting memories of Izanami's. And with the vision of the three-legged crow, everything about me changed. I guess seeing a creature so beyond otherworldly, so magnificent and unimaginable was enough to alter even the vampire legend that I was. That I'd proven myself to be long before becoming a glowing, floating, buzzing, black-eyed mist monster with a voice like the tumbling of a thousand civilizations.

With full realization of my abilities as a...goddess, I guess...I'd been unable to control things like my voice and strength.

But what haunted me were the lives I'd watched unfurl and extinguished so brutally. By someone who didn't exist.

No matter how many times I told myself that none of it was real, it hit me like a thousand funerals.

And beyond that, I saw that Roman had done the right thing, and believed he didn't.

Once I finally was able to come out of the bedroom, Nicholas tried to make light of it. "Finally. Jesus, El, I was starting to think I'd have to make a church for you or something, with the halo and everything," he said, pointing at the reddish-gold glow emanating from my body. "It's weird keeping a god in your cabin."

"**OUR CABIN**," I said. Nicholas winced at the timbre and crushing boulders *weight* of my voice. "Sorry—our cabin."

"That's better," he said, shaking his head with his finger poking at one ear, working his mouth up and down. "If you sound like that around Birch Tree, the place will crumble."

"No, it will not," I said with a laugh—my own laugh.

Not the laugh of a goddess who had changed the face of vampirism forever. I was still getting used to being *this*, so different from who I had been, and from everyone in existence, mortal or not. I was getting control back.

Nicholas took my hand, not tentative anymore. I'd felt his fear when I changed, but I didn't *take* it. I didn't need to consume it any longer the way I once had, to control it. It was never about control to begin with. It wasn't even about survival.

It was about living.

"You're sure you're ready?" Nicholas said. I couldn't stop looking at him, at how much like himself he was, the same as when we met. A civilized man of the woods with the aroma of baked goods and peppermint. "You haven't fed…"

"And I don't need to," I said, cupping his cheek in my hand.

After returning from my vision of the three-legged crow, seeing Sierra cradling the dozens of *tengu* that had given their souls for her to feast upon, I wasn't overcome with sadness. Not for long. What sadness I did suffer at their deaths was quickly eradicated when, driven by instinct and oneness with my companions, I dropped my jaw open in that straight-from-*The Grudge* manner that I hoped would go away soon, and I took a great gulp of air.

Every one of the crows was swept up in the cyclone of breath, and I took them all in, absorbing each of their stories, each of their souls, all of their lives, until they were part of me, and I was satiated. Until I felt at one with them. I hoped it wasn't a goddess thing that I'd have to do forever—but I thought it might be. A part of my life evolved into something incomprehensible to mortals. But not to me. The crows and I needed each other. We always had, when they were just black birds that followed me around all the time, and now when I was truly immortal. That which consumes me makes me stronger. And vice versa.

"I think it's time. I want to just go to the damn bookstore, Nicholas! It's been…how long has it been since I *read a book*, for crying out loud?"

"I know, I know," he said, nodding. "There's so much crap for you to read, all your favorite garbage."

"I don't read garbage."

"Prove it."

"Pr…prove it?"

"I know. You can't, can you?"

We drove to Birch Tree like regular people in the SUV that had been sorely neglected for a long time. It was kinda nice to anxiously wait for it to turn over, guess at what the grinding sound was when Nicholas shifted. Normal. Human. Zero fate of the world involved. We stopped for coffee at Black Bear, and I had to swallow back a lump at how much I'd missed it, how it took me by surprise that I needed the smell, the sound of our shoes on the floor, and autumn wind shutting the door behind us. The hiss and chugging of the pots and machines, and the friendly chatter, the smiles.

Light and careless, if just for a moment, for everyone inside.

Leaves rustled in with us when we unlocked the door to the bookstore and flipped on the lights. The silence greeted me like opening a book itself, soft and warm with the feeling of promise and peace. Nicholas had given his few employees the day off, knowing how we'd need this place to ourselves today, and probably not a little concerned that I would do something totally weird to freak everyone out on my first day in public.

This was the start of our new life. This was the epicenter, and while the rest of our world surrounded it, here we controlled how much of it we'd contend with. Here, we were quiet.

Nicholas slipped his arms around my waist, planted his lips on my neck. Not a hint of teeth, only lips. No crows beat their wings outside. No visions infiltrated my mind. My mist was as subtly comforting as a pair of fuzzy socks inside my boots—negligible until the moment I wanted to feel it. I reached an arm up, my fingers in his hair, and pulled Nicholas closer. I breathed in today's concoction, created just for me, just for what my soul desired: cardamom and autumn leaves. Vampire senses allowed me to go beyond that—a hint of warm animal fur, a fox. The soil around damp moss. The memory of the scent of red velvet cake. But I chose to stick to the top notes because I didn't always have to dig deeper. No, I could be right here, right now.

This was a purpose, too.

"It's almost opening time," Nicholas murmured into my neck, barely words, but I understood.

"Almost."

I turned around in his arms, tangled my hands in his hair, tangled my heart in his, tangled his limbs in mine, tangled us forever, or at least until just before opening.

~

We stumbled to our feet from behind the register where we'd ended up, Nicholas raking his hair back, me trying to make sense of clothes.

"I'll put the coffee on," he muttered, squinting hard as if he'd just woken from a dream. I felt like I had, too. More coffee would help.

The familiar clanking of the old coffee pot into the machine, the grounds being poured into the basket, the scent of it and Nicholas, and the spines of the books peeping out at me from the shelves—it was all I could ask for of eternity. Simple, constant, full of love and comfort.

That was not what eternity had in store for me, but here was quiet.

The coffee bubbled away while Nicholas and I put away a stack of books—or I put away a stack of books and Nicholas made a new stack of books by the window seat. Half the furniture in this place was stacks of books.

The wood floor took on a new life now that I could take the time to glance it over—the depth of the knots was like looking into other universes. I smiled to myself thinking of little universes under our feet, like the Dr. Seuss story about Horton. Another story, simple and full of love and promise.

I opened the door, the string of jingle bells clanging against the glass. Brown, crinkly leaves breezed in. I didn't brush them out. I was wearing my favorite green sweater that I'd taken from Nicholas when I was still human, best thing to both absorb and cozy up against the fall chill. We settled together on the small window seat that could go unnoticed by unfamiliar faces, curled up with throw pillows on our laps and chipped coffee mugs, and watched the leaves blow by. We read—him, classics that were so pretentious I wanted to die, and me some new werewolf series that I kinda loved, but kinda didn't. Thing was, I could read the whole series in two days and have the rest of my life to read "better" books.

The day breezed by without a peep of vampiric activity. With Lynch in Yomi, and Blue…part of Izanami, and Roman running from all he couldn't actually outrun, everything was remarkably quiet. Turns out every day isn't full of crises. Sierra had been quick to leave. I didn't hear from Kat's daughter and she didn't appear to me—but I felt her. I felt her growing. First as a tremble in my belly, as if she were turning, a baby of my own somehow, nourishing each other through unseen blood and blackness.

With Lynch's love, she grew. They both did. And the world was safe from him.

It wasn't this day, but it was one not long after; another one that passed with the *shush* of pages turning and the steam of coffee, peppermint brownie kisses and crow calls. On this day, Nicholas's blood flow slowed and his pupils dilated, just enough that I would notice. He took his hands down from behind his head, dropped the front two legs of the chair behind the counter to the floor, and stood very slowly.

I'd noticed nothing, I was so entrenched in being normal. I'd forgotten that normal had once included Roman. But here he was. He wasn't alone.

She was red-haired; no surprise there. All of Lynch's girls were after Kat died.

Roman smiled when he saw me, and despite myself I smiled back. The girl hung behind him, eyes darting wildly, as if some monster greater than herself would leap out from the bookshelves to attack her.

It was the same kind of homecoming that Roman always received after leaving us. We had a routine now, of hugs and murmured apologies, filled with love.

"This is Angelica," Roman said, putting a hand on her arm gently. She startled when we merely looked at her but his touch settled her. "It's okay to say hi," Roman whispered.

"H…hi," she stammered.

"Jesus, she's just a child," Nicholas said.

"No, not really," I said, neither of our eyes leaving

hers as she half-hid behind Roman. "She just feels like one."

"I wanted to come alone, but she—"

"We understand," Nicholas said.

With a swallow of hesitation and a glint of excitement in his eyes, Roman said, "There are more. They're at the mansion."

It was a Tuesday, which meant not many customers, and so we were able to talk for a while after getting Angelica comfortable with a warm blanket and some coffee. She winced when she took a sip.

She wanted only blood.

"She hasn't fed, huh?" I asked Roman in a hush.

"She won't. But she can't eat anything else, it makes her sick." Angelica dozed on the window seat, weak from lack of food, obviously, and terrified of us to boot. Roman leaned in but we all knew she'd be able to hear us if she wanted to. He told us how Lynch seemed stronger, more peaceful and at ease. He could tell because their connection was more powerful than it had ever been, that they could speak to each other in their minds now.

"Between the power of Yomi—"

"By the Power of Yomi," Nicholas said like He-Man.

Roman laughed, and I laughed with him, even though Nicholas didn't do this stuff for laughs. This was just who he was. Nicholas caught me staring at him adoringly. I rolled my eyes to brush it off.

"Chris gleans energy from Yomi," Roman went on.

"It's like he's finally found a home." His eyes shined. Mine had been shining since Roman called his offspring "Chris." It made sense—Chris hadn't ever fit in our world, or among humans. He couldn't abide by rules of good and evil because he was something else.

"Yes, he's home," I agreed. "And…Blue…Izanami… they're part of that for him. And the baby—"

"They call her *Chiisana Negami*," Roman said, smiling wide. "Little Goddess."

After that there was only laughter and love between us. We were all so *overcome*, and everything felt finished. Not over, but finished. Ready for our next mountain to climb. This one wouldn't lead to Yomi, not for me.

As Angelica stirred, we got back to business. Roman told us how Lynch led him to the girls he'd turned, and how most—not all, but most—came with him back to Ossipee to be part of our coven.

Our coven.

"They aren't all well-adjusted to vampire life, that's for sure," Roman said with the huff of a parent talking about the teenager they don't understand. "Angelica is the most…traumatized," he said with a glance at her. "But I don't know if it's from being turned or before. Something from her own life. That's the problem—we don't know what their lives were like."

"They could be nothing but trouble," Nicholas interjected.

"Or they could be hurt beyond repair," I said, more to

myself. Angelica gave off the aroma of a scared cat, one who couldn't truly see what they were afraid of.

"They belong to us, though," Roman said. "We'll take responsibility for them, no matter what. I will. That's my burd—my privilege."

Nicholas took his hand. "Finally," he said, and hung his head with relief.

For too many years, Roman had been a man of obligation. To Lynch, yes, but even before that to his wife, Emily's, family. Leading a good life without error. Helping these new vampires, this was something he wanted, and something not entirely *good* by the rules of the Lord probably. To see Roman accept the gray area made me grin.

"They're all at Lynch's house?" I asked, picturing who knew how many fresh vampire girls at that giant house. It was an MTV reality show waiting to happen.

"We sure as hell aren't offering up the couch," Nicholas said.

"Fair point. I suppose we'll…come meet them?" I said, looking to Nicholas.

But it was Roman who confirmed it with an eager smile. "I'll get them ready," he said.

We lost some, sure. Like any new fanatical group of heathens, we lost some of Lynch's girls. The eeriness of looking around at two dozen other women who looked just like them, watching them go through various phases of accepting life a as a Vampire of Fate, well…it did plenty of mental damage. And a lot of them had some already.

Roman ran the Great White Mansion like a bed and breakfast, making eggs and pancakes every morning, place settings for all of them whether they could stomach human food or not. "Jane likes the eggs, reminds her of babies," Roman said with disgust. Changed my view of an omelet forever. When we dropped by early, Nicholas would steal hash browns off one or another's plate while I leaned against the kitchen counter with a cup of coffee. The whole place bustled with the clanking of dishes, muted bickering, laughing, life and life after death.

A couple of the girls came to help at Birch Tree, but nothing serious. It was only to get them out of the mansion, away from the others, including Roman. None of them were drawn there the way I'd been, none of them *needed* it the way I did.

Winter came, like an old friend. Some of our newbies had never seen snow. It was something to watch, the half dozen of them out there, hair like streaks of blood on the pristine white, making me lick my lips. The Christmas lights went up overnight all around town— on the lamp posts, in shop windows, and Jingle Bells played on loop. *Elf* was on every other day, and I only missed the invite to Kat's family's house with a brief pang. Stockings went up in our cabin, and the cat was home more often than not. Roman still showed up a couple of nights a week and walked right in. We still ate cookies and drank cocoa, like we had when I was human and crashing here. I woke in the same bed as Nicholas now, and once again, every morning was a wonder.

We settled into a rhythm of being together: Nicholas and I, Nicholas and Roman, Roman and the coven, the coven and me, Nicholas and the coven… It was random bouts, random but consistent bouts of togetherness. We could comfortably count on it every day.

I had had family before. I had missed them every day of my life. But this was family, too. Not a replacement family, not a next-best-thing, but a real family. Equal. Comfortable.

And when it became too comfortable, and nothing was changing except for hunting techniques and confidence, and nothing grew but love, things naturally changed. We could never get *too* comfortable. That wasn't the *Shinigami* way, or whatever our way was now. We hadn't exactly named our new clubhouse for orphaned vampires, we'd been so entrenched in enjoying it.

My own scent permeated Birch Tree Books on this, another simple day. Vanilla, sugar cookies, cardamom. Nicholas smiled at me, breathed me in deep. The swirl of his eyes sped up—a more intricate pattern now, at least to me. The love in his eyes was thicker. Ever since I'd known what I would become, I'd feared I'd be too much of a monster for Nicholas to love. Of course, before that I was worried I wasn't interesting enough for him, too. Once I'd experienced bloodlust, though, once I'd become a mythical thing, it seemed impossible to me that we'd be able to have a happily ever after of our own. How could we go back? But it never became a question of knowing too much to go back—we'd experienced and changed enough to see what was important and choose it. I'd given Nicholas much more than just my love, when he'd had such conflict over taking lives, no matter what the circumstance. I'd given him the truth, and instead of just accepting who he was and what he had to do, I embraced it. *Became* it.

Shown him by example how to own his nature and love himself more for it. After all, I'd torn through blood and ashes to achieve the eternal life I'd longed for.

With head held high, Nicholas was well-fed and enjoying the chill sun streaming through the windows. It was strange for him still to feed on just anyone he found appetizing, without the assurance that it would do the world good to finish them. That seed of an idea, that *unmei nashi* were born to die by his hand, had been planted and watered so much that it took over the garden. At first, I went with him—always together—and I'd feed, tell him what the future might hold for his choice of victim. But he came to terms with what I'd learned long before, that nobody has it all good or all bad, and everyone has worth to someone and hurts someone. Now Nicholas had developed his own palette, a fresh taste. Turned out, it was one for the elderly, who'd seen enough of life and wanted it to come to a close. He identified with that, the need to feel *done*. Most of the girls at the mansion thought it was gross. Not all, though. One thoughtful, under-the-breath-humored girl who barely spoke to anyone voiced that wisdom and fullness of life tasted like magic. Nicholas took her under his wing right away. It was this girl, Lafinn, who was dusting stacks of books-turned-end-tables when *it* happened.

"I thought that shelf would be full until the end of time," I muttered to Nicholas as the couple we'd just sold a tote bag full of bad biographies to held open the door on their way out.

He slipped in with a murmured thank you and a head nod, met the couple's eyes as if they'd given him a hundred bucks, and raised a hand holding a bagel smeared with jelly to them. *Toasting*, I thought, and nudged Nicholas, who I'd shared the joke with silently. Just as the door closed, the bells jingling, the man dripped jelly down his shirt.

"Bad shirt anyway," Nicholas said, leaning over, but his eyes never left the man. Neither of us could look away.

Past the terrible polo shirt of wide blue, purple, pink and red stripes, was the kindest, most unassuming gentleman. A young guy, twenty-five maybe. It was his lips that caught my attention first as he mumbled to himself, wiping jelly off his shirt, then looking at his hand in frustration. He talked to himself out loud, which I loved at that moment. A deep, rich voice, and beautiful teeth.

"Calm down," Nicholas said, and only then did I notice how hard I was breathing.

He approached the counter like it was an emergency, wide brown eyes pleading. "Do you have napkins? Or like a towel? Or…napkins?" He nodded toward the coffee pot.

"That's a coffee pot," Nicholas said.

"What?" he squeaked, wrinkling his forehead, squinting at Nicholas. "I know it's a coffee pot. Are there napkins near it, man?" He waved his jelly hand, gestured at his ruined, horrible shirt.

Lafinn shot across the shop. I panicked inwardly that it was too fast, another customer would see, but I underestimated her. She'd shielded herself quickly, almost by second nature. Her creator had never been quite so prolific with it, but Roman had been a good teacher. Lips pursed, eyes bulged, she slapped Nicholas's hand away from a coffee-stained tea towel. "I'll do it," she hissed. Nicholas put his hands up.

Towel in hand, she turned around slowly, purposefully, giving herself time.

Creating herself for him.

With every millisecond, she transformed, Nicholas and I watching her create a thrall.

"You always said you didn't control the thrall, and I always said—"

"Shhhh."

Well, my scent was all mine and every time it drew someone in, it was because I had done it. Willingly. Purposefully. Without apology.

Lafinn's began with her heart. It glowed under her blue sweater, then reached up like the naked birch tree branches made of light. They touched her jawline, bringing a golden shine to her features. It struck the tendrils of her fiery hair, even glistened around her glasses. She turned more, and the scent came next. It didn't come in a wave, but more of a tingle, like spice sneaking up on your tongue. She was cinnamon and pine, orange and cloves. The darkness of the wee hours of Christmas Eve after the party and after the wrapping, when it's so dark all you can feel is peace and cheer and anticipation. She handed our visitor the towel, which he took in a haze. Her light stretched out to him, inviting him to her.

"You don't belong here," she said with a warm smile.

Thank you so much for reading **Crawling Back**. I hope you enjoyed it!

I have so much more coming your way. Never miss a release by joining my free newsletter where I'll be sure to keep you updated on upcoming books!

To sign up, simply visit
https://juliehutchings.net/

Thank you for reading CRAWLING BACK! If you enjoyed the book, I would greatly appreciate it if you could consider adding a review on your online bookstore of choice.

Reviews make a huge difference to the success or failure of a book, especially for newer writers like myself. The more reviews a book has, the more people are likely to take a shot on picking it up. The review need only be a line or two, and it really would make the world of difference for me if you could spare the three minutes it takes to leave one.

With all my thanks,

Julie Hutchings

Charity Blake survived a nightmare. Now she is the monster others dream about.

By day, punk-rock runaway Charity Blake struggles through a stream of dead-end jobs and the haunting memories of her past. But at night she is the Harpy, sprouting wings with black feathers, and claws made for tearing the flesh of her prey.

Having survived a lifetime of abuse and torment from a sadistic man who broke her spirit, Charity's physical manifestation of her grief and anger allows her to hunt down those like her abuser. Only this time, Charity isn't a helpless little girl praying for things to end. Now she is the monster, and hell hath no fury like a harpy scorned.

Power always comes at a price though, and Charity's inner predator craves to take over. Torn between a life with no feeling other than the sweet satisfaction at ripping evil apart or suffering through her days to stay with the two people she cares for most, Charity must choose between her human existence or the wild and feral freedom of a flying avenger.

A perfect read for fans of Joe Hill, Anne Rice, and Chuck Palahniuk, THE HARPY is the first book in the chilling and deeply disturbing world of the Harpyverse where victims become vigilantes and power is a thing to be played with.

Get your copy of THE HARPY today and delve into the deliciously dark paranormal horror everyone is talking about.